CLIMBING
MOUNT MERCY

By Colleen Kanten Carbol

Climbing Mount Mercy
By Colleen Kanten Carbol

ISBN: 978-1-989092-86-6
Celticfrog Publishing
Clearwater, BC

CELTICFROG PUBLISHING

Isaiah 54: 8
I hid my face from you for a moment;
but with everlasting kindness
I will have mercy on you
says the Lord, your Redeemer.

ONE

THE ANNOYING JINGLE of the cell on her dashboard sliced the quiet purr of the engine.

Kitty wanted to smash them both—the melody and the cell phone. Her knuckles tightened their grip on the wheel as her anxiety mounted.

Kitty continued to snub the sporadic demands of the phone. To ignore it was impossible. Lance wasn't about to give up—even though he must certainly realize there would be no answer forthcoming.

He had to know Kitty was at the wheel, since she had pulled out of the parking lot while his dismissive words still taunted her. "Go then, Miss High and Holy. Venecia Vale will soon return to me on her knees. Begging. And no promise from me that I'll take her back either."

The rental Ford Kitty was driving seemed to have a mind of its own as it blended with the traffic on Deerfoot Trail. Kitty had thought she was going west before taking that second turn and finding herself headed south—away from the city of Calgary. Still in Alberta anyway, she had time to figure out which highway would take her back to British Columbia.

Besides, what difference did it make which direction she took? Anything to get away fast from last night's confusion and stupor. Anything to leave behind some of the bad decisions that had been made these last foggy weeks.

The phone signaled its annoying demand—again. Lance was not easily dissuaded. Once out of the city limits looking for a pull-out, Kitty eased her vehicle into the first available space. She needed to release the tightness in her chest and breathe. She turned off the ignition and loosened her grip on the steering wheel. The cellphone clamoured yet again. She snatched it up and powered it off.

Relief!

Kitty stretched her legs and reached out her arms to ease the stiffness. Clenched and unclenched her fingers. Tilted her aching neck forwards, backwards and sideways, shaking out thick blonde hair that tumbled rebelliously down her back. Having barely taken a brush to it this morning, she wasn't in the mood to care what it looked like. The outside pocket of the battered old camera bag on the seat beside her held a lipstick and brush. She should probably use them.

Then her eye snagged the gleam of the gold-embossed briefcase thrown onto the seat beside her camera bag. The pompous words that mocked her. 'Venecia Vale, Photography' added nausea to her remorse. Who did she think she was anyway? How had her pride been allowed to lure her into pure fantasy? She threw open the driver's door and scrambled around to the right side of the vehicle. Unable to reach the offensive briefcase while on the driver's side, she certainly could from the passenger side of the vehicle, especially with the fresh air blowing on her neck.

Vehement satisfaction heated her chest as she grabbed the gold-inscribed portfolio and flung it over the backrest. It landed with a thud somewhere amid the litter and coffee lids on the floor that served as a garbage collection depot. That's where it belonged.

Venecia Vale's year-long pretense was over. Finished. Done. She did a couple of jumping jacks on the gravel shoulder of the road and scrambled back into the driver's seat where her camera bag waited.

Her old bag was enough to protect her precious camera. She patted the worn leather gratefully, glad in more ways than one to be on her way back home.

The southern route was as good as the more northern one. Gunning the car back onto the freeway, south toward Highway 3, she'd head to Vancouver, BC, via the Canada-USA border route instead of through Banff and Glacier Park, the way they came.

Maybe the change of scenery would allow her a fresh perspective of her chosen career. Perhaps, going this direction, her longed-for future would be visible through her own eyes —instead of Lance's. She needed new inspiration, new vistas at which to point her camera, throwing away the rose-coloured glasses she had donned less than a year ago.

"Go then, Miss High and Holy…" His words in her head sounded less scathing as Kitty contemplated the freedom ahead. 'Go' is exactly what she had done. An amused and naughty satisfaction pricked her at the thought of Lance having to order a cab, probably to the airport, now that the rental car under his name had been absconded.

Or he could forget to ever go back to Vancouver, for all she cared. Kitty could not have chosen to make a trip with a man of less integrity, a mistake she would not make twice.

Three hours later, abandoning the highway leading toward the US border, she made her turn to the West, trading four lanes for two. The strain between her shoulder-blades began to subside. It had been a long while, she realized, since her heart had cried out, "Help me, Lord!" The short prayer, persistently repeating itself, began to lift her weight and anger. Her mind slowly began to clear.

The miles dissolved behind her, along with her tension. As she drove through the changing scenery her chest emptied its heaviness. Already into the foothills, she'd be rolling through the Rockies well before dark. A blue-grey vista beckoning to her in the distance told her the Rocky Mountains were not far away.

Up ahead, a sign announced a coming gas station, and as another announcement flashed an invitation to Big Bob's Burgers. Kitty realized she was hungry. Was it Bob that was big or the Burger? She must have just made a joke?

Better not pass up this gas station; it might be some time before another would show. Kitty filled the tank, then ordered a big Bob's burger from the little drive-in. Bob was as friendly as he was big.

"Like some lettuce and tomatoes, Miss?"

"Love some."

Kitty grabbed her camera and clicked a few shots of the surroundings as Bob prepared the order.

He reached into his bin of crisp-looking lettuce. "Not from here, are you?"

"Just heading home to Vancouver."

"Nice camera. You a photographer, Miss?"

A photographer? Yes. Yes, she was. Kitty was taking back her photography. As of now. She smiled. "As a matter of fact, I am. I was thinking about taking some photos of this beautiful area. Do you happen to know of some spectacular mountain view I should look for? Guess there's really no end of possibilities."

"You're right about that, for sure. Me, I've only travelled to Vancouver a few times 'cause I'm mostly minding the burgers. But come to think of it, seems like I heard some travelers tell there's some great views in a big canyon somewheres over the BC border. Can't tell you exactly where it 'tis though. I'd just be guessing."

Kitty ordered his hot country coffee, grinned at Bob, and tipped him extravagantly. She scrambled back into the car, set the coffee into the cupholder and burned rubber back out onto the highway.

Uncharted territory summoned. Here was the gateway into her fresh outlook on life. Her new season.

Half an hour later the road began to climb, and Kitty realized gratefully that even though Lance had been allowed to misguide her passion for photography, he had not been able to kill it. She still felt that inescapable call. These towers of rock cliffs, adorned in evergreen pines and summer shrubbery, were already reminding her to prepare her camera.

The lowering sun glinting from the snowy peaks lit her spirit with hope. Sprinkled here and there with paint brush and other wildflowers, the mountain slopes called. Like a passenger on eagle wings, her heart soared ahead of her out across the sunset. This soul-song of freedom cried to be documented with an image of God's creation. Kitty had to get at least one good photograph tonight. But the sunset scene would need to be found quickly if it were to be shot before Kitty would need to locate a motel somewhere.

Highway 3 began to wind into steeper terrain. Each new switchback revealed breathtaking rock cliffs plunging beyond a wide-ranging chasm. Excitement mounted as the scenery stirred her imagination. Her sought-after poster picture might well be awaiting her in this continuously transforming tableau of the Rocky Mountains.

The purity of the vision that once motivated her—before Lance had befuddled her head—began to warm her like an ember from the past trying to find oxygen. Kitty wanted to shoot this grand specimen of God's creative genius today.

Finding a suitable place to pull over that might also have a view, was proving problematic. Attempting to find an available side road, her search became more resolute. In the distance, looking like a relic of the past, a small, weathered sign hanging at a tilt announced, "Private Property." She drove more slowly, searching more intently. Beckoning trails were few and far between, and she passed several before finding something that looked promising.

Unannounced, just before the curve ahead, a broad exit bordered by spruce presented itself. Yes. Now. She carefully lifted her foot from the accelerator, applied the brakes and turned right, off the pavement and onto the gravel. As she parked, an elusive quiet descended. A few cars had passed her while on the highway. Here in seclusion, the road sounds seemed to have expired altogether.

Lofty silent evergreens surrounded her. In the dusky distance, a twist in what looked like a logging trail invited investigation. The rugged terrain beckoned upwards. Well, sure. Why not? She might never again find herself with an opportunity as promising as this. She turned the key and eased forward onto the unknown trail. The gravel was rough under the wheels, but not yet threatening.

Kitty applied the gas with resolve. At this point she didn't need a 4x4 or anything more than this Ford Fusion to head upwards. Long afternoon shadows reaching across the road made friendly overtures. She didn't hurry, but she kept the tires turning. Somewhere up higher, the dense trees were certain to spread open for her to see what was beyond them: the sky, the mountains, the sunset.

Promising that her chosen career was not over, wisps of sunshine filtered through the boughs.

Kitty's heart leapt with expectancy. It had been months since she had experienced such a rush of hope. It was high time for a new folio of her photography—samples that were really, truly her. It was still possible to delete from her folio those shots she was less than proud of. Her eyes kept probing the towering evergreens for a shaft of light. The sun was still riding the tops of the pines, but it would soon give up.

There. A sliver of brightness lit the gravel ahead. Then another, further up. Yes! This was it—the break in the forest wall that would soon reveal the panorama she was hoping for. Another quarter of a kilometre and it was found. The evergreens thinned. The wild grass on the slope gave way for some blackberry shrubs and dwarf junipers.

The rear wheels of the Ford Fusion slid as she parked at the side of the road.

Breathless, Kitty jumped out of the car, slung her faithful camera bag over her shoulder and sprinted up the ridge leading upward.

A bright sky beckoned from beyond the ridge, but Kitty discovered that the way forward was a much steeper climb than expected. Bushes obscured what should have been a path, and the gravel skidded under her shoes. She grabbed at the bushes, gasping for air between each step. In the distance through the trees, she could glimpse her goal.

By the time the blue vista opened up, her arms were scratched by determination. Scraped hands or not, she had no intention of quitting.

The ground leveled off. With a cry of triumph Kitty flopped onto the top of the knoll and gloried in the panoramic distance. Never had any quest felt more worth it. A massive chasm lay below her, and beyond it in variegated colors, the mountainside spanned the view of her dreams. The orange and purple hues of the sunset crested through snow- tipped peaks, swelling her chest to the point of bursting, but she had no time now to indulge her senses.

The beckoning arms of a pine tree recklessly clinging to the edge of the cliff called her to pause. With good timing Kitty could include that leaning pine in her shot. This photo might even be a match for Tom Thompson's famous painting of the Jack Pine.

She struggled to find a flat spot for her paraphernalia and the perfect angle to catch the sun's rays. The precarious cliff side began its descent too quickly. Loose rocks slid from under her feet and tumbled over the edge, crackling their protest as they ricocheted toward the chasm floor. She needed to find a level area where the camera could stand. There. *This spot feels more secure.* She joggled the tripod.

Oops. Kitty grabbed the bush close to her, using her other arm to support her camera with as much strength as she could muster. Her arms began to burn. Just a little more. That should do it.

She straightened her back and took one last satisfied glance over the ravine and up at the sunset, balancing the view of the rocks with the tilt of the pine tree. Kitty leaned forward to check the viewfinder and held her breath in rapture. Perfection.

She gently pressed the shutter button.

A shriek escaped her as the edge of the cliff gave way. The camera toppled forward, and her flailing body followed. Sky moved around her in slow motion. Reason disconnected—until her body slid against the cliff side and rolled to an abrupt halt. Breath exploded from her chest as Kitty fought for long minutes to get air back into her lungs— and took grateful, gulping breaths, realizing she was not dead, probably not even hurt. She was not unconscious. Kitty was not even alone. Her trusty camera had accompanied her down the slope and landed with its legs sticking out in embarrassment beside her.

She inspected her limbs. Nothing broken. A long scratch on her arm was trying to bleed, but Kitty made a guess that the bruises she felt but could not yet see, might last longer than the scratch. Her head was intact, and it seemed that her brain was, too, though she might be questioned on that point. What had she been thinking? How had she let herself wind up alone on a cliff in the Rocky Mountains?

Kitty looked upward from her painful seat on the rocky precipice. The roots of the leaning pine were not far above her perch, but the mere seven or so feet above her head might just as well have been twenty.

Kitty looked warily downwards, not even daring to bend forward to check for the bottom of the gorge. Her heart pounded at the thought of edging over even a foot. The little outcropping that had stopped her plunge barely held her and her camera. To the left, she could see the extension of the ledge on which she sat following along the curve of the precipice. To the right, the ledge narrowed and became part of the rocky mountain side.

The sky beyond the ravine was changing colors. Infusions of grey told her she had undoubtedly missed her daylight moment. Watching the fading rays, she realized the gravity of her situation. In the hours leading to this moment, her motivation had been the adrenalin of fury as she responded to her recognition of Lance's attempted control. Yet now, only the humiliating recognition of her own impulsiveness remained. Her own heedlessness. Her own inept recklessness.

What good would her anger do her now? The obvious prospect was a chilly night clinging to the side of a mountain. Who would be likely to drive this remote road? Who could hear her scream?

She turned off her thoughts and listened. As dusk approached, the mountain silence was deafening.

Fear began to claw at her stomach. What animals were out there in the night? Kitty wished for her cell phone and the flashlight from the car. She wished she had a blanket from the car. She wished she were in the car.

Kitty looked up at the huge pine tree leaning above her head, its maze of roots clinging to the ridge above. Mercifully it was still in place; it hadn't fallen off the cliff. She turned again toward the ledge meandering on her left. Her breath stopped. What was that?

What could it be, out here in the wilds? Poised on the very ledge where she was trapped. What… Oh no!

No, it can't be. A wolf? *Oh God! Help me!*

TWO

THE ANIMAL STOOD still and wary perhaps thirty metres along the ledge. It was enormous.

Its pale coat was lit by the glow of oncoming twilight, and even at this distance the eyes shone like slits of silver. The pointed nose was testing the air. Its pointed ears tilted upward and toward Kitty's precarious position on the cliff side.

Kitty was paralyzed by unutterable terror, listening for sounds of warning.

Dryness numbed her throat and separated feeling from her body as the animal on the ledge appeared to lean in her direction. Even her prayer froze—until the huge beast suddenly indicated its intention. In the next moment, it sprang toward her.

Kitty could no longer contain the scream that cleaved her throat as the animal's legs gained traction. Its whining enhanced her panic, and she whipped her arms over her face, inhaled, and closed her eyes. Blackout seemed a distinct possibility.

The beast was almost upon her. Kitty could hear the uneven scrabbling of its feet before it leapt. She felt the motion of its body as it landed beside her and its fur brushed her arms. Kitty screeched with horror as a long, soft tongue lapped across her cheek. She hurled herself against the cliff side, expecting the teeth to find her throat. Instead, a series of whines accompanied the slurp of its tongue over her chin. She opened her eyes.

The animal stood there, white-gold in the twilight, watching her with quizzical amber eyes. A smoky black vee travelled below the throat and circled its face, upward like eyebrows. The huge paws straddled her motionless torso while a scratchy moaning rumbled deep in its chest.

"Yo, down there. Are you all right?" The big voice yelled from near the roots of the leaning pine tree. Even with the leap of hope in her chest, she couldn't respond. The animal's glowing eyes still transfixed her with speechless terror. What was the creature waiting for?

"Speak!" The tone of the worried demand from above her was both relieving and annoying. "You okay?"

Even with chaos scrambling her brain, it began to seem ludicrous that Kitty was still sitting on the ground looking into the face of this menacing beast in front of her while listening to the command of some kind of terrorist yelling at her from above. "Yukon! Off!"

The wolf flinched in instant obedience, backing up to flatten its front legs, lifting its rear behind it and wagging its tail like it wanted to play. Kitty collected her senses and looked upward, not prepared for the wild man that bent over the cliff. A half foot of dark hair bearded his face and helmeted him with a haystack of gnarled curls. The only features visible were the sharp protrusion of his nose—and two intense eyes that appraised her with less concern than they should have.

Kitty had heard of Blackbeard before now, but this couldn't be him. Maybe this was a Wolf Trainer. She felt a small surge of hope. And yet—she also felt the rise of an absurd anger. Anger at the animal as well as the man.

If this creature was obeying that maniac on the ridge, then why wasn't he letting her up? And why did his pal up there not do something?

"Don't be afraid, Venecia," said the deepest voice Kitty could recall having heard in recent times. Could it really be coming from the madman by the pine tree? "You are Venecia Vale, aren't you? Yukon won't hurt you."

"Yukon? You mean this… this beast trying to eat me?" Fury took away the fear and cracked sparks in her voice. The animal whined at her feet, respectfully side-watching his master above him. The apparition on the ridge roared with laughter. "Don't worry. Yukon doesn't care for sweets."

Kitty did not appreciate his joke.

"So why is he still guarding me?" Yukon inched forward as she turned. "He's gonna bite me if I move! And what makes you think I'm Venecia Vale?"

"Babe, I'm sorry." His voice softened, just a little. "I'll get you up out of there and then you can explain yourself."

"You can explain *yourself*!"

"Hey, it's not usually a good idea to leave your car available this close to the highway—let alone your identification. Never know who might run away with them!"

Suddenly he was gone. "Wait!" Kitty yelled after him. He had left her alone again with this animal who continued to watch her with inscrutable eyes. What did the bush guerilla call him? Yukon? Why would the creature's name trigger such a lurch in her chest? Ridiculous! Or was it the unearthly depth of the voice speaking the name that did it?

A little gurgle came out of the animal's throat, and she felt the soft head brushing against her. It whimpered. Kitty reached out a cautious arm and let its tongue slosh her hand. It licked her fingers.

Her hand was lured to the irresistible softness of the warm throat. "You're not really dangerous—are you, boy?" This animal was certainly not acting like a wolf from the wild.

"Okay, Venecia. Coming down." The sound of the bushman's voice returned. "It's easier to get you up this way than by trying to follow Yukon's skinny trail."

Kitty wanted to be afraid. She wanted to run; but could hardly do either. She wanted to scream but she had already done that. Her would-be rescuer threw a knotted rope around the leaning pine and began letting himself down to her narrow ledge. She squeaked in alarm, and he shushed her brusquely, like he would an impatient child.

Kitty wouldn't be shushed. "There's no room here for you. It's too narrow. Won't that tree break?" She held her breath as he began his descent. Shabby but classic western boots reached the ground first, followed by worn jeans. Kitty tried to press herself against the cliff as tightly as possible to make room for him. Muscles rippled under his shirtsleeves as he reached out to reassure her. A grin cracked open a space between the ragged mustache and the hairy bush beneath it, and as she peered into the fuzzy face Kitty realized with a shock that this was no old man after all. Just a wild one with penetrating, stormy-ocean blue eyes. And a kind one. Nothing like the Lance LeFevre from whom she had escaped.

"Up, Yukon," he barked at the eager animal who took off like a silver streak along the narrow ledge, up over the ridge above and back to the pine tree, to stand above them in obedient anticipation, watching its master rescue Venecia Vale. It held its head erect, the tail a frothy white curve over its back.

The mountain man picked her up by waist like she might have been an exhausted feather pillow. He boosted her over his shoulders and commanded, "Up you go. Just stand on my shoulders and you'll be more than tall enough to hoist yourself over the edge. Grab a handful of grass and you're home free."

It was so easy that Kitty giggled in surprise as his powerful hands grabbed the ankles of her leather boots and boosted until she flopped onto the grassy bank at Yukon's feet.

"You don't want your camera, do you?" The call from below teased.

Kitty shrieked. "Oh, my camera! Yes, of course! My poor camera. I'm so flummoxed I almost left it for the wolves!"

In moments her rescuer was climbing the knotted rope with two feet and one hand and passing her the camera with the other. He rolled up onto the grass and dropped the camera stand on the ground.

He stood up beside her and said, "You're welcome."

Embarrassment engulfed her. Kitty was still brain-dead. But it wasn't that she was ungrateful. She had just been so terrified of this... this Yukon brute—or whatever his name was. It had all just happened too fast. She raised her head to lock eyes with his blue ones—strangely compassionate.

It was not reproach she saw in them after all, though she must certainly be deserving of some form of reprimand. She had been rescued from a calamity of her own making. Yet he actually seemed to empathize.

Maybe he wasn't going to be as dangerous as he looked. Shame engulfed her. As her voice mouthed the words, "Thank you," he reached a strong hand to pull her to her feet. Relief coursed through her body, but her knees turned to porridge, and she crumpled to the grass. Yukon bounded to her side in canine empathy, sweeping her cheek with a wet tongue.

"Leave it, girl!" its master commanded. Yukon moved backward, instantly shamefaced. Kitty reached out her arms to surround the animal's warm neck, buried her face in the thick fur, and burst into tears. This animal would not hurt her. She knew that. She clung and wept, unsettled by a troubling familiarity. Her rescuer let her cry until only little hiccups were left.

Then the mountain man seemed unable to resist her need for comfort. He knelt on the ground beside her, put gentle hands on her shoulders and said, "Shh ssh... it's okay. I think you've had a lot for one day."

THE NONCHALANT RESCUER de-knotted and coiled his rope and threw it back into his Toyota 4x4 with relief. You never knew when a rope might be useful in this out-of-the-way place, but who would have thought it would be needed for such an unexpected rescue?

He had let Venecia collect herself on the ground beside Yukon. The dog seemed to have no intention of abandoning her. Yukon was defensive at times, but it was rare for her to be protective. Perhaps she wanted another member in the pack.

He could see the young woman's wary dark eyes watching him as he grabbed the remains of the tripod and draped her camera over his shoulder. Her arms were still wrapped around Yukon's neck. Yukon seemed happy to stay, as the shock of blonde hair fell over the dog's eyes.

The blonde got up unsteadily. He offered her his outreached hand and held tightly until she stopped swaying.

"He sure is an unbelievable dog," she said as Yukon made a graceful leap into the truck box. "I do still think he looks like a wolf though."

He smiled through his beard. "She is a good dog. She's the one to thank for finding you. It's doubtful I would have discovered you on my own without her help."

He wished he could have taken a picture of the shy surprise that showed on her face. His pride in Yukon swelled. He was glad the young woman didn't seem mad at either him or his four-legged sidekick.

Why was this blonde waif driving alone in the mountains with no company but a camera?

What was it about her that twisted his breath and yanked at the muscles around his heart? Oh, she was beautiful. So spunky to be as young as she appeared. Yet so guarded.

At that moment the shutter in his brain clicked, and the shyness of her eyes brought the past into blazing focus. He knew this woman! From a day when her hair had been a glinting espresso brown —and her eyes, even then, as deep as the dusk that had descended around them.

She spoke. "And who might you be? I don't think I heard your name."

He hoped she didn't notice his momentary hesitation. "Just call me Joe. That should do for now." He decided, impulsively, to save his first name for later. She didn't need to know just yet, that he was Geoffrey Joseph Armistad, her workmate from three years before.

An unreadable expression flitted across her face. What could she be thinking? Those gorgeous oval eyes swam in mystery and skepticism. But then, how could she be anything else but skeptical, being required to trust this wild-west caricature of himself.

She didn't seem to be too terrified, yet her demeanor projected a defensive wariness—at once both trusting and suspicious. He wanted to shake her—just a little. After that he wanted to hold her. She seemed so small, helpless, and homeless. She reminded him of the little cougar kitten that had once spat at him even as he attempted to rescue it. Except he wasn't sure he wanted to put this abandoned kitten back where she came from.

"Hey, listen. Why don't you let me run you up to my camp for a bite to eat. I don't think you're ready to drive yet. Do you?"

Uncertainty stalked her expression, and her cheeks paled. It was as if the sun had suddenly dropped into the gully. Actually, it had. Sunset was officially complete, and twilight had taken over.

"Don't be anxious, li'l one. It's not far. You'll feel better with some food in you."

Why did she look suddenly cornered?

Geoff hesitated. She did need his help. Undoubtedly, she was a feisty little trooper, but her eyes said more than she had spoken. Her white leather jacket, now sadly smudged, her denim jeans and the meticulous cut of her silky blonde hair labeled her a city girl—although she had been anything but that when he knew her back then. Her terrifying interlude on the ledge must have left her exhausted. He longed to be able to bolster her courage with a hot cup of cocoa, or coffee maybe, and some helpful words to send with her. If she left now, he would worry about her all night.

"Are you afraid of me?"

She had yet to smile at him. The tears had stopped, but apprehension still collected like murky pools in her eyes.

Suddenly the sun came out in the dusk. She smiled. The relief flooding his chest matched the relief he could see on her face. "You're not scared of me... are you?"

Soft laughter bubbled out from behind her lips as her smile widened. "No, I don't--think I am... This is a scary place at nightfall, but I don't think it's you I'm afraid of after all—or your wolf." She stretched out her hand to the dog straining to reach her over the side of the truck box. "I'm probably a whole lot more scared of myself right now."

"You think?" He watched her focus on Yukon.

"I guess anyone who is unstable enough to let herself fall over a cliff is a danger to herself and everyone else around."

He laughed from deep in his chest. "I think I can handle it. C'mon. Hop in the cab. We'll come back for your car a bit later. It'll be fine here. I need to find us some food first."

"Umm... I think... that is, I... Well, I didn't see a rest stop anywhere along the road... Is there maybe one coming up soon?"

As understanding whacked him in the head, he didn't know whether to laugh or to empathize. Solemnly he raised his arm and pointed his finger upwards into the stands of evergreens leading each other over the dusky hillside.

He smiled and handed her a box of tissues. "Take Yukon with you."

YUKON CONVERSED WITH HER all the way into the trees and back to the waiting Tundra, with soft moans and persistent whines prompting recollections of their earlier relationships --when Yukon was little more than a puppy and her owner was less of a wild man.

She scrambled into the waiting cab and tried to relax against the backrest. Her rescuer gunned the motor of the 4x4 as he expertly navigated through the rising switchbacks.

"You doing okay?"

She nodded. "I'm good,"

Comprehension had revived her numbed senses. Recollections she had put out of her mind for three years now trickled back into probability. The blue eyes of the Geoff Armistad she had known then, along with the voice that rumbled in her memory, shook her and verified her suspicions.

AS KITTY WATCHED his hands smoothly shifting the gears, all her uncertainty disappeared in the comfortable dusk of his truck.

Venecia. How did I ever get to be Venecia? I wonder if he could possibly know who I am? He surely can't guess I'm just Kitty. The funny little dark-haired Kitty Sampson he used to ignore a long time ago. In the presence of this man who I know is genuine, I can't ever be Venecia Vale again—not that I ever was.

Memory rebuked her. Why was hindsight always 20/20? Lord, I am so sorry. How could I have allowed Lance to influence me? Why didn't I listen to You long ago? I knew better; I was just in too much of a hurry, I guess. Too self-focused. Too easily influenced by compliments. Not willing to wait for You.

Geoff startled her when he interrupted her musing.

"Venicia." The name sounded like strawberry mousse on his lips. "I hope you're feeling less terrified now."

"Thank you, I am. Much less terrified. I think God must have sent you."

Yes, of course. Geoff had paid attention to the name on her briefcase and naturally thought that's who she was—Venecia Vale. And now Kitty would have to enlighten him. With this blonde hair and her new life story, would she ever be able to convince him—of anything? Especially since I'm not who he thinks I am—and I'm so not the little girl he once knew.

When Kitty realized she had also met Yukon as a puppy shortly after Geoff adopted the dog, reality hit her senses like a new birth. She had just taken a leap back into the other end of Time. Bringing with it a disturbing case of

Colleen Kanten Carbol

nerves and a fresh pounding that shouldn't belong in her chest.

"I'm really sorry that Yukon scared you," he said. "I'm kind of ashamed I laughed."

"You did?"

"You know I did." The light from the dashboard touched his grin. "And I have to add, I'm sorry I'm such a frightening looking specimen. You probably won't believe it if I tell you I do have plans to tidy up this mess of a beard."

How could she tell him she actually loved his goofy wild man demeanor? It suited him, this Geoff she had known so long ago. It was her turn to laugh. "That's quite all right. Once I got over my terror of both you and your wolf, your appearance gave me confidence. I could see you knew what you were doing, and I do thank you from the bottom of my heart for being here.

"By the way, what *are* you doing here? Is this where you live—or do you just happen to be out hunting?"

The trail was becoming rougher by the metre. The passengers swayed with the rising switchbacks. He handled the wheel with one hand while the other hovered near the gear shift, ready with an automatic rescue should she bounce out.

"Yes to both your questions. My rifle's in the back. So's my bow. I was out scouting around for game again. And yes, I'm living in these mountains right now."

"Mmm...in a house up the hill?"

"We...ell...Part of one...some of the time..." He turned to her, grinning. "You'll see when we get there."

Getting there in the quickly descending darkness left Kitty totally bewildered. She knew they were headed

23

upward on the mountain, but in which direction they had been turning, she had no idea. Geoff drove slowly, carefully. She felt sure that he would have been bombing around those corners had she not been with him.

"Don't be afraid," he said. "We're not close to any drop-offs on this part of the trail. Since it's almost dark, it probably feels longer than it actually is. But you're perfectly safe. If you can't trust me, there's always Yukon." He paused as though expecting a response to his humour. She didn't respond.

"We'll soon be there. You must be starved."

"Not starved. But I am getting hungry. It's been a while since I had that burger at Big Bob's."

"I wish I could offer you a mouth-watering partridge pan-fry or an elk steak tonight, but I think you may have to come back again for that. It's still too early in the season to hunt big game, so I'd have to beg mercy from Logan's freezer at his house where the take is stashed. Besides, I've been too busy to be hunting anyway." He glanced at her with that inscrutable look of his. "I even had to forget about that bird I was chasing when Yukon took off to find you."

"I'm sure glad she did." Kitty said.

Yukon picked that moment to reach her head through the cab pass-through, as though she were part of the conversation. Too choked to speak, Kitty turned toward the sleek head and patted Yukon's nose.

"Back, Yukon," Geoff said, very softly. Yukon moved back into the truck box with a whine.

In another three minutes, Geoff drove out of the bush and up onto a level area facing a copse of trees in the distance. Moonlight shone on the dewy meadow. Kitty could make out the shape of a small see-through frame in the distance. And nearer, a dark dome-shape she recognized as a tent tucked under a tarp.

Geoff pulled up to the side of the campsite and cut the engine. He hurried to reach the passenger door before she could open it and ceremoniously took her hand to help her down.

The mountain wilderness had not taken the gentleman out of him. She regained her balance as her feet touched down on scattered pine needles.

Yukon leapt from the truck box meeting her exuberantly, threshing her tail in excitement as though to say, 'Welcome! This is where I live. I hope you like it.'

"I'll show you around in a bit," Geoff said. "First I want to get our fire going."

He grabbed the ready kindling and piled it on top of the old ashes in the fire pit. While Kitty watched, he placed some bigger sticks of firewood on top and struck a match. He added two chunks from the tall stack of chopped logs standing nearby. The kindling crackled, the wood caught, and soon the blaze was lighting the rustic seating-area.

With a grin and flourish Geoff led her to her seat—a firmly rooted stump sculpted into a chair close beside a pine camping table. The second seat he placed beside hers was also a carved stump.

"Want some coffee?"

"I'd love some. Thank you." Unexpectedly relaxed, she let her gaze travel around the shadowy area he must consider his turf.

It had been a long while since she felt this content. The open frame in the distance, forming the shape of a small house, mutely called for inspection. Patience. He'd promised to show it to her. She tried hard to listen to the message of the enveloping darkness. A night bird called softly from the shadows; an uncertain chirp close in the grass sounded friendly. As a hint of a breeze began to cool the meadow, the pressure of the day began to ooze from her tense back.

Geoff had soon produced a piping cup of coffee, undoubtedly from a camp stove somewhere beyond her view.

"Black okay? I can only do black tonight—unless you'd like me to open some canned milk? I don't have cream around very often."

"Black's perfect. That's how I like it. Thank you."

As soon as she had taken the tin mug from his hand to let its steam fill her nostrils, he disappeared inside his tent. Within moments he came back, bringing with him a soft alpaca blanket. He snugged it around her shoulders.

Kitty shivered with pleasure and hugged it to her. "Thank you! This is so nice of you."

"I think we're going to have Yukon's favorite treat tonight," Geoff said. "Unless, that is, you prefer something else from my abundant store. Some canned chili? Apples? Mushroom soup and crackers? Next time I have company I'll be sure to have more to choose from."

"And Yukon's favorite treat is...? I'll bet it's hot dogs."

"I hope you don't mind." He sounded a little sheepish. "We can roast them on sticks. I have some special buffalo sausage from northern Alberta. Yukie and I have them for a treat once in a while."

26

"Mind! Right now, there's nothing I would like better. If you knew how long it's been since I've roasted hot dogs on an open fire, you would know how much fun this is and how excited it makes me feel!" Kitty probably sounded like a little kid, but she didn't care. It was the truth. So nice to come back to normal civilization. One more plate of caviar or liver pâté at Lance's invitation would make her barf. Besides, there was fresh air to go along with these sausages—sweet mountain air, laced with the aroma of spruce and other unnamed fragrances that wooed her senses.

Geoff neatly skewered a sausage onto a stick freshly cut from the willows behind the tent.

"Let me do it!" Kitty jumped from her seat to grasp the newly cut stick and begin cooking, watching the flames lick the curve of the chunky sausage.

"Wuuff," Yukon said, with her tongue lolling out in anticipation even before the coals began to lure the juices from the bursting skins.

The lazy night was scented and half-moon lit. There was no need to hurry. Kitty's curiosity had been tweaking her ever since they began the drive up-hill. She began to expose her curiosity while they let the sausages roast.

"So tell me all about this mountain life you're living…Joe." The leap in her chest told her she had almost forgotten to use the name he had given himself. "How long have you been out here?"

He grinned at her and pulled his beard. "About as long as it's taken this to grow." He chuckled again.

"My beard wastes no time. That makes it a few months now. Back a bit in the woods is my pile of cut logs. I've always wanted to build a cabin in the mountains with my bare hands and a chain saw—so that's what I'm working on. You can see it in the distance this side of the trees."

Kitty let her eyes drift upward to re-examine the hollow shape she had noticed when they drove up. The unfinished frame in the moonlight tweaked her imagination.

"Well…that sounds ambitious—and romantic…" The words escaped her lips before they reached her brain. She was glad her cheeks were already warmed by the fire.

"I have a long stretch of university studies ahead of me," he said, "and I feel like I just need a little sanctuary. More than that, it feels good to heave an axe and pound nails. When I got back from the East, my buddy Logan and I were chin-wagging and we discovered we both had the same daydreams. When I told him I wanted to find the side of a mountain he, told me I could buy into his. Sometime I'll tell you about its history with his family. We've got lots of ideas, but this little log retreat is where my role starts."

Kitty's breath became shallow and sporadic in the night air. She had so many questions she wanted to ask him, but she wasn't quite sure that Geoff was ready for them. Why should he be? She would like to remind him that Logan was her cousin, although telling him so could be a bit premature.

Tonight's brief encounter was not long enough to share everything he was drawing out of her heart.

"You said you've been East? Where? When… I didn't realize that you…" Her heart jumped again. What had she just intimated?

He appeared not to have noticed. "I had planned to start university a couple of years ago, but the company I work for, Caveman Construction, won a bid in northern

Ontario. They offered a ton of money in exchange for two years of my life. I couldn't refuse. The job finished there, and I'm back home now. It was a hugely educational and enjoyable couple of years. Makes my education plans much easier to implement—if I expect to graduate before I turn forty." Kitty recognized his playful exaggeration by the crinkle at the side of his eyes. "But I do plan to enroll for the fall—unless I discover I need a winter in the boonies." His arm swept an arc over the meadow and dark mountain peaks.

Kitty felt her exhilaration mounting with a definable tremor. It was thrilling just to be near this man who had rescued her, not only from to-day's avoidable fall, but from the misery that had been roiling around in her life in the years since she had last seen him.

That had been over two years ago, at the open house celebration just a few weeks after the breathtaking wedding aboard the *Lazy Lady*. She had thought then that she could never forget the thrill of that double wedding on that glorious day. Memories of the wedding-decorated deck and the individual beauty of the brides together, both her friend, Becky, and Becky's mother, Jennifer,

Kitty realized, feeling a wave of shame, that she had not been in touch with any of them, including her cousin, Logan, since well after the party. And for months she had not pulled from the back of her folio even one of the photos she had taken with such pride. Her cousin, Logan, and Becky, his bride, had been snapped well before the existence of Venecia Vale. Now she'd like to show those pictures to 'Joe'.

But she didn't want to introduce that briefcase just yet.

THREE

IT SEEMED SO LONG AGO—that day on the deck of the *Lazy Lady* sailboat when the real Kitty Sampson had taken those pics on her new camera. Geoff couldn't possibly remember her, could he? the insignificant server from Jen's Place?

Professional photographers had set up the wedding poses, and Kitty couldn't resist sneaking a few shots. Her cousin Logan was marrying her dear friend Becky. Jennifer, Becky's mother, would also pledge her vows to her own friend, Hank Larson, in a magical double wedding—on the very same day and in the very same ceremony.

Geoff had been chauffeur for both couples. Not the same Geoff Joseph Armistad who appraised her just now with his alarming mountain man demeanour. It was the other Geoff, the neatly groomed young man who had supported Becky and her mother, Jennifer, in their unique double elopement. The Geoff who hadn't known that Kitty existed. The Geoff she could barely remember and wasn't sure she even wanted to. That Geoff.

Fondly Kitty recalled Becky's long-ago comment about sharing her simple wedding to Logan with her mother's marriage to Hank. That meant more to Becky than a traditional fairy-tale wedding for her and Logan, alone. Kitty was glad she had those wedding shots to be proud of, taken well before the mishmash of distasteful photos now occupying her awful sample case.

Geoff leaned toward her, breaking her reverie. "Can I roast you another hot dog? Looks like Yukon doesn't want any more." Yukon lay close to the declining embers, snoozing like a disinterested wolf with her head in her paws. "Would you like some more coffee? There's lots."

Kitty shook her head abstractedly to both offers, her lips curving upwards.

"You seem deep in thought," he said.

"It's another world out here. I'm kind of overcome. It brings back memories…"

"What kind of memories?" He reached out and patted her hand. "Good ones?"

"The earlier ones are very good."

"And the more recent ones?" Shadows flickered over his bewhiskered face. "Like, how did such a gorgeous young woman happen to be driving all by herself on this lonely mountain trail? It sounds to me like a story there."

Kitty shivered. Her fingers felt hot where he had touched them. Did his words require an answer? Mixed emotions threatened to escalate into panic. How could she answer truthfully? Did she want to?

"Can you tell me?" He gently persisted. "It's your turn to tell me about you now, you know."

Kitty barely found her voice. "I don't think I can... not right now…please…not right…"

"I understand." His husky tone sounded regretful. "It's not very polite to interrogate a visitor. It certainly isn't any of my business."

Remorse washed over her. "Oh, it's not that…you've made your business welcome with your extraordinary rescue! I mean… It's just… You saved me tonight. I don't want to sound ungrateful, but I don't know where to start."

Geoff gently lifted her hand, placed it on his upturned palm and covered it with his other. "Don't apologize. I've no right to make you uncomfortable. I'm just so happy that I could be the one to rescue you from your mishap—and I've enjoyed this time a lot." He laid her hand in her lap. "You haven't mentioned your mother either. Does she live in Nanaimo too?"

Kitty pulled in her breath with a tight gasp. Mentioned her mother? She hadn't even thought about her mother, and the reminder was not welcome. A sudden chill stiffened her expression. "We can discuss some things, Joe, but let's not include my mother just now."

Geoff reddened and quickly suggested. "Maybe we've talked enough for one night."

Unexpected disappointment frustrated her.

Then he brightened. "But, hey, there's no reason you can't come back, is there? Unless you want me to put you up for the night."

The sudden leap in her chest subsided in embarrassed shame. This kind man before her certainly meant no harm by his generous suggestions—spontaneous, and possibly in jest.

Fresh hope flooded her shaky emotions. Maybe they *could* eventually pick up somewhere where they had left off so many years ago. Could she actually accept his offer to stay the night? He was a woodsman used to sleeping under the stars. He might offer her his tent. Even as Kitty's heart lunged with eagerness, a thrill of apprehension stabbed her. How far from an innocent child she had come.

Lord Jesus, help me!

As Kitty silently cried out to God, Geoff said, "If I promise to make myself more presentable, would you be willing to come back?"

Relief broke her tension. She smiled. "You're presentable enough just like you are."

The unreadable expression in his serious eyes, navy blue in the darkness, made her somehow uncomfortable. He had asked her if she was afraid of him. Kitty had told him she was more afraid of herself. He couldn't guess how she really felt.

The hefty logs that had flamed into such comforting warmth were turning into coals. As though just becoming aware of the night air, Geoff suddenly jumped forward for another armful of wood. He dropped the load down beside the fire pit and guided a couple of solid logs into the embers, creating a responsive crackle of sparks and a new shimmer of light over the campsite.

Kitty drew the alpaca blanket more tightly around her and slid off the stump onto the ground. She reached her arms around the stump as far as they would go, snuggling up to the coarse sensation of bark; it had been a long time since she'd been so close to the earth.

"I can't believe how good this makes me feel. Makes me think of my daddy. We used to go camping sometimes. It's all been so special I'm almost thankful my fall happened. I just wish this didn't have to end."

When Kitty heard no immediate answer, she turned her head to look over her shoulder. Geoff was closing the door of his truck. He held something under his arm as he came back to the fire. A wide grin showed through his beard.

"What...what's that?

The package looked familiar.

"Oh, I just brought it along from your car. I thought I might be able to persuade you to show me your pictures. This has gotta be Venecia Vale's work, doesn't it?" Geoff held her loathsome portfolio in his hands. "Gonna show me your photos?"

Kitty held her breath. Why did he have to go and bring that briefcase out here? These photos did not make her proud. Better to put the whole thing into the crackling flames than open those pages—even if it meant destroying the ones she was actually pleased with. But how could she refuse?

"Do you really want to see them? Right now? They're not my best work, and I *will* be taking more..." Her voice quivered.

"Aren't they as pretty as your briefcase?" His long fingers caressed the fine leather and traced the gold lettering. "Venecia Vale. Such an elegant-sounding name. She must be one important lady." There was gentleness in his smile. And admiration.

He set the case carefully on the second stump in front of her, turning it so the words, *Venecia Vale*, faced directly toward her. Kitty lowered her eyes at the accusation of the gilt letters. The apprehensive pounding of her heart almost choked her. He leaned downward, so close his beard brushed her cheek.

Geoff reached his finger underneath her chin and gently lifted. His sombre expression held her transfixed as her eyes met his. She felt her colour drain as the dryness of her throat stopped her voice. His eyes probed hers like a lie-detector. Kitty barely breathed, waiting.

Geoff took his hand away from her chin, allowing her to writhe in misery. Long seconds stretched under his piercing scrutiny. His eyes narrowed as he clarified his question. "*Are* you Venecia Vale?"

Kitty turned her face away from the force of his gaze and dropped her arms over the letters on the briefcase, letting her head fall in anguish over them. No words would come to the surface. Pain and embarrassment numbed her body and exploded in her head.

No, no, no! Her raging brain screamed. *No! Never. I'm not her! I never was and I never will be!* A shudder convulsed her shoulders.

Powerful arms lifted her to her feet from her position beside the stump. Those same arms surrounded her with a touch so gentle she wasn't sure he was still holding her.

"Kitty, Kitty. Give up already. You know who this is." She opened guilty eyes to meet his teasing amusement. "Did you really think you had me fooled? How long were you planning to play this game?" Geoff asked her.

Kitty collapsed once again on the stump chair, unable to face him. He brought her another coffee. She accepted it gladly, both to help prevent her shivers and also to give her something to do while she thought about what to say next.

The combination of triumph and wistfulness in his expression left her both defenseless and uncertain. Kitty wondered if what he saw on her face could be exposing her heart before him, and even she couldn't decipher what was in her heart. She wasn't ready to spill every anguished confession rising up within her. Some of it was almost too hard to acknowledge to herself, even when she knew she heard it.

Kitty, run away and find a place to hear what God has to say to you.

"Kitty…" Geoff said, "would you have left without telling me…anything?"

She had to respond. Her long silence was beginning to sound silly.

Cautiously looking up from her coffee mug she tried, "Geoff…I guess, if I had thought I could get away with it, I would have waited until…until…. Will you let me come back? Do you want me to? There's so much I could tell you. I want to explain it all to you when… when we have more time. When I can get my head sorted out."

He did not look convinced.

"All right then. Yes, Kitty. Of course, I want you to come back… if you want to, that is. I was hoping you would want to see me again. It's not like you owe me an explanation, though, just because you accidentally fell into my life. You must be plunk in the middle of living yours. It's a long time since we were both working at Jen's Place. You've moved on. Obviously way, way on."

His hopeful expression made him look like a vulnerable little boy searching her from behind a hairy mask.

Her voice quivered. "Geoff, I can tell you this. I'd rather be going back, instead of just moving on. Way, way back…." *Where had that innocent girl that used to be her… gone?*

"Strange how we've met up with each other again. Seems such a weird coincidence. Perhaps we should just go back to where we were before I landed in your mountain side?"

His blue eyes were soberly, darkly blue.

"You call this a coincidence?"

Kitty tried to face him bravely. "Well... I... Maybe our meeting isn't a complete accident..."

He smiled. His voice strengthened. "All right, then, Kitty. I think I hear you. We need to give ourselves some time. And we do need to get together again. I could come to you, but I have a feeling it would be more therapeutic to meet here, on this mountain, where we can give our concerns to God—together. With the last three years of non-communication behind us, we could both use the peace of Mount Mercy, couldn't we?"

"Yes." Choking tears threatened to stop her voice.

"Then, for tonight, it's nite-nite, little Kitten. I'll follow you back to the highway and point you toward the Short Stop Motel that's maybe ten minutes down the road. Would that be okay?"

She nodded, mutely.

He handed her a business card titled 'Silverhammer Construction, Logan Kovalik, Supervisor'.

"Here's your cousin's card with his new cell number on it, just in case you can't reach me immediately out here in the hills. I wrote mine on the back. You can call one of us when you're ready to return."

Geoff stepped closer to her, near enough to touch her hand. *He wanted to give her a hug;* she could feel it. He acted as though he considered himself the elusive Sasquatch and didn't dare.

He said hopefully, "In a few days then? A couple? Tomorrow?"

"I'll try to be in touch by next weekend," she said. "It's getting late. I think it's time I head down the hill."

Kitty saw the hesitancy in his arguing eyes. But he voiced no opposition. With a resigned smile he led her to the 4x4.

Yukon leaped up from her spot near the dying coals.

"Stay and watch, Yukon," he commanded the dog. "I'll be back." He threw a bucket of water on the embers. They hissed briefly, then died.

Kitty threw her arms around Yukon's neck. Burying her face in the soft fur, she struggled to hold back the tears. "Stay and watch, Yukon. I'll be back too."

Yukon whined softly and stayed obediently where she sat.

The drive down the rough road to her car felt much shorter to Kitty than their drive up. She wanted it to last in order to bask in his strength a little while longer. As Geoff helped her out of the truck, Kitty moved as slowly as she could, her reluctant heart echoing the pleading of her brain. The Fusion was waiting where she'd parked it. She stood hesitantly by the door. It was time to leave.

Kitty searched her pockets for the keys. Then dug determinedly into her purse.

The jangle of her keychain brought her head up to meet Geoff's grin. Her keys dangled from his finger. She'd forgotten them in the ignition when she climbed the hill to go for her sunset shot.

He opened the back door, reached inside for her jacket and turned to her. The softness in his eyes was so penetrating she had to look away. He helped her slip her arms into the sleeves, one at a time, and then lifted the jacket deftly over her shoulders. His warm fingers brushed her neck as he prevented her hair from snagging under the collar.

"Thank you," Kitty said, barely above a whisper.

Geoff went back to bring her camera with its camera-stand, and the embossed portfolio, from the truck. He placed them carefully into the trunk of her car as she watched, wordlessly.

He held the door open for her while she wriggled into the driver's seat, then helped her adjust her jacket as she settled in. Kitty shivered, clicked her seat belt, and wondered when she'd see him again.

He put the keys into her hand.

GEOFF WATCHED KITTY brush the silky hair from her forlorn eyes. She gave him a wan smile and turned on the ignition. The headlights spread over the rough surface and lit the bordering evergreens. Carefully Kitty manoeuvred the car off the rough shoulder and onto the logging road.

Geoff slipped into the lonely seat of his Tundra, turned the key, and the powerful motor rumbled to life. He drove around her car to guide the way back to civilization.

He felt as though his spirit were holding her hand as Kitty followed him down around the bends. At the bottom of the mountain he signaled, pulled over, and braked as Kitty arced around the Tundra and continued on the trail toward Highway 3. He strained his eyes to watch her through the black night. Kitty didn't look back, easing her car onto the highway headed east toward the small motel. No other traffic stirred on the highway, which now must seem dark and lonely to Kitty. Her car was not moving swiftly. He would have liked to at least follow her to the motel to be sure she was safe, but Kitty was a big girl in her determination. He watched from the distance until her taillights disappeared.

His thoughts were empty of everything except the unexpected new power of Kitty. Kitty, the inexperienced and innocent little girl he had once known—but had never noticed—and who today had crashed his heart's defenses with one glance of her velvet-brown eyes. Kitty, whose dark locks, often pulled up into a tidy knot, he had never even thought to touch. This new Kitty, with the now-blondecascade of hair he wanted to sift through his fingers; the slender body whose maturity had only created more curves and softness; the laughing girl who had become, in the intervening months, a woman he barely recognized.

This Kitty had shaken his world.

His ego rebuked him. "You idiot. How could you have missed seeing who she was back then when you had the chance?" Yet the message of his Father's voice inside him spoke even louder than his self-recrimination.

Then was not the time, My son.

It had taken a wrench of control not to reveal the explosion she had delivered to his core. He shocked himself with the surge of emotion he had subdued. For the time being, he must remain simply her acquaintance of the past—the inscrutable bearded rescuer he made her think he was. He must continue to be no more than the encouraging friend he had shown her; it was still way too soon to speak the depths of his heart. Furthermore, he wasn't sure he fully understood his own heart.

He remembered the long-ago evening at Jen's Place when Kitty had made bannock and shared with halting words the story of her faith. The memory triggered a rush of tenderness.

Kitty had been tagging along the day he brought Yukon, as a puppy, to meet their close circle of friends. He was astounded that he had never observed Kitty herself closely enough to remember the details. In the past three years he had scarcely thought about her, even vaguely. Until today.

Did she care? He had no idea whether or not he had meant any more to her, back then, than a piece of leftover bannock, but he hoped he meant something to her now. Time's passing must have created enough emptiness for both of them. Tonight, he would stake the future of his career on that heart-tug. He would be haunted by the loneliness in her eyes until she returned. And if Kitty gave him a chance, he knew he would never want to let her go.

If it were up to him. And if he managed not to scare her off.

Take care of her for me, Lord. Please bring her back to me so we can find a new starting place. Keep her for me until then.

He started the engine and turned his truck around. He drove up the mountain trail to home and Yukon.

FOUR

KITTY SQUINTED AT THE SUNLIGHT streaming through the ineffective venetian blinds of the Short Stop Motel. She was surprised she'd slept so long; her watch showed 7:20.

The sheets she had yanked over her head last night, sure she'd never be able to sleep, felt soft and soothing this morning. Kitty stretched, curled over, and stretched some more. What a perfectly luxurious night. Not even the hint of a disturbing dream played with her surfacing thoughts.

It was as though the presence of Geoff had been sitting protectively by her bedside watching over her the whole night through. Kitty remembered how sure, yet gentle, his hand had felt when he led her back to her car. She'd better forget about that. What uncalled-for fantasy!

The words from heaven that had spoken so strongly yesterday—when Geoff's questions began to jolt her heart—those words still sternly directed her quivering longings: *Kitty, run away and find a place to hear what God has to say to you.*

Sunshine spoke with the hint of happy freedom Kitty thought she'd lost forever. Still, within her she felt unmistakable words of caution, an insistent message from God. *Slow down, Kitty; listen for My voice...*

Geoff was back up on the mountain, but he had left with her his spirit and a continuous replay of the words they had shared by the fire. Last night a blend of emptiness and anticipation had awakened every pore of her body. Something within her felt very different. How had she managed to fall asleep with her mind in such exquisite turmoil? Even thoughts of Lance had been unsuccessful last night in trying to invade her peace.

Thank you, my Lord Jesus, that You have not abandoned me.

He never would. The fog was leaving her brain. God had given her the strength to leave Lance's inappropriate photo session on her own initiative. That dose of courage still coursed through her veins. There had to be hope.

Oh God, forgive me for this last year! Kitty wiped hot tears from her cheeks and fell on her knees beside the tossed bedcovers. *I need You. Kitty needs You. I won't ever again try to go it alone. I'm so sorry, Lord. Help me. Help me never again try to be someone I'm not.*

With unknown music rising in her soul, Kitty showered and blow-dried the professionally-cut layers of blonde hair. Visions of her bearded rescuer played in her head as she vowed to act on yesterday's new direction. Geoff's obvious concern for her lonely departure last night would warm her new life forever—whether or not she ever saw him again.

The shrieking laugh that swept through her soul was unexpected, but it was quite clear whose laughter it was. Venecia Vale was far too deeply ensconced in the heart of Kitty to allow her to find freedom so easily. Venecia had earned her position and had no intention of easy relinquishment. Lance's silent arrogance filled the space around Venecia's emerging regret, and Kitty realized her misery might be only beginning. Perhaps God had no intention of letting her off so easily.

Kitty was uncertain how many hours it would take her to drive to Vancouver. She needed to start now, wanting to locate an agency immediately to return the rental car that rightfully belonged in Calgary. She realized how impulsive her act had been, but Kitty would do it again in a heartbeat to get away, even if she did have to figure things out later—like she was trying to do now.

Last night Kitty hadn't cared. Now, it was beginning to make her heart do a slow dance of dread. The first link to her regrets that needed to be severed was this rental car.

The GPS mapped the road ahead. With her hands on the wheel of a car that was not hers, time was truly of the essence. The first thing to do was find a rental office in Vancouver that would accept the return of the vehicle. The sooner, the better.

After that she had an important call to make—a change-of-accommodation plan that could not be postponed.

Only after she'd accomplished both the car return and the phone call could Kitty indulge any unlikely fantasy. Geoff had indicated he would be waiting for her return to his mountain. Thinking back, perhaps a more imaginative choice might have been never to leave at all, to pretend that Geoff's mountain was the secluded island of the Blue Lagoon. She could happily be lost forever in Paradise, never to return to the reality of Lance's demands.

How silly. Life was lived in Reality.

Furthermore, her first priority must be to get away and find a place to hear God's voice.

Kitty put her foot on the accelerator and kept it there for hours—with only one brief rest stop—until the passing of miles between mountain ranges finally led her over the Port Mann Toll Bridge. A blend of anxiety, elation and hope kept her alert the whole drive. She was nearing home. Strangely, Kitty wasn't yet feeling very tired—or hungry; seeking a coffee was only a good reason for a pause.

Kitty took the next exit off the highway. There'd surely be a Timmy's or Starbucks coming up. Her stomach was at last beginning to recognize a long absence of food. There must be a drive-in somewhere along here soon.

At the curve of the next right turn, the shrieking wail of a police car suddenly split the air. Kitty eased over, wondering who was in trouble with the law this time. Feeling a surge of pride that her traffic record was clear, Kitty edged along confidently.

The whirling demand of the police siren came nearer as she shoulder-checked to see which car he might be hailing. She couldn't tell. As Kitty eased over just a squeak more, the noisy police car careened ahead and pulled over a few yards in front of her, slowing down with decisive intent. His lights continued to blink authoritatively.

Kitty stopped. Nobody else did. Who was he after anyway?

A broad stretch of uniform stepped out of the squad car. And he was coming her way. What was going on? As he neared her vehicle, she lowered the window—just in case—even though it made no sense.

Intimidating, mature eyes glared at her from beneath a pair of greying eyebrows. His square jaw was stubbled with 5 o'clock shadow.

Without an explanation the officer said, "Your driver's license, please."

The expression on his imposing face did not change as he repeated, firmly, "Your driver's license, please, Ma'am."

"What on earth for?" Kitty sputtered. "Did you just pull me over?"

Sternly stoic, he said more slowly, "Lady. I asked you for your driver's license. And you may as well pass me your automobile identification as well."

Kitty fumed with the injustice of this interference as she pulled the rental information out of the glove box to accompany her drivers' license. The officer returned to his car while Kitty waited—watching the traffic go by and drumming her fingertips on the dashboard. Finally, he returned, looking very sombre.

"Kitty Sampson, correct?"

"Yes."

"Alias Venecia Vale, correct?"

Kitty felt her colour drain and her brain protest.

"No." It was the first thing that entered her thoughts and the only choking word that would come out. Two days ago, her answer would have been a haughty yes.

"Are you telling me that you are not Kitty Sampson?"

"No, I am not!"

The sudden darkening of his features dragged her back, struggling to remain in the present tense. Kitty swallowed deeply and cleared her throat.

"What I am trying to tell you is—that is, what I mean is that I am not Venecia Vale. Not anymore." She kept her voice even. "Could you tell me, Officer, what this nonsense is all about?"

"Lady, I wouldn't sound so flippant if I were you. We have been notified that you are driving a stolen car belonging to EverReady Rent-a-Car in Calgary, Alberta. This is *that* car, is it not, Miss Sampson?"

Kitty drew in a startled breath. "Yes... it is from EverReady." Her bravado began to fail. "But it's not stolen. You already know it's a rental. I'm just on my way to return it." She tried hard to hold her head up. *Was that concern in his eyes?*

"It was due yesterday, correct? In Calgary. You have it in your possession. I think you better follow me to the station."

"But that's ridiculous! I didn't steal it." Her voice squeaked painfully. "I just wanted to get back home. I'm so sorry it's late, but now I'm here and all I have to do is find out where I need to drop it off!"

"That *would* be a good idea," the officer said, sarcasm scorching his tone. "Looks like someone should help you with that before you decide to have the serial number changed."

"I told you, I'm not stealing it!" Suddenly her fighting spirit collapsed, and tears spilled over. Furiously Kitty wiped them away with her jacket sleeve. She repeated in disbelief, "How can I be stealing it when I'm returning it?"

"To where are you returning it?" he asked patiently.

"Well... as soon as I got a coffee I was going to find out where I..."

To accompany his exasperation the tiniest hint of a dimple flickered momentarily in his stubbled cheek. "Lady, why didn't you return it in Calgary where you arranged to?"

"But I didn't...." she protested. "Someone else arranged ... he was supposed to take it back..."

"So you did steal it then."

"No, no. I only borrowed it." He didn't appear to believe her protest. "Truly. Just to get home to West Van. Did the rental agency notify you?"

"No," he said.

Seething fury and frustration drowned her. How *could* that rat back in Calgary, with all his pretense of class, have reported her as a common thief?

"Then it's not stolen, is it? I was too tired to carry on until after my night at Short Stop Motel. So, I left early in the morning to get back home to my own little relic and return this one."

"Come on, lady. Can't you do better than that? If you knew it was a rental, why didn't you return it before you were accused of absconding with it?"

"I couldn't," she whispered. "I needed it. I had to get away... from..."

How in the world had she allowed herself to trust a man so suave and calloused? How typical of Lance. The Lance she should have seen through—seven months ago— the first time his flattering words conned her. Who else but Lance would have sicced the law on her?

The officer's softening expression communicated uncertainty, as though he recognized the possibility of some missing pieces to this story.

"Miss Sampson, I should have seated you in the back of my squad car long ago. You must realize that this is a serious accusation. You need a better defense than your pretty smile."

Her heart was thudding slowly. Would he take her to jail?

"Officer. Sir. Can you tell me if it was the rental agency that reported a theft—or was it an individual?"

Turning thoughtful, he hesitated, scrunching his tight mouth to the left, and Kitty jumped on the silence. "I thought so. That scum bag."

"No... I mean yes, the agency agreed the car appeared to be stolen, but..."

"Do you have the name of the person who made the report?"

"We have yours..."

Kitty took another chance. "How about this?" She turned her pleading eyes on him. "If you could help me find an agency where I can turn this vehicle in, I will happily pay the fine or whatever they want. And then I will be rid of him! Forever!"

The stoic demeanor of the officer softened. He closed his mouth and stood still in thought. He lifted his cap and scratched his head.

"We...ell... Maybe I'll try to see what I can do." He consulted his phone. "Follow me," he said. "Don't make me regret this."

Kitty wanted to jump out and hug him but wondered what rules he might be ignoring to help her. The daylight nightmare was over. She relaxed and followed him to the rental office.

Kitty turned in the keys and paid the bill, no longer threatened with jail.

Outside the rental office, Kitty tucked her credit card back into her small bag and turned to the police officer with a smile that seemed to rattle him even more than the unprecedented events of the past hour. She still wanted to hug his ample midsection.

"I can't thank you enough, Mr..." *What was his name, again?*

"Officer Robert McCain, Miss Sampson..." He appeared to be searching for words. "I want to apologize for the misunderstanding, Ma'am. I think this has been a sort of comedy of errors. You made a bad mistake taking the vehicle out of Alberta—but if the rental agency is happy, so am I. Unless, of course, someone else presses further charges..."

Dark fury spat from her eyes. "He just better not try..." Then she relaxed. "Officer McCain, I'm so sorry for my bad attitude. Please forgive me. I'm afraid I brought it with me from Calgary."

Robert McCain's paternal expression conveyed worry. "I'm on duty, Miss Sampson," he said sombrely, "so I can't suggest a coffee, but I can certainly drop you off where you need to go—if you give me the address."

Sunshine broke over her face. "Oh thank you, Officer! That would be so awfully helpful."

Fifteen minutes later his police car pulled quietly up to an older home in downtown Vancouver.

He carried her suitcase up a short flight of steps to the door. As Kitty felt for the key at the bottom of her bag, Officer McCain reached into his wallet.

"Here's my card." The concern in his eyes gave her courage.

With Geoff so far away on his mountain, it felt good to have a friend—even as unlikely a one as this officer.

She held out her hand.

"Thank you, Officer McCain."

McCain nodded his head, turned on his heel and strode back to his car. On impulse, Kitty followed after his retreating uniform. She stopped when he turned.

"Just had to say it one more time. Officer McCain, thank you."

He tipped his hat and disappeared into his cruiser.

FIVE

THE HEELS OF KITTY'S BOOTS QUICKENED on the cement sidewalk like they belonged to a child coming home. As she skipped up the stairs where her suitcase waited, the sparrows chirped their evening melody from the maple tree in the front yard. Above the door, a time-worn wooden sign welcomed her. "Auntie Bee's Nest."

Kitty picked up her suitcase and pushed the door inward, her heart singing a new song. One she hadn't heard for a long time. She felt almost like herself again—almost as free as she'd been in Nanaimo on Vancouver Island, all those months ago—though Kitty now felt like she'd aged seven years.

At the far end of the hallway Kitty turned the key in the lock of Room Five, the small accommodation she'd moved into when she followed Lance to Vancouver. She dropped her suitcase and briefcase beside the single bed.

Thank you, Lord, I'm safely back.

She couldn't wait to let Auntie Bee know that there would be no move to The Ridge after all. No need for that extravagant room Lance had insisted she would want once her new business started paying her what she deserved for her "specialty art photography." Besides, he'd told her, she'd have lots more privacy on the ridge.

Privacy. Right.

Kitty pulled her phone from its pocket in her purse and dialed the realtor to register her cancellation of the rental agreement. Lance had chosen its high-rise elegance for its prestigious address and the magnificent view over

Vancouver harbour. He had even placed a non-refundable deposit on it so she could sign the lease at her pleasure—next month or earlier. How gullible she had been! The concerned receptionist on the other end of the line gave her a small amount of flack, but not enough to convince her that she was passing up a "very rare opportunity with a long waiting list."

"Thank you very much, ma'am," Kitty said. "Feel free to turn the suite over to whomever you please whenever they want it. You can apply the deposit to the new renter. I will not be needing it, next month—or ever."

Kitty felt not one flicker of regret.

Done. Now she would be able to sleep.

She grabbed an apple from her small fridge. After her week away on Lance's promised first "specialty photo-op," the milk smelled sour, but the orange juice tasted all right. Time to pick up some fresh groceries tomorrow.

A familiar knock signaled her to open the door for Bertha—otherwise known as Auntie Bee. The smiling landlady opened her plump arms to Kitty's hug.

"So nice to see you, child. Hope you had a good time. I noticed you even had a police escort tonight... Are you okay?"

Kitty laughed lightly. "That's a whole other story. He was a really nice guy." She found her purse and rummaged around in it. "Here's his card. Enter it into your contact list or take a picture of it and keep it on your phone, in case you should ever need help."

"But aren't you home a little early?" Auntie Bee never failed to check up on her. Six other roomers lived in Auntie's Bee's Nest, but Kitty always felt favoured.

"I'm so glad to be home, Auntie Bee. I can't tell you how glad. Guess what, I'm not going to be leaving yet. I've decided to stay here for a while longer. Right where I belong."

Bertha's mouth fell open. She clapped her hand over her suddenly flushed cheeks. "Oh no, Kitty. No. I'm so sorry." She sat down.

"Wh... what is it, Auntie?"

Remorse spilled over Auntie Bee's gentle features. "It's too late, Child. You gave me your written notice, remember, or I might have waited. I thought you were certain. Someone called the same day the ad came out. I've rented it for the beginning of the month. He's paid me for two months plus a damage deposit. I have no choice. I am sorrier than I can ever tell you."

Shock and resolution settled over Kitty's face in the same grim moment. When her voice finally returned Kitty encircled Auntie Bee with her arms. "It's okay, Auntie. I wasn't thinking at the time, and it certainly wasn't your fault. It just means that my plans will have to change again, and very quickly. I'll really miss you this time."

She had two weeks to find another place.

Then a thump in her chest shocked her with its warning. If homelessness was staring her in the face, she'd be better off getting out of here now, before Lance got back from Calgary. Tomorrow should give her enough time to pack her few things. Misgivings at being around here even one more day began to flutter in her chest.

She'd start as soon as she'd had some rest.

KITTY DROOPED MOMENTARILY on the well-used couch that came with the apartment —trying to pray.

Even with only a few possessions, it was hard to get going the next morning. But there was no time to waste. Sorting and packing, she kept up a one-sided conversation with her Heavenly Father about what steps to take next. Yesterday, determination to put Lance behind her had given her a surge of adrenaline that brought courage. That was yesterday. Now, she wondered where her inspiration had flown. Without her familiar room to collapse in, it would be difficult to gather another boost of hope big enough to handle her new mess of worms.

Her prayers reflected despair, as ugly memories of Lance's scandalous expectations flooded back, and shame sank into her belly. Becoming Venecia Vale had taken her to a place across a river from which she now struggled to return.

Venecia Vale. Lance had come up with that handle. Probably from the same self-aggrandizing archives where he had dragged his own 'Lance LeFevre.'

"You really need a name to suit your status," he said. "Something imaginative, artistic, and elitist. 'Kitty' just isn't going to cut it." So, Venecia Vale she'd become.

Despite her hope of his sincerity, he'd baited her with his interest in her photography.

Kitty soon discovered that mentoring her photo art was not as high on his priority list as he had pretended.

Venecia Vale's leather case lay where Kitty had kicked it under the computer desk. May as well tackle that job now. Salvage what she could of what belonged to the real Kitty and burn the rest. Kitty lifted the briefcase and unclasped the latch, closing her eyes against the gold engraving. Maybe Auntie would lend her a paintbrush to get rid of the name *Venecia Vale*.

From the back pocket of the briefcase Kitty withdrew her prized pictures of the double wedding aboard the *Lazy Lady*. The smiles of beloved people beamed out from the photographs she'd taken that day. For over a year she'd kept in touch with them—until Lance walked onto the scene and she removed herself from their lives. Shame and regret enveloped her.

She'd left the old Kitty behind—in more ways than one. With her now-blonde hair, even her cousin Logan would probably not recognize her if he passed her on the street. Could she ever bring back the old Kitty, with her trust, and especially her innocence?

Lance had insisted that she'd never achieve recognition as a photographer with her old look. "You can't win any favour going out there looking like you just walked off the plantation."

To think that she'd let him get away with saying it, let alone listened to him. He said if Kitty were to become a credible photographer, she needed to look the part. What unmitigated cow excrement. Kitty had only believed him because he spent his questionably-acquired money on her. Wined and dined her among his elitist so-called friends. Told her she had what it took to be published in the slicks. Kitty so badly wanted his flattering words to be true. With his guidance she could *be* somebody.

Fool, fool.

She pulled out the first photo for which Lance had been the director. With her own expertise Kitty had made the woman look classy, even though the flow of the shawl that shimmered over the model's curves hinted at her lack of clothing. Then the next. And the next, each incriminating picture charging her with the photographic temptation to which she had submitted.

"They're just beautiful bodies," Lance had said. "Pays big bucks. Just get a little more practice, so you can feel at home in the part." And he had patted her reassuringly where his hand should never have gone. Right then she should have known he was bad news. Suddenly an urge to share it all with Auntie Bee gripped her chest. But it was unlikely she'd have the opportunity.

Lance had first spotted her on Vancouver Island in Nanaimo, at the coffee shop where she'd been serving tables during her college break. Jimmy, her employer, was always happy when she snapped a few photos of his customers so he could show them proudly on the walls of his "gallery."

"It's good advertising," her boss said.

Kitty had a deep desire to make her photographs not only beautiful, but educational. For some of her school assignments she had scoured less savory neighborhoods for evidence of need—many of them children. Among the faces that laughed were others who reflected hunger, loneliness, and pain. The nearby world needed to know. A few of her models reached Jimmy's art walls.

Lance glanced at the folksy display. "This is your future," Lance said.

"Hold it right there." Kitty had focused her lens on Lance's handsome smirk and made a professional click.

"Thank you, sir. Welcome to Jim's Gallery. May we post your photo?"

"You are fabulous," Lance said. His eyes roved over her photographs and then over her. "Honey, you are going to waste here."

His work was in Vancouver, he told her. If she moved to the city, he would personally train her to become the most famous photographer in the country. Willing models to sit for her —both adults and children. Paying models. She'd allowed herself to believe him. She'd aced her subjects at photography school. Why take more training when she had Lance? The memory sickened her.

Kitty pulled out the old photos and lingered over the wedding shots she'd lovingly snapped Those familiar faces almost brought tears. It was months since she'd seen any of them. Deliberately ignored them. And who was Geoff, anyway? Only a face among forgotten photographs.

Suddenly, there *was* Geoff, smack in the middle of her life.

Kitty placed her photos carefully back in the case, in front of the earliest ones she had taken of Geoff and Yukon as a puppy. She yanked out the more recent photos from the front of the briefcase. They nauseated her.

In a few scathing moments she consigned them to obliteration, ripping them one at a time, slowly, deliberately, into small pieces of revenge.

Kitty had failed to take out her kitchen garbage before leaving last week. She found a big orange refuse bag and emptied into it the malodorous garbage, then added whatever banana peelings, smelly take-out cartons and other unmentionables she had recently accumulated and stirred it all with the biggest spoon she owned. On top of that Kitty drizzled from her fingers morsels of photography like she was decorating a compost cake. To complete her concoction Kitty spilled over it the contents of a bottle of hot sauce she'd tried last month and disliked, added the empty bottle to the mess and knotted the top of the plastic bag. Satisfied, Kitty carried it out back to Auntie Bee's garbage bin.

Her kitchen drawer held one sturdy bread knife. Would it be strong enough for this next job? Kitty attacked the gilded words on her briefcase with a mighty sweep, cutting and scraping. *Venicia Vale* did not stand a chance, even if Kitty must demolish the whole briefcase. When she was through, the leather folder looked like a refugee from the dump. And *Venecia Vale* would be remembered no more.

But now Kitty was tired and ready for rest. She'd have a clearer mind in the morning. And she'd be able to reflect on some new ideas she'd begun to consider for her immediate future.

Kitty took a shower, slipped into her pajamas, and slept for the last time in Room Five.

SIX

EARLY IN THE MORNING, a teary Kitty hugged Auntie Bee good-bye.

"I want to give you a special phone number," she said, with a hesitant smile. "After I've caught up with some relatives I haven't seen for a while, I'll be driving to a place near the border of Alberta. I may even be there for a while."

Bertha's wise eyes twinkled. "Kitty," she said. "I think you're holding out on me. That Lance fellow you once told me about...is he extra special to you?"

"Horrors, no! Never as long as I live! That rat is poison."

"Oh... Well then...?"

Kitty pressed hands to her unusually hot cheeks. "It's a long story, Auntie Bee. But I will tell you this. In the mountains way far from here, I accidentally ran into someone I knew a few years ago." She drew in her breath. "Geoff is a good friend, and I'm going to visit him. There's a nice motel called The Short Stop that's close to his campsite."

Auntie Bee wrapped Kitty in a reassuring hug, winked, and let her go. "Keep me posted, honey."

Kitty drove away in Lizzy, the twenty-two-year-old sedan she'd left behind when Lance picked her up a lifetime ago. The trunk and back seat accommodated her few belongings. With Auntie Bee's permission she abandoned the only piece of furniture she owned, an ugly old armchair that was too big to handle. She needed her computer, of course.

Lance had told her to give her rags to Value Village and promised her a whole new wardrobe, so Kitty had few clothes. The camera bag Geoff had rescued sat close beside her in the front seat. Her shredded briefcase in the back seat kept company with a pillow, her sleeping bag and a comforter, and an old but working cooler that held a can of salmon and the few remaining contents of her fridge. A small duffle bag of can't-throw-aways fit into the trunk of the car.

Kitty picked up coffee and a breakfast muffin from the Tim Hortons's closest to Riverbend Park and drove to the still-deserted playground. Letting her eyes scan the quiet ball field, she willed her mind to relax. Prayer was swirling around her, but she didn't really expect any talk-back from God. Everything felt too confusing for her to even listen for an answer. She just stayed in the car trying not to think while she finished her take-out.

Kitty, find a place to hear God's voice.

All right, then. She'd better pay attention. This was as good a place as any.

As Kitty took the last bite of her breakfast muffin the tears began to slide down her cheeks. She choked on her last swallow, coughing between gasps. Never had she been more miserable, more alone or more sorry for herself—even after her Daddy had died over a year ago.

His physical heart had given up, but his big spiritual heart kept Kitty strong. He reminded her from his hospital bed, "You are in God's care, my precious." It was true. His parting love filled her with so much hope Kitty knew she'd be all right.

Yet how easily she'd let her daddy down —as well as her Heavenly Father, Who cared for her even more. It was too long since she'd talked to Him and listened to His voice.

Forgive me, Jesus. I know I walked away. I need to turn around.

More tears fell. They washed some of the condemnation from her soul as a familiar voice whispered in her heart. *It's OK, Kitty. I'm here. I've seen your mistakes. They're forgiven. I'll help you tell the truth, and I'll help you make better choices. Just let me.*

Kitty wept in the quiet of God's presence. She gathered up the wet tissues and considered her options. She would never again make a move without discussing it fully with her Heavenly Father.

She decided to go find her cousin, Logan. Kitty slipped the key into the ignition.

If she got lost on the way, she had Logan's new phone number. Thankfully, the *Silver Hammer Construction* card Geoff had given her rested somewhere in her purse. She rummaged around, pulled it out and entered the number on her cell phone.

Kitty remembered where the foundation had been poured for Logan and Becky's home in Maple Ridge. She was familiar with the streets that would take her there although she couldn't recall the house address. Logan and Becky's second anniversary party had been held in a small condo they occupied temporarily after their marriage. On the day of the party, they had excitedly shared their plans for building a house.

Now Kitty stared in awe toward the end of the street.

A West Coast home rose from the empty lot her cousin Logan had proudly shown her earlier. Logan had been her hero for as long as she'd known him —which was just a few years after the glorious day he had tracked her and her daddy down. Kitty's mother, Logan's Aunt Olivia, had left her and Daddy well before that, and she'd stuffed that bitterness deep inside and out of sight. Anyway, her daddy had loved her enough, and the Lord had loved her enough to keep her from thinking too many painful thoughts about her absent mother.

After he'd caught up with her, Logan had always looked out for her and had shown unfailing kindness for her as an irresponsible teen.

Kitty pulled up in her scruffy Chevy to the green lawn sloping from the front of a rock-trimmed dream house. She'd always wondered what kind of place Logan would build for Becky after they got married. Now she just wanted to sit here and breathe in the beauty that he had created.

An expert landscaper must have been employed to design the plantings and shrubbery that greeted her. Or maybe that was Logan's touch, too. He seemed to be a master at every trade he attempted.

A wide porch sheltered the double glass door entrance. Kitty closed the door of her car and tip-toed up the walk. Would anyone be home? How shocked would they be to see her? Holding her breath, she timidly rang the bell, almost relieved when the answer was slow in coming. Then quick steps neared the door, and someone swung it wide from inside.

Kitty was greeted by stunned silence. Becky's dark eyes widened in puzzlement before she squealed.

"Kit-tee!"

Becky gathered Kitty into her arms and rocked her back and forth in a hug that threatened to be endless. "Look at you!" She stepped back. "I can't believe it's you."

Neither could hold in the giggles. They twirled each other around the big entrance until they had to stop to brush tears from their eyes. Becky pulled Kitty into the living room and dragged her onto the sofa. "I'm so happy. I'm *so* glad it's really you. It's been nearly a year since you disappeared! How and where *have* you been?"

Kitty found her voice, laughing. "Oh here, there and everywhere."

"Well, after while you'll have to tell me where that was. Right now, we better have tea—or something. Had lunch yet?"

Becky must have seen the answer in Kitty's face. She stood, reached for Kitty's hand and led her to a bar seat in the kitchen. "I'll show you around after I've fed you."

The cozy comfort of Becky's big home filled Kitty with awe. On the house tour, her friend kept up a constant chatter with stories of building incidents, their plans for one day positioning a nursery, the colour choices they had to make. The high basement was to be finished later for a family area. Becky extolled the successes of *Silverhammer Construction*, Logan's company.

"How's UBC going?" Kitty asked. "Still chuggin' away at your studies?"

"Oh sure. Going great. I'm not trying to carry a full course, though. As Logan says, I've got lots of time to get my degree. It's a long commute to the campus, so two days a week keeps me busy enough at that. Anyway, I love taking care of our home."

Becky didn't even ask Kitty if she wanted to stay, simply commanded her to bring her things into the bedroom that was available for company. As Kitty set down her suitcase her eyes filled with tears. "I... don't know what to say. I can't just plop down here with no explanation."

"No, of course not," Becky teased. "But you can make your excuses later." She laughed as she flipped Kitty's blonde hair through her fingers. "And I mean all of them."

"Just relax and unpack while I prepare dinner," Becky said. "And don't come down till I call you."

BECKY KNEW LOGAN would be home at 6:30. Otherwise, he would have called to warn her. What fun it would be to surprise him with his cousin's presence. Becky was still reeling from the shock of seeing Kitty after these long months.

Kitty had attended their wedding over three years ago. Kitty was a dark brunette then, with straight hair either pulled up in a ponytail or allowed to hang down her back almost to her waistline. Once Becky had discovered that Kitty was Logan's cousin, she had always felt like Kitty's big sister.

At the two-year anniversary party, a year ago, Kitty had looked very little different from the teenager she was when they still worked together at Jen's Place. Kitty had always carried such a happy air of innocence about her. They were only three years apart.

Today she was still Kitty. But with her new hair colour and sophisticated cut she seemed to have grown up overnight. And something besides her hair had also changed; there was a new reticence about her. And yet Kitty did seem relieved to be welcomed into their home.

Becky was thrilled with the pleasure of receiving her unexpected guest. Yet, something tightened her heart with another concern. Kitty needed a friend.

"Hey, Sunshine! I'm home," a deep voice called from the mud room.

Becky heard Logan drop his tool belt at the back door and ran to throw herself into his arms. Today he had been working at the jobsite instead of the office and the scent of sweat and dirty man greeted her. It made her just as happy as his spicy office fragrance—maybe even more, so earthy and masculine.

She nuzzled his dusty nose with hers. "Hurry up with your shower. Dinner's in the dining room tonight. We have company."

"We do? Who?"

"You'll see."

Becky's signal to Kitty coincided nicely with Logan's arrival at the table. He turned his head at Becky's announcement, "Here she is—our long-lost photo-girl."

Kitty stepped carefully down the staircase, wearing a fresh lime-green shirt tucked into jeans, her blondehair hanging long and loose. She smiled hopefully. Logan watched her for thirty seconds, then with a whoop he met her half-way up the stairs with his arms extended. Becky sighed with satisfaction. Logan's cousin was back.

"Kitty. Kitty-cat! Thank God! High time you showed your tail around here. It was soon time to send out a search party. You practically dropped out of existence. So did your phone number!"

Kitty hung her head. "I know. That was bad of me." She looked up with a child-like remorse. "I won't do it again."

Becky's visit to the farmers' market earlier that day had readied her for dinner preparation. The three of them soon demolished almond-crusted chicken and a huge salad.

Before Becky got up to turn on the coffee, Logan reached to the sideboard for his Bible. He offered Kitty an explanatory smile as he opened it.

"Becca and I were just reading in the '*Book of Philippians*' yesterday," he said. "We usually do a short reading together after dinner. We left off in the fourth chapter. I'll start with reading verse four again.

"Rejoice in the Lord always. Again I will say, rejoice!"

KITTY WISHED SHE WERE back in the guest room.

Rejoice? Without a home, without a job, with months of wasted living to account for?

Becky came back to the table and sat down between them, taking Kitty's hand and giving it a loving squeeze.

"Let your gentleness be known to all men," Logan read. "The Lord is at hand."

Oh dear! Gentleness? Seems like a long time since I've had any of that.

"Be anxious for nothing, but in everything by prayer and supplication, with thanksgiving, let your requests be made known to God…"

But Lord, how can I not be anxious? You know I have been asking for Your help out of this mess I've made, but... You want me to be thankful about it?

"And the peace of God, which surpasses all understanding, will guard your hearts and minds through Christ Jesus."

Peace. Yes. It actually has been beyond my understanding how You've helped me lose some of that darkness I've felt around me. I guess that's what I've been sensing, desperately needing... peace, even in the middle of the opposite. Kitty had read those scriptures many times before, but tonight they burned her soul.

"Finally, brethren," Logan read, "whatever things are true, whatever things are noble, whatever things are just, whatever things are pure, whatever things are lovely, whatever things are of good report, if there is any virtue and if there is anything praiseworthy, meditate on these things..."

His voice continued on to the end of the chapter, but Kitty was mesmerized by the words that had been making her heart beat faster. *True, noble, just, pure, lovely.* Her thoughts had been far from these beautiful things for so long. There was no mention, either, in anything Logan read, of anger, hatred, or revenge.

Is this the message You've been wanting to speak to me, Lord? Could she conquer the disappointing weaknesses inside her? How was she going to make a fresh start?

The room was very quiet. Becky went back to the kitchen where the coffee had been perking, bringing back with it to the living room a tray of cream, organic honey and cups.

"This one's yours, Kit," Becky said, pointing out an elegant mug decorated with the words, "love, joy, peace." Kitty hugged it in her hands before allowing Becky to pour her coffee.

"Doctor it however you like," Becky said, pointing to the coffee table.

Seats were quietly chosen. Coasters were located. Cushions were adjusted. Legs were crossed and uncrossed.

The pregnant pause indicated to Kitty that it was time to explain herself. Besides, the moment felt right. Her whole being was surrounded by the warmth of these two she loved so much. God's Word had come alive again. True, noble, just, pure, lovely. Everything she had always wanted to be in spite of her recent failures. Right this moment, the word *true* spoke the loudest. She owed them her story. Just how much of it, she was not quite sure, having failed to communicate with them for over a year.

Logan sprawled in a recliner that must have had his invisible name on it. He stretched one long leg over the footrest and gazed solemnly at Kitty's profile.

"I don't suppose you've talked recently to Becky's mom, have you? Or Hank?"

Kitty turned, responding with a forlorn half-smile. "You know I haven't...."

He sat in quiet appraisal.

Kitty drew a deep breath. May as well be the one to broach what they all must be thinking about. She'd better do it before someone asked what had happened to her hair.

She took a deep breath. "So how do you like my hair?"

"It's gorgeous," said Becky. "It is."

Logan's lips smiled a one-sided little twist. "Can't disagree with that."

"What made you brave enough to do it?" Becky asked.

Kitty's face fell. She set down her coffee and breathed in.

"I did it for a man."

"Oh, Kitty." Becky's voice was soft and sad as she set down her coffee.

Then she brightened. "Well, I did something unexpected with my hair once, too. Cut it. Short. That was also for a man. Taught him a lesson, too." Logan ignored her teasing reference to an incident long past. Today Becky's dark hair had been allowed to grow again. A soft mantle of dark curls fell past her shoulders.

Logan seemed stern. "Was your experiment worth it, Kitty?"

Kitty's façade collapsed. Colour drained from her cheeks as a barely audible "No," escaped. "No, I like blonde, but I certainly don't believe it was worth it."

Kitty began to unburden her soul. Over her next three days of sporadic confessions, Becky and Logan wiped floods of her tears. They encircled her with their arms and their prayers and convinced her that life was not over.

It eased the heaviness of her story when the discussion turned to her trip back from Calgary.

"You what!" Logan snorted incredulously. "You got trapped on a ledge with a wolf?"

Now Kitty could giggle happily. When she revealed that the wolf's name was Yukon, everything fell into place.

Once they were able to stop laughing and digest her story, Kitty found the next more probing questions uncomfortable. The tingle in her cheeks rose from blush to burning. Her words choked her.

It was then Logan's demeanor took on an air of paternal gentleness.

"Geoff's expecting you back?"

"Yes."

"When?

Kitty could barely raise her eyes to Logan's teasing grin.

"I promised him I'd try for this weekend."

Logan raised his eyebrows. "Has Jennifer been filled in on this interesting story?"

Kitty turned from his probing eyes. "I'll be sharing it with her as soon as I can get to her place. Can't do it by phone or email."

"No. I wouldn't think so." Logan agreed, a serious tone in his voice, but there was a twinkle in his eyes.

SEVEN

YUKON COULD FEEL excitement in the air by the way her master's electricity spoke to her.

Yukon was happy with that. She was hoping they might be going to find Kitty again. She desperately wanted her back here on the mountain. It was just too wonderful that Kitty had been waiting for her on the ridge the other day. Yukon hoped she hadn't scared Kitty with her wild enthusiasm. She'd always felt deserted after her master left Kitty behind so long ago. To see her again, to hear that soft voice, to feel those arms around her neck sent familiar shivers through her whole body.

Kitty belonged to her and Geoff, especially now, since she'd returned so briefly to tease them with her presence. Besides, when she left, Kitty promised that she'd be back.

Geoff whistled and Yukon took one long, practiced leap into the truck box.

JENNIFER CAME RUNNING out of the house when she heard Geoff cut the engine. She threw a hug around his neck as he grabbed her and swung her with powerful arms.

"Hi, Ma." Emotion vibrated in his voice. He tried to rough up her cheeks with a beard too long and curly to have any bristle-power. "It's been quite a while. I love you just as much."

"Me too." She grabbed both his hands, pulling him halfway down the sidewalk. She dropped one hand and turned into the back yard, calling to her husband, "Hank, look who's here."

Yukon complained loudly from the open truck box.

"C'mon, Yukie," Geoff called. "It's okay." Yukon flew from the box and crashed at Jennifer's feet. The dog responded ecstatically to Jennifer's pats, but at Geoff's signal, quickly heeled beside his left leg.

Hank came from behind the workshop looking as pleased as Jennifer felt. "Hey, you ol' bushwhacker." He hurled his wiry five-foot eight frame at Geoff and caught him off-guard, nearly knocking him to the grass. Geoff regained his balance and braced his feet in defense. He whacked Hank with alternating fists to each of his shoulders. Hank sprang forward with a bear hug to the waist. Soon both men were clapping each other ferociously on the back, finishing their antics by grappling each other to the ground. Hank managed to land on top, probably with Geoff's giving way to allow it. They were, after all, separated by twenty years.

Jennifer and Yukon were used to these two. Yukon looked obediently bored. Jennifer laughed aloud, scratching behind the dog's pointed white ears.

"Hello yourself," Geoff roared. "Why haven't you grown some hair, you bald-headed baboon?"

Jennifer shook her head. "Will you two never grow up?" She hoped they never would, these two who could easily have been father and son -- although their silliness made them look more like brothers. Since Geoff had walked into Hank's Rustic Diner five years ago, when Jennifer had been working there as a server, she and Hank had been part of his life. Their mutual love for this young man overflowed their grateful hearts.

Geoff followed Hank as he sauntered through the back door of their home. Jennifer watched them, the smile in her heart warming her face. She'd had a hunch that Geoff would show up soon. It was about time for him to emerge from the boonies for some of Hank's cooking.

They sat outside on the back deck, chatting while Hank barbecued the buffalo burgers Geoff would be expecting.

"How's business at the diner?" Geoff asked. "Busy as ever, I suppose?"

"Even busier. Sometimes I actually have to go back to work, wear my chef's hat and fill my old spot. People just seem to keep hearing about our buffalo burgers and country cooking. They keep coming back for more. As it is they're often waiting in line so long I don't get to go home until close-up."

Hank was obviously proud that his Rustic Diner had become so firmly established, but he revealed his jesting as he backtracked. "Actually, the diner is well staffed, and really, I am rarely required on the premises unless I am so disposed. Even if you had not informed us you were coming, I would have been home grilling just for my Jennie and me." Hank grinned at his self-adopted son. "I am honoured to be cooking your burger tonight. We have been anticipating your arrival for some time."

"Are you sure you wouldn't like me to go clean up before we have this feast?" Geoff asked, ruffling the edges of his beard. "I'll have to get professional help for the haircut, but I can certainly get rid of this facial fur all by myself."

74

"Nah," Jennifer said, affection warm in her voice. "Let us admire you for a while first. You can try out our new guest room later."

"You're not going to let me stay in Hank's old quarters above the Diner?"

"Nope. Not this time. Now that our house is finished, we can keep you close by until bedtime. That way you can fill us in on your progress out on the mountain. Are you ready to move into that cabin yet?"

"Not a chance." Geoff pulled out his iPhone and flipped to some snapshots of the piled logs in the shelter of his wooded haven. His tent was pitched nearby. "Not much more to show you yet, though most of the logs are cut to length. It's about time to get them pulled together. I'd like to get to lock-up before winter."

While Geoff recounted stories of his progress, Hank stacked two hot buffalo burgers on Geoff's plate and set another platter beside the huge salad bowl in the middle of the table. He placed two burgers on the grass where Yukon lay, jaws drooling. "Here you go, girl. Glad you came to visit."

Hank took his place at the pine table. "Want a hand, out there on the mountain?" he asked. "The diner will be somewhat quieter once summer season has slowed down— maybe another week. Shouldering a few logs might be beneficial to me. You could use some help. Especially since Logan is so busy these days, he won't likely be available.

"…Sure…" Geoff cleared his throat, "Hank… That'd be great," he said. "I do have a bit more stuff to get ready, though. When do you think you might come?"

Hank laughed. "Oh, any suitable time, I presume. I am not planning to go to the ranch until early October—to celebrate Thanksgiving with the family. Jennie and I can hit the trail to the mountain most any time. We'll take the camper and intrude on your paradise for a few days if you don't mind. My trustworthy Suzie should be able to handle the diner for a short while when traffic slows down."

JENNIFER PUZZLED at Geoff's unusually long pause. "Yeah, maybe…"

She had expected an exuberant "Yeah!" at Hank's offer. What was keeping him so strangely silent? She studied the furry face for some explanation. His deep-set eyes were gazing into the fire pit. It wasn't sadness she saw. Not worry. Not… No… it was embarrassment. His cheeks were brighter than the distant flames should be colouring them. Geoff had something else on his mind. He looked like he knew something he wasn't telling them.

"Shall we eat?" Jennifer said.

Hank bowed his head and thanked the Lord in loud, grateful praises, both for the steaks and their much-loved visitor.

"Amen."

The food made a welcome diversion from the abandoned conversation. It would all come back into focus soon enough, Jennifer thought.

Geoff plied them with questions about the Rustic Diner, its staff, its organic menu, its appreciative patrons. He asked about the ranch back in Alberta where Hank's family raised buffalo and grew vegetables and kept a few hectares in organic oats and wheat. It was not difficult to engage Hank in his favourite subjects, including his praise of his darling Jennie and his praise to God "from Whom all blessings flow."

Jennifer wasn't sure what made it pop into her head. She broke in, "Geoff, you haven't by any chance heard anything of Kitty lately?"

Geoff looked up from his buffalo burger, startled in mid-bite.

Aha.

"Kitty almost dropped out of the world since her father's funeral," Jen said. "She visited after we moved in here, but when I tried to get in touch with her in Nanaimo last spring, she was no longer living on the island, hadn't even informed her pastor she was moving. Of course, it's highly unlikely that you would have heard, since you were working in Ontario during those days."

"Ah… well. Yes, I was. Then. At first. Not exactly… but"

His cheeks were telling on him. His expression was so unlike the Geoff they knew that Jennifer and Hank both put down their forks and examined him with quizzical smiles. Jennifer could read him like a book. She knew he had something to share.

"Okay, Geoff. When did you see her? Spill it."

Looking like a teenager coming in past curfew, Geoff sat up very straight in his chair and cleared his throat mightily.

"Couple of nights before last," he said. "But it wasn't my fault. Yukon found her."

Yukon perked up and came to stand beside her master. Geoff reached down and scratched the dog's ears absentmindedly.

Hank burst into a howl of laughter.

While she waited for Hank to be done, Jennifer's expression gave Geoff an eloquent go-ahead. *Tell the story, Geoff. We know there is one.*

Geoff reacted as though he had actually heard the words. Awkwardly he began trying to explain himself. "Hank, it wasn't exactly a joke to find her next to killing herself falling down the canyon below. I had no idea who Yukon had discovered. I didn't have a clue what this crazy blonde photographer was trying to do, all by herself on our mountain."

"Blonde?"

"Kitty didn't even look like herself. I didn't know who she was."

"But you did figure it out," declared Hank astutely.

"Well, sure. Eventually."

"You remembered at last how cute she was, right?"

Geoff protested. "Hank, you know I hardly remembered the girl from Jen's coffee shop, even if she was Logan's cousin. The only thing I had on my mind in those days—besides my new shepherd-cross puppy—was helping you two tie the knot on the same day Logan and Becky did. That was as much excitement as I could handle."

"Uh-huh. That was then. And this is now. Now you know who she is, correct?"

"Well, sure. But that doesn't mean—it doesn't tell me—I mean I don't..."

Jennifer slipped out of her chair and gave Geoff a little hug, then went to Hank, and for him added a kiss with her hug.

"Aw, Sweetie," she said. "Don't be so hard on him. I know he's a big boy, but can't you see he's just dying for some fatherly advice? I'll get the dishes. Some guy talk will do you both good. I'll bring dessert later."

Much later.

EIGHT

KITTY HIT THE ROAD AGAIN, ready to settle in for a long drive.

Today just after sunrise, she said goodbye to Logan and Becky, certain they were suspicious of the tremor in her voice when she reminded them that she had a standing invitation at Mount Mercy. Logan had laughed in his loving way, warned her not to get caught in the blackberry bushes or fall off another cliff, and told her to give Geoff his best.

Squeezed in Becky's tight hug, it had been hard to let go, but Geoff's mountain called.

Kitty took her place in the driver's seat, teary-eyed, and rolled down the window to wave good-bye.

Having been parked so long at Auntie Bee's, she suspected her Chevy needed service soon but was pretty sure it could be counted on for a few more miles —at least long enough to get her back to Geoff and his wild territory.

Every nerve sang inside her. If that's as far as her old car could take her, she really didn't care. The only thing in the world that concerned her today was getting home to Mount Mercy and Geoff and Yukon. Even if it were for just one more visit.

Home? How could she even presume to think of Geoff's mountain as home? Well, she couldn't help it, when that's how its every blade of grass, every spreading pine branch and every friendly little bush and flower had begun to call. The place to which she was returning felt like home. Geoff felt like home. The acceptance of it as truth shocked her.

Even if Geoff tired of her in a few hours, she had to get back to find out. He had, after all, asked her to return. Although, after he heard the rest of her story, it wouldn't surprise her if he just wished her a good life and said, "Nice knowing you."

The grey stretch of asphalt beckoned eastward. As Kitty drove, her soul found more freedom, as though the invisible bars of her cage had begun to disintegrate with an unexpected wave of a magician's hand. That magician was Geoff.

In her chest a memory quivered. She still saw the sad upturn of his lips behind his beard, the slow wave of his arm as she had pulled away. He wouldn't have acted like that when they met at Jen's Place so long ago. She had to find out if Geoff might actually learn to care about her. Did he see her today as any more than a child who knew how to make bannock?

Kitty paused briefly at a rest stop and thankfully devoured the sandwich Becky had insisted she take with her, then revived, drove on.

Hour by hour she wound upward into the higher altitudes, passing towns and villages familiar from last week. The spruce trees bordering the switchbacks on Highway Three called her name in Geoff's persuasive baritone. Her heartbeat quickened with every kilometre.

Her heart jumped as she recognized the Short Stop Motel where Geoff had sent her to be safe that night. She was very close to Geoff's cabin. Better grab a quick supper at the motel before reaching her destination.

Just fifteen minutes after leaving the motel she saw the gravel pull-off she was looking for. That was it! With her heart skittering like a bunny in the bushes, she veered off the highway in exactly the same place she'd stopped last time to think. Now she could think some more. And she did need to breathe. Her headlights shone eerily into the gloom.

Once Kitty regained her calm, she put Lizzy back into gear and moved upward, soon passing the place where she'd parked and made her near-fatal decision on the cliff-side. This time she wasn't afraid, even though it would soon be dusk. She'd follow the ruts up to Geoff's campsite. If he wasn't there, she would park and wait until he came back and found her.

A short time later, Kitty hoped she'd taken the right trail. Should it be this winding? Her foot clung to the accelerator, which seemed to require more pressure with each new curve. Had the road really been this steep?

The motor growled. She didn't remember on her first ride up the mountain in Geoff's truck hearing any sounds similar to the grinding that was coming from under Lizzy's hood. Could she have gotten off the trail? Or taken a wrong turn? There didn't seem to be any other choices as she pushed her tired rear-wheel drive up the increasing grade.

At the next curve the tires spun, and with one long groan the car stalled. The dash lights flashed their warning.

"Don't panic, Lizzy. We're going in the right direction."

Kitty shifted to neutral, eased off the brake and allowed the car to roll slowly backward to pause at the last level place on the rutted trail. She turned the key. It started. Then she pulled the gearshift into low and stomped determinedly on the accelerator.

"Don't give out on me now, Lizzy. The campsite can't be too far...." With all her might Kitty willed power into the vehicle as the tires grabbed and pulled forward.

For thirty more seconds.

Lizzy tried valiantly, spun out, and refused to move another inch.

Now what?

Kitty turned off the motor and dropped her head onto the steering wheel in disgust.

At the same moment, her eardrums were met by a plaintive yowl and excited barking. Startled, Kitty looked up through the windshield. Joy swept over her, then propelled her from the car where Yukon met her with a dance that would have become a leap were she not so well trained.

"Yukon." A deep voice from the clearing stopped the dog, now yelping her welcome at Kitty's feet. Kitty stretched out her hand to the grateful moaning, dropped to her knees and wound her arms around Yukon's soft neck. She lifted her eyes. In the distance Geoff stood watching them.

Geoff.

Looking like he had three years ago. Dark wavy hair. Deep-set eyes so blue they made the sky jealous. No bushy facial hair. Clean shaven strong chin. Broad shoulders draped in denim.

Long-gone memories of Jen's Place flooded back, and with them unbelievable shyness that whimpered and curled back into her belly. This was reality. This was her fresh start.

Thank. You. Lord.

Geoff just stood there. Had he too travelled back in time? He still wore jeans, and he carried an axe as though he had just been using it. His smile started slowly and spread like sunrise over his face. He set the axe against a tree trunk and held out his arms as Kitty slowly walked into them.

His hug was tight and short. His smile lingered.

"Kitty. I was afraid you might not come."

Kitty had not called or texted him to announce her arrival, she wasn't sure why.

"I guess I could have let you know I was coming. I wanted to surprise you...but not quite this way..." She made a grimace at the tired old car.

Geoff's lips tightened, but he couldn't hold in his laughter.

Kitty felt too embarrassed to join in. "Is it still okay for me to be here?"

He stood quietly appraising her for a long time, slowly shaking his head.

"Kitty, it's more than okay. Welcome to Mount Mercy. I'm thankful you got this far driving that relic. You are one brave lady. Yes, Hallelujah, you're here. I had to go back to Nobleton to clean up and get a real shower, but I've been counting every minute since I got back. So has Yukon."

Yukon stood beside her, wanting to lick her hand and knowing better. With her quiet obedience, the creamy-toned dog conveyed the message, "Yes, I believed you when you told me you'd be back."

Kitty wiggled her fingers, and Yukon's tongue licked her hand gratefully.

"We heard you coming," Geoff said. "I ran like a madman and almost beat Yukon down to the clearing. I knew a car could never make the climb. You need a 4x4 to get around this corner. Good driving." He patted Lizzy's fender. "I'm surprised the old gal made it this far. I can see we're going to have to work on a road as well as a cabin."

Kitty smiled contentedly. "Well, I actually had fun trying to get this far."

Geoff grinned at her. "You staying over? You won't be going any further tonight, will you?"

"We...ell...I don't suppose...."

He laughed. "You bring a pillow? You can have my tent. I've been wanting to try out the cabin floor since I got the boards laid."

Shyly Kitty confessed, "Well, I did bring my sleeping bag."

"Okay," Geoff said, "if you would give me your keys, I'll just back your car up a bit and park it out of the way." Kitty's car cooperated.

That done, he grabbed her suitcase and shouldered her sleeping bag. Kitty grabbed her pillow, and the three walked together up to the campsite.

KITTY WASN'T SURPRISED when Geoff hinted that he usually turned in early and rose with the dawn. She assured him she had eaten. They would reminisce a bit, drink a cup of cocoa and call it a day.

"I want to show you around tomorrow. We have lots of climbing to do, so you had better get a good rest. How does that sound to you?"

"Perfect."

"You up for a pre-dawn drive?"

Kitty made a pretend gulp and nodded her pleasure.

"Okay," he said. "Let's figure out where your bed is going to be then."

He gave her the choice of a ride to the Short Stop Motel or sleeping in his tent. After being assured that Geoff would be comfortable on a spare camping mattress, Kitty happily dragged her bedding into the one-man tent and planned to snuggle in for the night. Her heart had relaxed, and her fear was gone.

Thankful that tonight's reunion had been light-hearted, Kitty was not in a hurry to begin explanations to Geoff. Not yet. Logan and Becky would be praying for her, and she wanted to collect as much strength from those prayers as possible before Geoff started expecting answers to the questions he had begun to ask last time.

"Want to get a quick look at what I've been doing while I've been waiting for you to get back?"

Kitty nodded enthusiastically.

"Okay. Let's take a few minutes for that before we hit the sack. Just to give you an idea where things are at."

Kitty stared out into the shadows, shivery with delight.

"First, though," Geoff said, "let's grab a cup of hot chocolate to take along. It'll take only a minute on the gas burner."

He picked up a flashlight, and they carried their tin mugs as he led her toward the dusky log walls of the cabin. Kitty clung to his arm as they stepped up two risers.

Geoff proudly pointed out the already-completed cabin floor where he'd sleep tonight. The new planks felt smooth under her feet.

"I've decided to use a few things ready-made —like these floorboards." He swept the flashlight across the finished floor. "I'd've had a big job slicing those trees in half lengthwise —so I took the shortcut."

"Makes sense to me." Kitty said.

Log walls now firmly enclosed the frame that Kitty had glimpsed from a distance last week. Open spaces cut into the walls promised windows and doors to come. Supports for a deck stood in place, but a wide opening between the deck and the cabin walls needed explanation.

"I'm going to cheat there, too," Geoff said. "Sliding doors."

"Good plan." Kitty looked upward. The top of the cabin was still open to the darkening sky.

"But what if it rains tonight?" she asked.

"Not a problem. My truck has a water-proof cab. Don't even think about it."

Kitty felt only a moment of misgiving before trusting him when he said he'd be okay, rain or shine.

He turned from the log walls toward a side path that ran along the far side.

"Come on," he said to Kitty. Yukon bounded ahead of them. "You need an introduction to a very important amenity of civilization."

Just a few steps down the path, nestled around the corner in a pine grove stood a very small log building, barely wider than its plywood door, and twice as tall as it was square. He opened the door to the outhouse with a welcome flourish.

"Madame," he said. "For those important calls. No land line, but comfortable seating."

Kitty peeked shyly past him, correctly guessing that the open-air windows, placed in the walls just beneath the roof, must be one explanation why the fragrance in there was surprisingly pleasant. As Geoff swung the flashlight up and down and around the tiny building, Kitty saw that he had placed an essential-oil air freshener on the wall, as well as a hand sanitizer. A battery-operated lantern ready to be switched on, hung close to the door.

Kitty grinned her appreciation. "This place really is up to date, isn't it? Most versions I've seen elsewhere don't even come close."

"I'm glad you approve," Geoff said. He led the way back down toward the campsite. "It comes with an extra flashlight, in case you didn't bring one."

Kitty inhaled her relief. "Oh. no. I forgot about that!"

Geoff patted her arm. "Not to worry for a second. There's also one in the tent, in the pocket to the right of the door flap—just in case."

GEOFF MOVED HIS sleeping bag into the cabin while Kitty gratefully made her bed on the cot in the tent. He quickly returned, reached into a tent pocket on the side wall and pulled out his Bible.

"C'mon." He led the way back to their seats by the fire and opened to the Psalms. "For some reason I need the words of the Twenty-third Psalm. I'll read for us tonight.

You can read for us tomorrow." He grinned. "And you'd better still be here tomorrow night."

Kitty smiled in wonder. So he kept his Bible right beside him in the tent?

A sharp little shock of pain reminded Kitty she hadn't even thought to bring hers; it was still packed in the duffle bag left at Logan and Becky's. Come to think of it, her Bible had not been foremost in her mind for many months. The thought didn't so much make her feel guilty as it made her feel lonely. She'd missed so much comfort these past months ignoring God's loving messages to her.

After Geoff finished reading, he smiled as she glanced at him before turning toward the tent. He waved as Kitty stepped inside the tent flaps.

Kitty slipped between her blankets with the words he had read still caressing her ears, "Surely goodness and mercy shall follow me all the days of my life, and I will dwell in the house of the Lord forever."

NINE

KITTY'S EYES WERE STILL HEAVY as she rolled over in her sleeping bag the next morning and stretched languidly, wondering in the groggy recesses of her mind why she wasn't still asleep.

Birdsong? A faint melody, familiar, yet not quite recognizable, filtered into her wakening senses. It must have been part of a dream slipping away as she reached toward consciousness.

Was it a chipmunk outside the tent that signaled "new day?" Or was it the blended aroma of coffee and bacon in the crisp air that brought her fully awake? Either way, Yukon was already talking to her outside the tent as Kitty tossed her shirt and jeans back on, instant energy surging through her. She grabbed her hairbrush, pushed back the tent flaps, and stepped through the canvas door into a world touched by an indigo sky promising dawn. She stood tall, then drew into her delighted lungs the crispness of the pine-scented atmosphere.

In the distance, Geoff emerged from behind the cabin carrying a lantern and an armload of wood. He looked like he'd been awake for hours. He grinned at her.

"Good morning," he called. "I hope you slept well. You look fresh as a baby."

"You can't even tell what I look like," she said. "But yes. Best sleep I've had in months." Kitty bent at the waist and flung her mop of hair forward over her face. Silvery in the dawn, it fell almost to the pine needles around her boots. She made a vigorous downward sweep with her hairbrush.

It must be this fabulous mountain air. With a quick twist of her wrist and the help of a scrunchie, she flipped her hair into a high ponytail, ignoring the tendrils that refused to be captured.

"Breakfast is almost ready," Geoff called. "When we're done, I want to take you on the first phase of your tour. I know it's early, but there's a sun about to rise that will take your breath away."

"Something else was trying to take my breath away this morning as I was coming to life," she said. "I heard a sound... something like a little trickle of music from heaven. Were you whistling or anything like that?"

Geoff smiled self-consciously. "Maybe you heard my recorder. I've decided to teach myself to play an instrument. Since there's usually no one around to laugh but the squirrels, I decided to give it a shot. This morning I felt so lighthearted I had to go into the woods and join the birds. Hope it didn't disturb your sleep."

Kitty laughed. "I want some more of that disturbance as soon as you dare."

"Well first, I dare you to eat my apple oatmeal."

Geoff waved his arm toward the two surprisingly comfortable stumps beside the folding table and set the cinnamon in front of them.

As they ate, excitement skittered up and down her spine. Kitty could hardly wait for the sunrise Geoff had promised.

"I love this concoction," she declared, scraping the bottom of her tin bowl.

When they had made a quick finish of breakfast, Geoff spooned the deliberate leftovers into Yukon's dish to flavour some dry kibble. He swished the dishes in a blend of water from the storage tank and the water steaming in the teakettle. It was obvious he didn't need Kitty's help, but she'd watch and learn for another time.

He rinsed the last plate and turned it over the edge of the frying pan drying on the tray. He wrung out the dish cloth and hung it on the nearest branch. "Ready to head out?"

"As ready as that chipmunk I heard by the tent this morning." Kitty grabbed her denim jacket.

An ATV she hadn't noticed before sat next to the cabin in the silver-blue chill of pre-dawn, shrouded by the last minutes of grey night. Yukon had already found the front seat.

"Get in the back, Yukon," Geoff ordered. "Kitty gets the front seat today."

Geoff looked as pleased as a first grader on his way to Disneyland when he reached out his arm to boost Kitty up into the passenger side of the ATV. He clipped her into the seat belt and sprinted around to the driver's seat. Turning on the lights, he roared out of camp and onto the twisting trail that wound through the upper terrain of Mount Mercy.

Geoff could have been born in an ATV Kitty thought. In her experience, this bouncing back and forth, jarring and rolling, was a first. Breathtaking. Thrilling. She tightened her hold on the grab-bar as the four-wheeler flung her backwards on the first steep ascent. As he revved the motor to give the tires a grip in the rocky ruts of the road, he turned to catch her momentary spasm of terror. His boisterous laughter turned her concern into exhilaration.

"You okay?" Geoff's smirk faded.

"I'm good," she yelled back, loving his concern.

"You sure?"

She smiled, nodding, then shrieked with laughter as the ATV veered wildly toward the deep rut on the right. A leafy branch slapped her face.

"Sorry, Kit! This road is pretty narrow."

"Road?"

"Are you hurt?"

"Of course not. I didn't expect it to be this much fun though."

They scrabbled along for several minutes, and slowed down at the next wide curve that took them deeper into the trees.

"Look, Kitty. Up there to your left."

The Ranger growled to a crawl and Kitty squinted through the trees. All she could make out in the dense forest were more evergreens, the tips of their branches touched by the first glimmer of lavender rays. Geoff braked, switching off the motor.

He came to the passenger side and reached out his arm. "Out you go. See what you can see."

"What am I looking for?"

Geoff reached behind her head and gently placed his hands on either side, tilting her face upward.

"Look way up into that tall stand of pines. Check the middle of the tallest ponderosa paired with the spruce beside it. Maybe ten metres. See anything unusual?"

She must be missing something. Tallest pine. What was a ponderosa? Check the middle of it. What should she be looking for? A bird? An animal? All she could make out were more branches.

Then a ray of dawn attempted to trickle through.

"Yes! I do see something now. Hiding between the branches. It's sort of grey-looking. Kinda wide." Her excitement mounted. Geoff laughed softly. Kitty squirmed, turned her feet, ready to follow. As soon as her toe reached a pine-needle-covered slope before them, Geoff was there to take her arm.

He led her a few yards under the green canopy before he stopped beside a broad tree trunk fitted with skinny log steps, spiked to lead upwards into its branches.

"I get it," Kitty said. "I'll bet there's a tree house up there. Can we go up?"

Geoff nodded, clearly pleased. Kitty grabbed a rung and lightly made her way upward toward the opening in the log platform above her head.

Kitty giggled with delight as she poked her head through the hole, hearing Geoff's chuckle behind her. She slithered through the opening and onto the platform barely visible in the last moments of grey night. Dry log walls about four feet high surrounded a roughly square log floor, transporting her to a world of young imaginations.

This ancient fortress could only have been built by teens or children-at-heart.

Peek-a-boo spaces. A scattering of tin utensils. A tarp, that might once have served as a roof, crumpled against the far wall. Two big stumps toppled like overturned chairs. Some worn garden tools lying on the floor. A low pile of dry pine boughs dumped in the corner, higgilty-piggilty like everything else on the floor.

Above the log walls, daylight was beginning to penetrate the pines surrounding their hideout. Kitty turned wondering eyes on Geoff.

His expression was triumphant. "Your cousin and his brother built this when they were only fourteen- or fifteen-year-old kids. How do you like it?"

"My cousin Logan built this?"

"None other. He told me his dad got them started on it."

Kitty breathed in with deep awe. She closed her eyes as a dreamy smile played on her lips.

"No wonder I love him so much. He's always been the same darling carpenter. And so adventurous."

"Logan is pretty special, isn't he?"

"One of a kind," she said as she investigated the tree house.

"And," Geoff said, "he's also taught me everything I know about building with wood. I know a few things he doesn't, but my great carpentry skills I've learned from him."

Geoff turned toward the surrounding treetops. Kitty followed the direction of his gaze over the hide-out walls and gasped. On the horizon where the evergreens parted, sun had broken over yet another distant mountain range. The valley sang with color, almost as though this was the very spot God Himself had designed the rainbow.

A breathy "Ooh…" escaped her lips. She stood silently enthralled for several minutes. Geoff did not break her spell. Her soul swelled with praise to the One Who made it all.

"What does this do to you, Geoff?"

"Makes me know from deep down inside that God is in control—of everything I give Him—no matter what."

"Yeah," she said. "I can see why."

"I didn't always feel that way," Geoff said. "When my mom died, I lost what little faith I'd had, until Hank and Jennifer became my new family. Now I've learned to believe in His love again."

Kitty turned to face him. "It somehow feels more true up here, doesn't it?"

He met her eyes with blue intensity. "It gives me great hope."

A little shiver of anticipation washed over her. She didn't dare ask him what particular "great hope" he meant. Could this hope have anything to do with her?

Silently they returned to the ATV.

As they bounced back toward the campsite, Geoff's brow furrowed as if deep concentration had claimed his thoughts. He paid more attention to the ruts than he had on the way up. He seemed so focused he must have something very serious on his mind. What was he thinking about? Why was he so quiet? He stayed in that same mood all the way back to the parking spot in the cabin clearing.

By the time Kitty got her curiosity under control, Geoff was back to normal and automatically picking up kindling twigs in the surrounding brush.

"Did the ride wear you out too much for a walk this afternoon?" he asked her as she trailed behind him.

"Never! Especially if it will be as much fun as seeing the tree house." Her excitement was still high. "Where do you have in mind? I'm up for it." She picked up a small armload of twigs to match his. "Where are we going?"

"Like I said, for a long walk." The mystery in his voice told Kitty he was planning another surprise. "Let's put the kindling over here ready for tonight."

They quickly finished a lunch of cheese, crackers and a shared can of beans.

Kitty felt fresh energy skittering through her as she tried to be helpful putting things away. Geoff grinned at her.

"We'd better take some food with us, too," he said. "We're likely to get hot and hungry again before we get back."

"You *are* being cagey, aren't you?" Kitty accused.

"Oh, by the way," Geoff added, "you'd better grab your swimsuit."

Kitty looked up in surprise. "But I don't have a swimsuit with me. I left it in my storage trunk at Logan and Becky's."

He grinned. "Well, you better figure out how to make do."

Her eyes flashed him a suspicious side-wise glance that made him laugh.

"No, sweet lady, I won't be spying on you, and we won't go skinny-dipping, either. Besides, you've got Yukon."

Fire flamed in her cheeks, and she dropped her head.

"Why don't you just grab a pair of shorts and another T-shirt. I brought an extra towel. You'll love it up there, I promise. And I'll make us a couple of sandwiches."

Kitty scooted into the tent and changed into shorts, then stuffed another pair and a T-shirt into her backpack, along with her sunscreen. Maybe Geoff had some mosquito spray. She felt as light-footed as a kitten.

ot be disclosed.

Kitty was glad Geoff had left his noon-day blue funk behind him. She worried that he might have begun thinking about the questions he had implied last week. As in, why Venecia? The subject was bound to come up sooner or later, but the longer she could postpone it, the easier it would be to face her emotions. At least, she hoped that would be the case, then shoved it out of mind. No need to concern herself with the answers just yet.

Just as Geoff had assured her, Kitty did love it up here. Loved getting here, too, stumbling around the hummocks and dips and over the branches and broken logs hidden in the scrub brush. Geoff led the way following a faint animal trail and continued to encourage. The trip wasn't as long as she'd expected, but it did veer off the logging road enough to confuse her sense of direction. And the trail rose upward so quickly her shirt was soon damp with exertion. Was the sun hotter up here?

Yukon bounded ahead. The dog knew where they were headed.

Geoff paused mid-step, his face alight. "Listen."

A faint trickle sounded through the trees. It grew louder as Kitty stepped cautiously forward. Around the last bend its origin was clear. It was the sound of rushing water.

"You're hearing it now, Kit. 'The invitation of Mercy Falls'."

The breeze carrying the splashing music of the falls already felt cooler. Yukon took off at a lope, and Geoff took Kitty's hand as he hurried after the dog. Kitty's excitement mounted as she imagined the falls beyond the clusters of evergreens and the scatterings of bushes thick on the rising mountainside. Still clutching her hand, Geoff tugged her toward the top of the incline and paused. The narrow river rushed through the gully a few feet below them.

The emptiness and the wildness thrilled through her. How much she needed this, after all her undesirable urban experiences. Kitty swept her eyes in every direction, feeling secluded by shadows and trees, by the rushing echo of the river, and the promise of the new day. Awed silence stilled her.

Some ten metres higher up through the cleft in the mountainside, a restless waterfall tumbled to the base of the rocks and cascaded into the churning water. Yukon let out a demanding bark.

"Okay, girl. Go." She bounded down the slope and into the water with reckless joy.

Kitty stopped and stared upwards in awe. The view of the falls was magical.

"So this is Mercy Falls."

"One step of them."

"You mean there's another?"

"There is an 'upper' Mercy Falls, but it's so high up and so far away I haven't been there myself —yet. I caught a bare glimpse of it when I first explored the mountain, but it's not visible from here. This 'lower' falls is what we usually call Mercy Falls. Yukon and I, we love it. You will too."

Geoff dropped his backpack and slipped off his T-shirt. He smiled at Kitty and pointed her to the blackberry bushes edging the stream.

"It's going to be ver-ry refreshing," he said. "But I think you'll enjoy it. Yukon and I will be busy if you want to change shirts. Come when you're ready."

Kitty ducked behind the bushes, slipped out of her runners and changed her top for the one she'd swim in. This was going to be fun.

Geoff's feet were already wet when he reached out his arm to her. She took his hand and carefully stepped down the bank, squeaking in alarm as she dipped her toe into the area of quieter water along the shore. As Yukon paddled toward her, Kitty threw herself into the deeper water, caught the dog's neck. and they both submerged in the icy pool.

She surfaced with spluttering laughter, pushing her long ponytail out of her eyes. Certain Geoff didn't know she was a fish in the water, Kitty caught his foot and pulled him into the swirling stream. When his head bobbed up, she pushed him down again. He grabbed her arms and pinned them to her side.

"Naughty, naughty mermaid! You are in trouble."

Kitty wrenched herself free and began long strokes toward the falls as Geoff and Yukon followed. None of them stayed in very long though. The glacier-fed stream was not lake temperature.

"The towels are on the blanket over there." He pointed to a sunny spot on the grassy bank. "Go ahead and warm up. I'm coming."

Yukon, having had a wild shake a little too close to Kitty, knew better than to claim a place just yet.

"Yukon! Let me dry off!"

Geoff swam a couple more laps between the pool and the falls and then joined Kitty on the blanket.

Kitty wrung the water from her ponytail as well as she could, then loosened it and combed her hair free to dry in the sun. Geoff's chest looked bronzed and muscular. He appeared joyously more relaxed than he had earlier.

Yukon put her nose on the edge of the tartan blanket with pleading amber eyes that gratefully responded to Geoff's gentle pat.

"Good girl, Yukon."

Geoff pulled out the empty tin cups from his backpack and set them down on the blanket. He took several steps forward, upstream. Grabbing a branch for support, he leaned over the flow and caught the cold water in the canteen he'd brought.

He passed it to Kitty. "Like to fill our cups?"

He dug into the pack for cheese sandwiches, apples, cookies, crackers, and more cheese.

Enough food for a family. Which they were, of course; Yukon was a hungry family member, too.

As she ate, Kitty's gaze drifted magnetically upward toward the cascade of water continuing its playful dance downstream. She found it hard to pull her eyes away from this river that had tumbled for generations.

"Apparently," Geoff said between bites, "one of Logan's distant relatives nearly drowned in this river when he was just a little kid. He'd been warned of the risks of being up there alone, but the fearless eight or nine year old didn't pay attention. He got too close to the call of the water and was pulled in. The river had about worn him out as he clung to a weakening branch. Story has it that he was saved by a wolf that snugged him by his shorts back to the shore. Some versions say it was a cougar or bear." He paused. "Could you believe that, Kitty?"

Intrigued, Kitty took her time before saying slowly, "I think I could."

Geoff nodded. "Yeah. I think maybe I could too. I like to pretend it's true, anyway. We know the ravens fed Elijah. And the book of Revelation tells us that someday the lion will lay down with the lamb. Why not now? Strange stories have been told about animals before this."

Thoughtfulness descended over them as they quietly enjoyed the sandwiches. The white noise of the stream calmed her exuberant mood. Geoff pulled three apples from the lunch bag, as well as a ziplock sack of chocolate-covered nuts.

Kitty bit into the apple, savouring its crispness as she looked up beyond the falls, high into the distance. The mountainside rose in majestic sweeps of rock and color. Was this, then, all an important part of Mount Mercy? A fluffy white cloud hovered near the peak.

As though reading her mind, Geoff said, "You're looking at the top of Mount Mercy. Folk tales have it that God lives up there. What do you think?" He turned to her. Kitty grinned at the twinkle she saw in his eyes, laughed lightly.

"Well, of course He lives up there. Doesn't God live everywhere? He must be up there, too. Just like He is here—with us, right now." She turned questioning eyes to Geoff.

"Yes," he said. "I love the wilderness, just like Logan's parents and grandparents did. I can't help but feel closer to God smack in the middle of His creation than anywhere else. I especially love the mountains. This one, in particular."

Geoff stood up and turned in a semicircle from east to west. "It reminds me of the mountain Moses climbed. I don't suppose I'll live here all twelve months of the year—but I would be happy to. Whoever named it Mount Mercy must have heard it from heaven. I can't help but feel myself being merciful up here—just because God Himself is so merciful to me. It's in the sun that shines. In the breeze that's blowing.

"Even when I use my rifle, I pray that God will make it merciful to the animals He has provided for our food. One-shot mercy, clean and quick, and our grateful thanks."

The sacredness in his words made Kitty shivery. She nodded, enthralled.

"There's lots more folk tales about this mountain." Geoff said. "Funny how they can raise faith inside a person."

"Tell me." She settled back on her elbows.

"One tale is about a young woman, grief stricken when her lover dies in battle. She climbs way up to that mountain peak you're looking at. Folklore has it that she planned to throw herself off the highest cliff into the river below.

"Then we're told she heard a clear 'No!'—from the cloud. 'Do not cut your life short. I gave it to you. I made you. You are mine. Go back down that mountain. Take My hand, and I will walk with you through all your valleys.'"

Merciful, yes.

Geoff paused. If there was more to the story, he didn't say. Kitty could not take her eyes away from the mountain top. Where God had shown His mercy. Where He had stopped a foolish girl from doing something crazy.

TEN

IN THE LONG PAUSE, sadness trickled into Kitty's mood.

"You warm enough, Kitty?" Geoff threw Yukon a third sandwich. "The swim didn't chill you too much, did it?" His brow wrinkled with concern.

Kitty tried to smile at him. "The swim was beyond wonderful. So is this place. I love it. Thank you for bringing me here."

"You seem kinda quiet…"

A tendril of hair fell over her cheek. She brushed it away to hide the tear that had escaped.

"It's just… I wish…"

"You wish…"

"I wish it was as easy to wash away the past from the inside as it is to wash away the dirt that sticks to the outside."

"Kit-tee." Geoff's smile collapsed in empathy. He leaned toward her. "We've all got a past. A past that God has thrown into the sea of His forgetfulness. And, like my pastor once said, God has also posted a sign that says, 'No fishing.' I don't have to remind you of that. Besides, you have no past to compare with mine. You must know that."

Kitty smiled, as brightly as she could at the moment. "Let's not talk about it, 'kay?" She stood up. "So they called this waterfall Mercy Falls…?"

"Yes. No one seems to know where the name came from. Maybe it had something to do with the wolf story.

Maybe it just matches the name of the mountain. It's been known by that name forever. But I like it. Don't you?"

"I do. Just what I desperately need—God's mercy."

"What *we* need," Geoff confirmed. "Would you like to head out then? We'll take another route going back."

"Sure." Kitty slipped behind the blackberry bushes and changed back into her dry clothes. The sunshine had almost dried her hair—and was improving her mood, as well.

She patted Yukon's head. "You're nearly dry too, girl,"

Geoff rolled up the blanket and put it back in his pack. He collected the small amount of trash from their lunch and added that to his pack. He grabbed Kitty's backpack and slung it over his shoulder with his own.

With a pretense of annoyance, Kitty claimed her backpack from his shoulder and strode ahead. Geoff grinned. "Better be sure you know which way to go."

She stopped, made a face at him, and waited. He laughed and took the lead.

They followed the natural curve of the path. Kitty, reoriented, trailed behind on her own as Geoff tramped ahead, his stride purposeful.

She had just caught a distant glimpse through the trees of the cabin walls and campsite to which they were returning when Geoff said, "Let's take a break."

With no advanced warning a sharp premonition struck. This break meant more than a drink of water. Confession time had arrived.

Yukon brushed against her legs and licked her hand.

"THIS IS CLOSE to another of my great thinking spots," Geoff said. "There's a little ledge right over this knoll where Yukon and I often sun ourselves." He took her hand and led her to a natural seat at the edge of the gully.

Kitty let him help her slip out of her backpack. He pulled the blanket from his pack and spread it on the grass. "There's water in the canteen if you like." The thermos still held a small amount of coffee. Geoff poured the last two half-cups.

He plunked himself on the moss beside the blanket. The height and muscle of him sitting tall and relaxed made her feel smaller than usual. Yukon curled up at Kitty's other side as they drank their coffee in silence.

Geoff was through with postponement. Kitty realized with a lurch that this interrogation promised to be five times as difficult as she had anticipated.

She'd brushed off the foreboding reality of her unspoken words.

His steely eyes bored into hers. "Kitty, are you ready to share your story with me? I know you want to, so why not just tell me why you look so sad?"

Kitty took a huge gulp of mountain air and tried to begin. She choked and swallowed. Then choked again. Where to start? She considered Geoff's quizzical smile when he had noticed the mutilated brief case in her car.

"How come you changed your name?" he asked. "I'd sure like to hear how my sweet Kitty Sampson turned into Venecia Vale." Tenderness tempered his curiosity, his urging voice more gentle than his demanding eyes. She studied her feet, unable to stop the trembling of her lips.

"Kitty, it wasn't your idea, was it?"

Kitty shook her head, biting her lower lip, looked up at him, trying to speak, before looking away again.

"Did someone tell you to change your name?" She nodded. "Why?"

"He didn't like it." The words sounded harsh to her ears, forced from her with sheer effort.

"Didn't like it! Kitty is an adorable name. More kittenish, even, than kitten. And I seem to remember your real name was majestic. I can't remember what you told us that day... What...."

"Keturah. It's a Bible name, and he laughed at me."

"Keturah." Geoff breathed the name like a blessing, the syllables soft and reverent. "Keturah is a name filled with the precious fragrance of God."

Kitty snorted. "Right. I can still hear him saying in disbelief, 'Keturah Sampson! You must be kidding? We can't have such a magnificent photographer sound like a little Metis mouse, now can we?' And I never even corrected him to say I was proud of my Metis heritage!"

GEOFF'S INDRAWN BREATH was the roar of a lion. Rage rose up inside him, and he clamped his jaws over his words—words that had not reached even his thoughts for years.

He leaped up, turned his back on Kitty and faced the distant mountainside with raised head while his clenched fists cut into his palms. He stayed silent for long, gulping breaths until he could replace his smile and turn back to her worried face.

"Shall I beat him up?"

Kitty laughed nervously even as relief broke over her face. "He's not worth the effort."

"But he treated you like... like..."

"A bug? Yes, he did. And I let him. When I couldn't hold in the tears, he turned on the charm and told me how wonderful I was and convinced me I would love being Venecia Vale. What makes me so furious now is that back then I allowed him to treat me like that. A mouse.

I believed him. I let him do it. I deserved what I got."

"No way!" Geoff bellowed. He grabbed Kitty's hand and lifted her to her feet. "C'mon. This is enough for now. Let's head home."

"*Home.* I like that," she said.

He threw on his own backpack, slung Kitty's over his arm, and turned toward the shortest route to the cabin. Painful though it had been for both of them, Kitty's heart had opened. It was a start.

Following behind him, Kitty spoke hesitantly. "He did have me brainwashed though. I thought for a while he was right. It actually did make me feel a little like royalty when he started taking me to fancy places and acting like I was special to him. Presents, clothes, stuff to make me beautiful for his personal backdrop. I never even questioned where he got his money from."

"Stop, Kitty." Geoff whirled toward her. "I suppose he wanted you blonde, too?"

She dragged her feet and leaned against a handy tree trunk.

Kitty looked embarrassed as she tried to stifle a nervous giggle, pursing her lips before her response. "We...ell, no. That was actually my own idea. I wanted to

shock him—blow him away with my new confidence. So…
I got brave and surprised us both. Was that awful?"

Geoff could not hold in his chuckle. This was a relief.
At least she had a little of her own spunk left after this jerk
had stomped on her. He reached for her hand and slipped his
fingers through hers to urge her thoughts forward.

"Kitty, my dear, you are something else. You surprise
me at every turn. I'm kinda lonely for that original brunette
I knew, but I certainly understand why you would decide to
go blonde. Whatever made you think you needed that
klunker to get ahead? You were a great photographer when
you were just seventeen—a natural. What'd you want him
around for?"

"I don't know," she said in a small voice.

As they reached the campsite, Geoff set the backpacks
on the cabin floor.

He picked up the armload of kindling they had
gathered earlier. Kitty followed him to the fire pit.

"I wasn't using my brains," she said as she turned her
face toward the distant trees. "That's why I let Lance tell me
what to do. And I wasn't listening to the whisper of the Holy
Spirit in my heart. I just let myself feel helpless and
insignificant. When I saw what looked like admiration in his
eyes as I photographed one of the customers at Jimmy's
place, I was flattered. I forgot who I was—God's
daughter—and...."

Geoff dropped the kindling he was still holding.
Furrows deepened between his brows.

Kitty took another breath. "When he said, 'You are
amazingly talented,' I was smitten. He noticed me. He made
me feel important—for all of a few weeks—and I was

hooked. I just knew my success lay with him. I actually believed it was my talent he was interested in."

"And then…" Geoff turned from the fire pit and stood to look at her.

"Let's make this story as short as possible. I decided that my hobby of photography didn't need any more formal training. I could succeed with Lance's help in setting up my shoots. He was no artist, certainly not a photographer, but he somehow knew where to sell my photos. I quit my great job at Jimmy's Family Cafe and…"

"Then…"

Kitty drew a huge sigh. "First, he humoured me. He loved my customer shots on Jimmy's walls. Then he took me to his studio and began to direct the shots. Soon I was doing 'folk variety'. Then I was doing 'art' shots for him—starting with nursing mothers. Pure sweetness, right? Then rear-view nudity. Then tasteless six-packs …" Her voice broke and the tears began to trickle down her cheeks.

Geoff felt pinpricks of denial rolling up and down his spine. This couldn't have happened to Kitty. It must have been a nightmare. She couldn't….

Get a grip, dude. She isn't enjoying this, you know.

Geoff wanted to hug the hurt from her small frame. He wanted to hold her with the ferocity of one of those mother bears roaming this mountain. What he wanted to do this jerk who had absconded with her innocence had no words. Instead, he patted her shoulder, encouraging her to continue the catharsis of confession.

Kitty wiped her eyes with the back of her hand and fiercely continued. "Lance bought tickets for a late afternoon flight to Calgary for some aristocratic photo-op he'd been talking about. I felt quite upper-class as we drove from the airport in the rented car to our fancy hotel.

"I gradually discovered his plan was to get me to shoot porn. I still can't believe I went along with it as far as I did. I'm so ashamed I could die. Logan and Becky prayed and prayed for me, but it won't leave. I'm dirty."

Geoff grabbed her arms and shook her. "Kitty, it's all over. By God's mercy, you're done with it. God has made you clean. I knew that when I saw your briefcase. You struck her from your life. Venecia Vale is no more. You can forget her."

"I can't. I can't!" she wailed.

"Yes. You. Can. Starting right now." He led the way back to camp.

But even with Geoff's certainty, supper was a quiet occasion.

Geoff hugged her, gently. "Thank you, Kitty, for today." His voice was husky and tenderly dark. "I'm so proud of you. That was difficult for both of us, but I know we'll feel lots better tomorrow. I'm asking God's Spirit to heal us, totally. Tomorrow is a new day and we'll be new, too. You'll see."

Geoff sat in silence long after Kitty had zipped up the tent flaps and said "good night." He communed with his spirit; he talked to God. The assurance that Holy Spirit spoke back gave him calm and allowed his hope to renew its certainty. The love in his heart for Kitty tonight was more real than the deluge of unpredictable emotion he had experienced last week.

Today's reassurance of his feelings was simply a quiet reminder. Self-control washed over him with waves of gentle warning. Kitty needed to remember who she had been and that she was still the same Kitty.

Slow down. Don't move so fast. Take the time you need to get to know each other.

Geoff dialed Hank's number. Maybe it was a good idea, after all, to invite him up here to help. Help with more than hoisting joists.

ELEVEN

GEOFF HAD TALKED to God long into the night. Heavenly comfort brought him nearly back to normal. This was another day made by the Lord, and he didn't intend to waste a moment longer in regret. Let the sun rise.

He lifted the corner of the tent flap and let Yukon notify Kitty that it was time to get up.

Geoff took his time preparing flaxseed waffles and eggs over-easy. Coffee was hot and ready when Kitty emerged from the tent, giggling at Yukon's antics and rubbing her eyes.

The walk he had promised for today should not be physically demanding. His plan was for friendly communication.

"How did you sleep last night?" he asked.

"No nightmares," Kitty said. "But I did dream about that girl on the mountain peak. I thought I was her, and then I woke up. To a wet nose stuck in my ear." She reached out and scratched Yukon's neck. The dog gave a satisfied "woof."

Geoff wasn't sure if she was just pulling his leg.

They were still sipping the last of the coffee when he reached for his Bible. "You want to read for us this morning?" he asked her. "We missed it last night, didn't we?"

Kitty took the Bible as though not sure what to do with it. He hadn't intended to embarrass her.

"It belonged to my mom," he said. "She had other versions around the house, too, like the *NIV* and the *New*

King James, but she told me she liked this old *King James* version best. I didn't know the difference then." He smiled ruefully. "I didn't read it for years. My mom died when I was still in my teens—and I still don't like to let it very far out of my sight…" His voice was fading back into memory. "I read it now though," he confirmed, "since I've discovered the truth in it. It's always in my truck, no matter where I am."

Kitty fingered the worn leather reverently. "It's beautiful," she said. "It's old, isn't it? … Older than the one my daddy gave me." She looked suddenly embarrassed. "I always seem to forget to bring mine with me."

Geoff let that go.

"Want me to pick something?" he asked. Kitty hastily handed him the Bible.

"These last few weeks I've been mostly into the Psalms," he said. "That King David was such a normal guy. He yelled at God and pleaded with Him just as we all do. David actually did worse things than I've ever thought of, and yet God called Him His friend."

Geoff flipped a few pages near the middle of the Bible and placed it back into Kitty's hands. "Here," he said. "Psalm 103 starts with 'Bless the Lord, O my soul, and all that is within me bless His holy name.' How about you start here?"

Kitty re-read the first verse and continued until she came to verse 8, "The Lord is merciful and gracious, slow to anger and plenteous in mercy…" Her voice slowed as she appeared to digest the words. "He hath not dealt with us after our sins, nor rewarded us according to our iniquities."

She took a deep breath, then continued, "For as the heaven is high above the earth, so great is His mercy toward them that fear Him. As far as the east is from the west, so far hath He removed our transgressions from us." Kitty glanced up at Geoff, her eyes holding unshed tears. "Look how many 'mercies' there are in this chapter."

"Yes. The words, 'His mercy endures forever' are written in the Book of Psalms so many times I stopped counting the repetitions."

She choked as her voice faded. "As a father pities his children, so the Lord pities those who fear Him."

A tear trickled down her nose. "Does that mean I should be afraid of Him?"

Geoff smiled benevolently. "You already know what it means, Kitty. To me, it means His love and His authority are exactly like those of the kindest Father we can ever hope to have."

Kitty closed the Bible, stood slowly, and handed it to him. "I'll do the cleanup this time," she said, still appearing lost in thought.

"Sure," he teased, "as long as you don't get in my way while I make the sandwiches for lunch."

He put the Bible in his truck and returned to the kitchen area and began spreading butter on slices of sourdough bread.

"This is fun," Kitty said.

"Ham and Jarlsberg cheese today," Geoff announced as he tucked their picnic lunch into his backpack. "Doubt if we'll need anything more this time than I can fit into my backpack."

Kitty skipped ahead of him, following Yukon's waving tail.

"This way, Yukon," Geoff called.

When Kitty giggled and caught up, he said, "Today we'll take a different direction. I want to show you where the rest of the timber for the cabin is going to come from. It's not very far. There's a nice little spring on the way where I get my water supply. We can have a water break there. It'll be a nice place to stop for our lunch on our way back, too."

Yukon bounded enthusiastically ahead of them, chasing squirrels and other creatures that challenged her from the shadows.

By the time Geoff set his backpack on the grass beside the promised spring, they were both thirsty. Geoff reached into the backpack for two tin cups, then filled them directly at the glittering mini waterfall. He passed Kitty a cup, watching her expression.

"Oh!" she gasped. "This tastes like it came straight from heaven with ice in it!"

"I've always thought that, too," Geoff said. "There is no water to compare with a mountain spring. This is another of my favourite places to relax and let God heal me."

"Maybe it can fix me, too." Kitty said after she swallowed her last sip.

"I know what can fix you, little Kitten," he teased. "A couple of counsellors."

Kitty sent him a blank stare. "You think I need some counselling, then?"

"Both of them."

As he grinned, she got it.

"Hank and Jennifer! They're coming here!"

He nodded, and Kitty lunged into his arms, squealing as she hugged him. "Yay! Hank and Jen are coming! How long have you known this?"

"Hank offered to help with the cabin the other day, and I let him know last night we were ready for him. Not sure when they'll get here, but I know they can hardly wait to see you."

A shadow flickering momentarily over her face made his thoughts pause. Then she smiled. He wondered what secrets she might be longing to share with Hank and Jennifer.

"Time to roll," he said. "Another hidden treasure on Mount Mercy awaits your viewing before we pull out our sandwiches."

Five minutes further up the trail a clearing opened to reveal a huge pile of logs mostly hidden by the brush that had grown up and over it.

"This," Geoff said proudly, "is the stash of logs that's been drying for aeons, just waiting for our cabin."

KITTY STARED OPEN-MOUTHED. She hadn't known what to expect. This stack of lumber was impressive.

"Look at the length of these," Geoff said, placing his foot on an old-growth log that had to be at least twenty feet long. "I counted the rings. This one's a hundred years old. Some of these giants are easily twenty inches at the base. I have a special use for every one of them—even these three and four-inch ones. The smaller logs will be mostly for the roof and the loft, the bigger ones for posts and beams.

"Tamarack," he said, pointing to the lower rows of the stack. "They're hardier and more long-lasting than some of the others. There's alder in here, too, for the cabinets. And cedar —so I can cut my own shingles."

Kitty leaned against a sturdy tree.

"I love their ashy color," They reminded her of the platinum of Grama-ma Nora's treasured old sugar bowl.

"They get this grey sheen from being stacked up here for so many years."

He pushed through the brush to the other side of the stack. "This pile was once bigger and taller than it is now. The missing logs are already part of the cabin."

"Did you and Logan cut these?"

Geoff chuckled. "No. Logan and his dad did—a long time ago. Logs need to be seasoned for a year or more; these got the royal treatment. They've been here for close to ten years."

"Incredible," Kitty said. "I bet there's a fascinating story here."

"Logan's Dad had plans for a cabin when the kids were little, but the logs didn't get cut till Logan was in his teens. And they haven't been used until this year. We'll have to bring a few more down to camp before we're finished— though there's still a big stack behind the cabin." He waited, as if he expected Kitty to be impressed.

She was. She pursed her lips and nodded. "I've always wanted to live in a log cabin,"

You said that about the treehouse, too," Geoff teased.

Kitty giggled. "Both true. I'll just have to come visit you again later when you have it all finished."

She'd visit him.

Much later? When it was all finished? Just to celebrate his accomplishment? Probably that's all it would ever be. Was she crazy to think that he would ever want her to live up here with him?

Kitty leaned forward and patted several of the close logs affectionately. "I love you, logs. You've gone through a lot of weathering and waited a long time to become so beautiful." She looked at Geoff, reflectively. "This makes me think of how beautiful my Grama-ma Nora is; she's weathered, like the logs."

Geoff chuckled. "You sound like you're missing your grandmother."

"I could very well be," she said. "It's been a while."

Geoff nodded understandingly.

"When do you think you'll have the cabin ready for lock-up?" Kitty asked.

"Shouldn't take us too long," Geoff said, "once Hank gets here to help."

"I want to help too!" And she meant it.

"We'd better hurry, then. Get you back to the tent for some more rest so you'll be geared up for toting logs. We won't let you hoist any of these big ones, though."

Kitty tossed back at him, "You'd be surprised how strong I actually am."

Smiling, Geoff turned back down the trail. "There's one more view to take in." He led them along a narrow trail that curved gently to the right.

"We'll follow this deer trail," he said. "It's not far. The sunset reflects on this side of the mountain with a different pallet of colors." He took her hand to help her over the rocks cluttering the rising path. "Look. This is Sunset Ridge'"

Kitty took big gulps of appreciation when they halted to view the valley spread below them in the morning sun. An entirely different artistic touch had wielded this brush. Geoff must have been here multiple times, yet his glowing face revealed the same breathlessness Kitty felt, as her gaze took in the panorama before her.

"God's creativity is so astounding," Geoff said. "*Mount Mercy* has so many facets it will take us years to explore them all. Early loggers logged this side of the mountain first, Scandinavian-style." He pointed into the deep forest. "If you look hard, you'll see the stumps where the logs were selectively chosen. But you have to look hard. This way, they kept Mount Mercy's forests intact."

"I love it," Kitty said.

He seemed reluctant to leave the view as he turned back down the trail they had come.

"And just see what else I have to show you." They walked quietly for several minutes before Geoff stepped a few feet off the trail and Yukon stood quietly by the trunk of a tall spruce. "Tell me what you see." Kitty followed his gaze upwards, searching its branches.

"Not another treehouse, is it?" she teased. "I don't see any steps up this trunk."

She squinted into the sun-drenched forest behind him, then returned her gaze and looked upward. "I see something up there! But what is it? ... Hey, that's a camera, isn't it?"

Geoff hoisted himself upward from the single 2X4 nailed low on the tree trunk. He reached above his head and unhooked the camera from its support to bring it carefully to the ground.

"Come," he said, patting the log nearby. "Sit here beside me and I'll unveil my treasures."

For ten minutes Geoff entertained her with short video clips that made her gasp. Forest creatures walking in the dawn across the very path they were on. Several elk. A five-point buck. A bear and her cub. Two wolves, passing the tree together in the dusk. An owl swooping in and out of the frame. The outline of two more deer, with their white tails bobbing...

The light of the camera's flash glinting on the eyes of a fox.

"And these were just in the last few days," Geoff said." I'm expecting a moose one of these times... maybe even Sasquatch." He laughed.

"I'm speechless," she said. "No wonder you want to build a cabin out here. What a way to be close to creation. It makes me want to forget about everything else."

Geoff reached up to replace the camera on its hook, then stepped back onto the path. Five minutes later they came back to the spring waiting at the bend.

He took the canteen from his backpack and filled it to accompany their lunch.

"Let's sit here on the grassy edge," Kitty said. "I want to watch the water rippling over the rocks."

Geoff joined her on the grass. He pulled out their food and placed it on a small cloth.

"Good thing I bought some more canned ham the last time I was in town. I'm going to have invent a better cooling method if I'm going to be able to keep more than just cans in my pantry."

KITTY FINISHED HER SINGLE sandwich well after Geoff had polished off two.

He stretched back on the grass, in his hand an apple with a bite missing. His other brawny arm relaxed over his head. His face reflected the contentment Kitty wished she felt.

She could stay right here looking at his wavy hair and his beautiful strong nose forever. He caught her watching him and she reached up to the warmth on her cheek. His smile began with the deepening blue of his eyes and their inscrutable questions. Her blush flared, accompanied by a revisiting despair that stole from her the beauty of the moment.

Muscles rippled when he sat up. His smile prickled her toes as she leaned back to watch him stand. He reached out both hands to hers and pulled her up beside him, tightening his grip just enough to indicate that he was in no hurry to let her slip away. His eyes were filled with longing as he wrapped one arm around her waist and let his free hand sift through her pale hair.

Kitty closed her eyes. His feather-light finger circled her face until it rested on her chin, pressing down gently, tenderly, with what she was sure was firm intention.

Too soon, Kitty. Too soon. You haven't finished your story yet.

She was sure he'd be sorry if he took the next step and kissed her before he knew the rest of her story. She'd be even sorrier. He'd probably hate her forever. Sudden certainty changed Kitty's mood. They were both here and now, together, in Geoff's self-named "fix-it place." When Hank and Jennifer got there, when would she have another moment alone with Geoff?

Even as tension clenched her belly, Kitty made her decision. She had to get the rest of her confession told and over with.

Kitty took a deep breath and, using every ounce of her will, gently pushed at his chest.

Geoff stepped back without letting her go. "Kitty," He said hesitantly, "may I ask you something?"

Unrealistic hopefulness leaped inside her.

"Like…what do you want to ask me?" She swallowed.

He looked shy. "I was just wondering if you would go with me, sometime…to church?"

To church?

His invitation was so far away from the subject on her mind, Kitty couldn't help but snicker. "To church? You mean here? On the hillside? Vancouver? Nobleton? What is your question?"

"Well, there's this small country church a few klicks from here. About a dozen or so families worship there every Sunday. I've been there just once. It's called Mercy Chapel, but it makes me think of the 'little brown church in the Vale.' My mom often sang that song when we got home from church—even when we didn't sing it *in* church. This little church, not too far from Mount Mercy, is old-fashioned and sweet and filled with welcoming people. The idea just popped into my mind 'cause you seem so old-fashioned and sweet to me, too. Will you let me take you? Someday? Some Sunday when we can?"

Sweet and old-fashioned? Me?

His eyes pleaded with such yearning she could barely nod or speak.

"Sure," she said, losing track of her thoughts. "One day I…"

She'd lose her courage if she couldn't be resolute. Kitty brought the conversation back to where her brain had begun to stutter. "Sure, you can take me to the church sometime. Right now, I think I'm thirsty for some more of that magical water." She moved firmly away from his nearness and stepped toward the spring, trying not to watch the sadness flickering in his expression.

He stood silent for long moments. Hopeful joy drained from his face like a little boy suddenly rebuffed.

TWELVE

"HEY, YOU NEED SOME MORE WATER? Sure."

Geoff picked up the canteen and held it under the water flow.

He passed her a cupful and was suddenly enlightened by the unspoken words in her gaze.

"What are you thinking about?" he asked, feeling uncharacteristically tentative. He thought he knew the answer.

"You must have a small idea what I'm thinking," Her sad, worried expression reminded him of yesterday. He waited, studying her sombre face.

"I'm afraid you... just... might be thinking about... Venecia Vale, again?"

"And you are right," she said, apprehension in her tone.

He groaned. "I thought you were ready to forget her. I hoped..."

"Don't you want to know any more about her at all then?" Kitty asked. "Can you actually forget everything about me that easily?"

Her question stabbed his conscience, but he knew his expression had given the answer. How could he explain how desperately his heart wanted to go forward?

"It's just that... I thought we wanted to put her behind us...forget her."

"Yes. Absolutely. Except..." Kitty hesitated, "there's more to her story."

Geoff sighed. "Okay. I get it. If it were up to me, I'd just drop it and forget it all. That's what I'd prefer to do. But if you need me to work through the rest of it, I understand. I think."

"If I don't tell you now, won't it come up later? Then what? Or does it even matter? Maybe you don't really care… if …"

"Kitty…." He moaned. "Don't do this to me." He reached for her and hugged his arms around her. She stiffened.

"My story isn't done," she said. "If I am going to be able to forget it, I need to tell it all… if it makes any difference to you."

If she had punched him in the gut, he would have felt less trauma.

He dropped down on the sun-warmed grass and patted the spot beside him. "Okay, Kitty," he said. He had difficulty controlling the hurt in his voice. "I'm here now. Let me help you put this behind you—behind both of us."

He took her cold hands in his, with desperate hope that she could hear the faith he had in her. She looked at him with tears threatening to spill over.

"Kitty, what happened before you left Calgary?"

KITTY, TOO, WOULD LOVE to let it all go. But she could not. Not yet. Reaching for the words she wished she could leave unspoken. She began slowly…

"Lance had taken me on his 'training shoots' a couple of times before," Kitty began. "Back then he'd rented separate rooms. This time his actions seemed more proprietary. He laughed at my reminder about separate bedrooms and told me I was a big girl now. Didn't need to be shy anymore, he told me. 'Besides,' he said, 'I can sleep on the sofa-bed if you insist.' He was such a liar."

Kitty had been given a few makeup tips from the hairdresser. When she came back with her new blonde look two weeks before the shoot in Calgary, Lance couldn't seem to stop complimenting her. That night, when she should have insisted he book a separate room for himself, he poured some wine. He poured smooth words as well. He told her she had enslaved him. He didn't even try to keep his hands off her. She remembered beginning to feel her new magnetism. That was before he began acting like he owned her.

"I think I liked the feeling of power I had over him."

"But that wasn't my Kitty!" Geoff blurted. "That was Valencia Vale. We're trying to exorcise her."

Kitty dropped her eyes.

She and Lance had shared the pâté, cancelled the dinner, and didn't leave the room 'til it was time for the early shoot.

"I'd only had a little to drink," she said, "and I could still think. What was happening was headed where I didn't want to go. Lance laughed at me. When he ignored me, I got mad and he got rough and I got scared. We were both mad when we headed for the shoot.

"Lance turned on the charm the moment we walked into the dimly lit studio setup. If I hadn't been wound up so tight, I would have used my head sooner and quit the place before he even got started talking to the attractive models he had engaged. I just kept trying to refuse his sloshed advances. We didn't actually finish that night's shoot 'cause his drinking got in the way."

Geoff squeezed her hands, urging her to continue.

Kitty still seemed to hear Lance's slurred laughter in the studio as he gradually directed the poses —from graceful to X-rated. When she became more un-cooperative with her camera, he just swigged some more —more than she'd ever seen him drink.

"I managed to keep my glass almost full, even as he coaxed and coddled. He wandered around with the booze bottle, whatever it was, waving it at the models with his unsteady hand. He turned to refill his empty glass and fell on the floor."

"I can still hear his slurred words to the models. 'You better go ahead, you two, and fin'shup. We'll have to shoot the good stuff tomorrow.' He struggled to get to his feet. 'I'm gonna take this cute camera-chick back to where she needs to go,' he said as he grabbed a handful of me where his arm ended.

"I practically carried him back to the room as he leaned on me trying to keep his feet moving. He could hardly even walk. I used my key to open the door and tried to pry him off me as we entered. He grabbed me, pulled me onto the bed, landed on top of me, slobbered on my face, then promptly fell asleep. I must have, too. In the morning I realized I could have been sipping more wine than I thought. Come to think of it, it had a funny taste. It wasn't until later that I—after—well, I wondered... He... I'd never tasted that kind of booze, whatever it was. He..."

"Kitty!" The explosion that shattered Geoff's expression rivaled the eruption of a calving iceberg. Fury froze on his face and his voice cracked. "Kitty. You could be dead by now. He raped you, didn't he? And he drugged you, didn't he?"

Kitty dropped her head in her hands. Geoff leaped to his feet.

"Kitty, do you want me to kill him? I think I'll kill him."

She raised her eyes, shocked to see the naked hatred on his face. His body held him as tightly as his expression, the tension in both ready to let go.

Kitty shook her head slowly. "He's not worth it. I did leave him behind, remember."

Geoff turned and walked out momentarily into the trees.

When he returned, after the few minutes that threatened to make her feel abandoned in outer space, he brought the old Geoff back. But his voice was harsh.

"Go on."

"Okay. When I woke up next morning, I saw Lance sprawled out, hanging half off the other side of the bed."

All through the night she seemed to have been still shooting the weird poses floating around in her nauseous brain.

"My head was pounding. At first, I drew a blank about the evening before. My brow was still sweaty when I woke up. Next day I still felt a bit woozy even though we had been dead to the world till nearly noon. I wanted coffee, but there wasn't any. Lance sagged on the far side of the bed. He grunted in a dozy stupor. The room reeked of liquor—and what else I don't know. I still had most of my clothes on.

All I had to do was add my top while holding my breath. Or I could choose a shower. I decided to risk three minutes."

Lance had flopped over and thrown his arm across the bed, fumbling uncertainly in the spot where she had lain. His eyelids struggled to lift, revealing pupils that were clouded and threatening.

His words were slurred. "Where d'you think you're goin', Miss Vale? Get back here in this bed where you b'long. We haven't even got star'ed yet." He clumsily rolled out of the other side of the bed, swayed, and fell to the floor. Kitty hadn't expected him to rise any further off the carpet than his wobbling knees.

"It took me two more minutes to rip a few things off the hangers, grab my makeup case and curling iron and throw them—and I do mean 'throw them'—all back into my suitcase. My heart was banging like crazy. Good thing he'd emptied his pockets on the dresser earlier. I grabbed the keys to the rental car and headed out toward the lobby. Lance had pulled himself to a slump against the night-table.

"He was still so drunk I didn't expect him to stagger after me to the parking lot. But he did and actually managed to stay on his feet —at least until I had started to drive away —swaying back and forth and still jeering as I slammed the car door.

"You know the rest."

Now Geoff looked like he was the one who'd been drugged. He stepped forward, awkwardly patted her shoulder, and zig-zagged down the path past the outhouse and toward the roofless cabin. He didn't even meet her eyes. She was glad. She didn't want to see the disgust that must be on his face.

A thousand fishhooks were imbedded in Kitty's chest. The same kind that Geoff must be feeling. How would they ever get past this? Thinking that some kind of story-confession like this could make it better was only wishful thinking. How could someone so strong, so kind, so brave, so gentle, ever see her again as anything more than a yukky, half-peeled, decomposing banana rescued from the garbage bin? Faced by the spoken reality of her sins. Kitty shuddered. Why would he even want to touch her, to hug her again, let alone take her into his home as his wife? She must be crazy. She didn't deserve an honourable man like Geoff Armistad. She took the short walk back to the outhouse with the window.

GEOFF HAD TO DO something about supper, but the contents of his belly churned. He obviously had much less grit than he supposed, stumbling through meaningless motions like a new-born zombie. He was certain he'd had something planned for tonight's meal well before they began their climb this morning. Now numbness immobilized both his brain and his body. Maybe he needed just a bit more time for normalcy to return.

Kitty's story was roiling inside his stomach. He felt as though he had been swept clean of everything a man carried inside his skin. Kitty's confession had spilled out of her in remorse and tears. She needed his compassion, not detachment. She needed tenderness, not the remote aloofness of his frozen righteousness. He had assured her that he would understand. That he'd support her. Yet, it was not in him to pretend he had answers. Right now, shock had rendered him incapable of diagnosing himself, let alone Kitty.

Was he experiencing a change of mind? A hardening of his compassion toward her simply because Kitty's inexperience had caught her unaware?

Oh God! What kind of man am I? The worst kind of Pharisee Jesus ever named? Forgive me, Lord. Help me. You know I love her. Fix me! Take the memory of this intruder out of her life.

But, Lord, especially take him out of mine.

He wanted to fall down on his knees and wail beside the spruce boughs, but he didn't want Kitty to see that kind of emotion. Not just now.

He knew he could act the truth if he used some faith. Faith in God. Faith in himself. Faith in Kitty. He stood straight and attached a smile to his face as he walked to the fire pit toward Kitty, huddled with her arms around Yukon.

"Know what you feel like eating?" Geoff asked.

Tears were still damp on her cheeks, but she returned a wan smile. "How about hotdogs?"

He nodded and walked to the cooler and stared at it.

The dog whimpered at his back. Neither Geoff nor Kitty was showing her much attention. That something was amiss was clear to Yukon.

In the middle of a whine, Yukon's ears sprang to attention. She took off like she'd sensed a rabbit and yelped in wild welcome, bounding straight toward the sound of a motor.

Geoff didn't bother to call her back.

On the lower flats beyond the campsite, someone was parking a truck and camper.

Who else but Hank?

Geoff had to get a grip. Hank knew him too well. Ever since he'd first met Hank at his Rustic Diner, Hank could zero in on him like a spotlight. He ground his teeth and willed Kitty's last words out of his ears. But it was no easier to forget her words than to expunge the pictures in his imagination.

His boots crunched firmly on the rocky side of the blackened fire pit. Hank and Jennifer stepped cautiously from behind the camper to greet Yukon's wild welcome. Geoff forced as natural a grin as he knew how as they sprinted toward him with outstretched arms.

KITTY BROKE INTO A RUN and flung herself at them.

If her blonde hair had surprised Jennifer, she made no indication. Kitty was sure the tears that ran down Jennifer's cheeks were turned on by joy, not sadness.

"Kitty, Kitty! Our long-lost little girl." Jennifer's hug almost left her breathless. When Jennifer let go, Hank took his turn to embrace her with his own paternal lack of restraint.

"Kitty Sampson," Hank said. "We have been missing you—so much!"

Kitty saw with thumping certainty that Hank spoke for both him and Jennifer. Regret pierced her that she'd knowingly excluded her friends these many months.

Hank and Geoff clapped each other on the back with their usual boisterousness. Kitty observed their affection with awe. They often reminded her of two little boys. They had been friends for so long. Today, they could almost be father and son.

IT WAS STILL EARLY evening when Geoff brought out cheese and crackers from his easy storables to go with water still icy from the spring. The idea of hot-dogs was forgotten. The subject of Kitty's new blonde guise was carefully avoided.

As was their regular habit when making a visit, Hank and Jennifer had brought dinner supplies with them —bison steaks from his ranch in Northern Alberta, vegetables and salad fixings from their Nobleton garden.

It wasn't long before Hank elected to barbecue the steaks, while Geoff pretended to supervise. Kitty helped Jennifer with the zucchini and sweet potatoes.

"I was certainly relieved when you called and didn't make us wait any longer," Hank teased. "I had feared you might not invite us 'til Christmas!"

Geoff wanted to find a witty comeback to offset Hank's ribbing. He couldn't. His brain was too aware of the elusive sorrow on Kitty's face—while he tried to present his own nonchalant, convincing self.

They lobbed cheerful small talk back and forth as they ate around the evening's campfire, enjoying Hank's generosity. Yet, a tentative uncertainty hovered between the awkward spaces.

"I'm glad you're here," Geoff said sincerely.

"Me too," Kitty echoed with a noticeable catch in her voice.

As the sun closed down and night shuttered the day, they agreed it was time for turn-in.

Hank kissed Jennifer lightly as he turned toward their camper. "See you in a minute, Jennie-love," he said. "You go tuck Kitty in."

Jennifer headed toward Kitty's tent. Yukon followed Kitty.

GOEFF'S HEART HAD felt all evening like it held five pounds of sawdust. As he watched Kitty's spirit slump deeper into the bog, he felt the stabbing guilt. He was sure it was his own shallow reaction today that was contributing to her sad expression. He would have to figure out how to cheer her up in the morning before Hank and Jennifer started asking more questions. Even though he had earlier suggested to Kitty that she could use a couple of counsellors, he hadn't really expected her to need more than a hug and a prayer. He himself should have administered that much at the spring. A huge apology was in order. He could have acted like the man he considered himself to be. Not some piece of dried-up scat.

God, forgive me.

Even as he prayed, he felt his Father's arms around him.

KITTY CLICKED ON THE LITTLE LED LIGHT hanging near the tent flaps. Jennifer, close beside her, followed her into Geoff's borrowed tent.

Kitty turned and flung herself into Jennifer's arms and wept.

Jennifer's tears joined hers. "Let it all go, Kitty. Whatever it is, just give it to Jesus and let Him give you peace."

"I don't deserve peace," Kitty mumbled. "I don't deserve God's love. I shouldn't have disappeared. I should never have got myself into such a mess."

Kitty felt the hug tighten as Jennifer gently insisted, "The Lord understands the whys, and He was beside you every step you took."

Kitty's words were interspersed with small sobs. "You know... the steps... I took?"

Jennifer loosened her hug. "Not really, honey. Becky told me what you said she could share. She told me you had gone blonde. I got the general picture. I know you and the kids prayed together. I know how troubled you've been. But I also know you are a daughter of the Lord. I know you love Him. And you know how much He loves you. He's already covered our sins. We don't have to keep on begging him over and over again."

Kitty stepped out of her jeans and into her pyjamas. "But how come He didn't stop me from making such awful mistakes?"

Jennifer smiled sadly. "I think it's because only a cruel God would take away our power of choice. He's not a tyrant. Is he?"

Kitty buttoned her pyjama top. "No—oo ... But ..."

"He's really our gentle Papa, isn't He?"

"Ye...es..." More tears pooled in her eyes and ran over.

"He never says, 'Go away,' when we talk to Him, does He?"

Kitty shook her head, her face woeful and tear-streaked.

"Some time," Jennifer said, "whenever you want to, you can talk to me about it. But in the meantime, trust Him to help you make the right decisions from now on."

"Jennifer…" Kitty hesitated. "When you tell the truth, do you always have to tell it all?"

Jennifer only smiled, urged Kitty into her sleeping bag and tucked it around her shoulders.

Jennifer gently settled Kitty back into the sleeping bag. She placed a light kiss lovingly on her forehead.

"Know His peace," Jennifer said softly. "Sleep in love.

THIRTEEN

WITH CLOSED EYES Geoff sagged on his sitting stump in front of dying embers. Each knee supported an elbow. His Bible hung heavy in his left hand while his head rested in the other. Yukon lay on the ground beside him, her head on his boot.

Geoff had no wish to rekindle the wood fire that had blazed so comfortingly half an hour ago. He didn't feel like being warmed up. He didn't think anything inside him could be consoled anyway, so crushed was his spirit in its weak humanity.

The firm hand clapped on his shoulder belonged to Hank.

"What part of the Holy Word are you savouring tonight?" Hank asked in his insightful manner.

Geoff looked up with a wan smile. "I was going to try for a Psalm, until I realized that without my lamp flashlight I couldn't see it, anyway."

"I love the Psalms, too. As a kid I memorized quite a few of them."

"Me too. Even as a wild kid, Mom managed to get some truth into me." He looked wistful. "I wish she were still here. She'd have been proud of me these last few years—at least up to now."

Hank squatted down in front of Geoff. "Believe it. She would be proud of you right now. I can empathize with your struggle, buddy. Women aren't always easy for men to figure out, just as we are a problem for them. Geoff, you are human. But God is good. He's got your back."

Geoff drew a deep, silent breath as they both rose to stand in front of the barely glowing campfire.

"How about Psalm 37?" Hank said. "I've never forgotten a sermon I heard on three short verses of that Psalm. I try to remember it every morning." He grinned, his grey eyes asking for permission. "Let me preach it to you? It's not very long. I won't even need a flashlight."

"Shoot," Geoff said.

"Here's what to do first," Hank said. "This is your part. Delight yourself in the Lord."

"I can do that."

"Second, commit your way to Him."

"Done that," said Geoff.

"Next, trust also in Him. Just trust."

"I'm trying hard."

"Then," Hank said emphatically, "here's what God does. Do you remember?"

"What?" He could make a sarcastic guess. Didn't a sermon always have a good conclusion?

Hank added the emphasis. "You do the trusting. Here's what God does: *bring it to pass.* He'll give you the desires of your heart. He didn't say *when*, but He did say he would."

Geoff was quiet for long moments. With guarded hope, he said, "Hank, do you really think it's possible?"

Geoff couldn't see the eyes of his mentor in the dusk, but the tone in Hank's voice sounded like the truth that must be shining in his eyes.

"I, of all people, should know." Hank said. "For years I allowed memories of April to impede my path—until that long ago day on Juniper beach when God used *your* words to slap me silly. Waiting for Jennie took me a lot of time and dismantled a lot of pride. Took a lot of patience, too, but I persevered. And God let me have her. He led us to each other." He laughed aloud.

"Geoff, Kitty told Becky her story and we're filled in enough to understand her fears. She'll come back to herself. And, I'm sure, she'll come to you, too. You're in love with her, are you not?"

Geoff hung his head in defeat. "Utterly and completely. But I sure haven't acted like it."

"Here's the conclusion of the sermon, then, from verse six. He's going to *bring forth your righteousness as light.*"

"Hank, tonight I feel about as righteous as a rotting fencepost." He placed his Bible on a stump beside him.

Hank gave him his moment, then continued, "furthermore, He will also *bring forth your justice as noonday.*"

Geoff laughed harshly. "Justice! If you want to talk about justice for me, I'd be indicted as a felon!"

Hank put his hands firmly on Geoff's shoulders.

"You're hardly that. After hearing Kitty talk about some of her concerns, I can see why you'd feel like becoming one, though."

Geoff groaned, ran his fingers through his hair and pounded his fist into one hand, then the other.

"Our Father loves us in all our ways, anyway," Hank said. "Our unpredictable feelings don't count for much. But His feelings for *us*, do. You and Kitty will both get through this. That is my promise."

Hank's faith was infectious. Geoff admitted to himself that Hank could be right.

"All right," he said. "Tonight, I'll take your word for it. Tomorrow I'll take your muscle with me over to the cabin and we'll put a big dent in that pile of logs."

KITTY AWOKE TO THE SOUND of the chainsaw buzzing in the distance. A glimmer of dawn peaked through the tent flaps. She sat up and rubbed her eyes, feeling more lighthearted than last night. Maybe it was the comfort of knowing that Hank and Geoff were working together over at the cabin. Or the fact that Jennifer was nearby.

Actually, she remembered Jennifer *had* blessed her with love and peace.

Could she keep it with her?

Kitty poked her sleepy head through the lifted door flap. Jennifer was already puttering about the camp kitchen with her shoulder-length hair pinned loosely back. No men and no Yukon to be seen.

The chainsaw roared again from the cabin over the rise.

Kitty pulled on yesterday's jeans, yanked the brush through her hair, flew to Jennifer's side and hugged her with breathless anticipation.

"Important things are happening at the cabin on the hillside," Jennifer said.

"C'mon, then," Kitty commanded, feeling like a child in her eagerness. "Let's go see what the guys are up to."

Jennifer smiled at her enthusiasm. "I've already seen where they're putting those rafters," she said, "but how about you go take a boo and let them know their sausages are nearly ready."

Jennifer reached into a carry bag and then tossed Kitty a camera. "Do me a favour and document this for me."

"You got it. Should have thought of that myself."

She didn't need to be told twice. The fragrance of sawdust called.

As Kitty scrambled up the hillside, Yukon greeted her exuberantly and accompanied her, tail a-wagging, to the construction site.

A long-seasoned log rested between a set of sawhorses, and Geoff grinned at her as she approached. He wielded a long saw like he was a hefty Spartan warrior.

"Hey, that thing looks dangerous," Kitty yelled.

The shrieking voice of blade grinding through wood quieted as Geoff flipped the switch. He set down the chain saw and blew the dust off his face with a puff of his lips.

"Couldn't do much without my trusty Husqvarna 450," he said, as it idled noisily at his feet.

Hank, balancing above them on the scaffolding, waved at her as Geoff turned off the saw. Kitty lifted the camera toward the log rooftop, grinned at Hank and clicked, then turned it on Geoff as he took a stiff pose.

"Hey." Kitty made a wide sweep with her arms. "You guys've already got a lot done. This is going to be way higher than I thought."

Geoff proudly described their progress. The loft rose twelve feet into the air on a 12/12 pitch. "I'm afraid I cheated a bit. We're using ready-to-go rafters and joints from Home Renovators to simplify part of the work. And before this day is through," he said, "we'll be ready for windows!"

"You'll need to replenish your energy a few times then," Kitty said. "Jennifer says to tell you your sausages are ready."

"HEY GUYS," JENNIFER SAID as they neared. "Perfect timing."

Jennifer beamed contentedly while the men washed the grit and sawdust from their hands in the basin she'd filled with warm water. Hank's buffalo sausages sizzled in the cast-iron pan as Jennifer brought them from the camp-stove to the folding table overlooking the campsite.

Both Kitty and Geoff sounded playful as they pulled folding chairs from the back of the camper. Jennifer eyed with relief their lighthearted switch from last night's gloom. *Thank you, Lord!*

The clouds that had hung low last night flitted away with today's sunny morning. She saw the shy glances Kitty turned on Geoff. Her heart bubbled with joy at the adoration evident in Geoff's blue eyes.

Geoff slipped his arm over Kitty's shoulders and guided her to the breakfast bar.

Hank hugged Jennifer and lightly kissed her lips. "Thank you, Jennie," he said. "You make a better breakfast than I do. Sure glad we escaped up here so you could be in charge. Your hash browns are absolutely the best."

Jennifer only smiled. It wasn't very often that she did the cooking for her chef-husband. It was fun—sometimes.

With plates heaped, they sat down together at the table, held hands and offered their thanks to God for the provision of the beautiful day to work in and all His blessings.

Geoff picked up his fork and said, "Funny how much better I feel after the chance to swing an axe or a hammer." He smiled directly at Kitty. "And after a good night's sleep. Right?"

"I slept like a baby," she said. "Thanks to Jennifer's blessing over me." Kitty exuded the enthusiasm of a little girl. Her shiny ponytail bobbed as she spoke.

Hank stopped with his fork halfway to his mouth and set it down again. "Yes. Isn't God good? I didn't expect to sleep much last night either, but I did. There's a passage of scripture I love that tells us His compassion never fails. His faithfulness is great. His mercies are new every morning. I am so grateful for that! It's in the book of Lamentations." He picked up his fork, thoughtfully. *"New mercies every morning."*

Kitty laughed, self-deprecatingly. "Lamentations! Yes. That sounds like the book I should read."

"Kitty!" Geoff said sternly. "Today is not the day to lament. It's a *new* day. Today is the day we are accepting His mercy. Lamentations talks about mercy! We're going to forget misery and rejoice. We're going to start the Mercy climb." He reached over the table and patted her hand. "Are you with me?"

Yesterday's pain was palpable around the campsite. Empathy bound all four of them together.

Kitty dropped her gaze toward her scrambled eggs, then lifted eyes that had brightened with hope and smiled tremulously at Geoff. "All right. I'll try."

THE MEN COULDN'T WAIT to get back to work. Their progress had given them momentum, and food had given them motivation to make more progress. Kitty helped Jennifer tidy the open kitchen as together they enjoyed listening to the activity at the site.

Kitty let her imagination take her past the meadow, up the rise to a finished cabin. She pictured little curtains on the newly installed windows, an old-fashioned comforter on a wide bed. Cupboards —maybe pine —stocked with non-perishables, and a little cooler holding freshly-bagged game. A wood stove, maybe. An iron frying pan. A little table on which to place the plates of sizzling elk steaks. She could help with wilderness tasks she'd only heard about.

If she were invited to learn.

All of a sudden Kitty felt tired.

She should feel elated, but she knew she couldn't stay here forever. After Hank and Jennifer left, she'd need to get back to civilization and leave Geoff to his wilderness. If Geoff's longing eyes told her what she thought they did, then maybe he would actually come find her. Was it possible that he, too, felt this magnetic pull that made her want to cling to his side every time he approached?

Jennifer's gentle words broke the silence.

"You're in love with him, aren't you?"

Her cheeks warmed, but honesty called for a simple answer. "I don't know. I can't help it, Jennifer. I can't get any other picture in my mind except Geoff. I can't think of anything else all day." She hesitated. "I guess you know most of my story. I feel like I have to find some time to clean myself up —to make myself worthy of him." Her heart checked her again. "Besides, I haven't even spilled all of it yet. I don't know how to do it. God's got to help me."

"Come on, Kitty," Jennifer said. "You've been taught the Truth all your life, living with the man of faith who raised you. You know the Gospel. You know it's not something you *can* do. Only Jesus can. You already have the Cross of Christ to put your trust in. You're forgiven already."

She put motherly arms around Kitty. "Let it go."

"I'm trying," Kitty said. "It's just the pictures in my mind… It may take a little while…to…"

"His Grace is huge. You'll be done with the memories and the impressions soon. All of our sins are in the sea of His forgetfulness. Our loving God is merciful." Jennifer gave Kitty an extra squeeze and dropped her arms. "We all need that mercy. Including Geoff. He's not perfect either, you know.

"However, I do understand that you can't just hang out here in Geoff's tent, moping. Want to hear my idea?"

Kitty drew in a hopeful breath. Any new idea sounded good to her today.

"You probably know that Hank and I have an empty suite. It's where Hank used to stay above the Rustic Diner— before we built our house. Would you like to live there for a while?"

Kitty gasped. Hope and excitement burst from her. This miracle was too much to expect in the middle of her turmoil. Her eyes widened and her lips dropped open.

"Jennifer." It was almost a prayer. "Do you mean it? Could that be possible? How would I pay for it until….?"

Jennifer took Kitty's shoulders and sat her down on the stump by the silent campfire. "Hank and I have been discussing this," she said. "Hank says we could use some more help at the Diner. Want to work for us for a while— just until you get your bearings and get back into your photography? We'd love that. We'd get to see you for a while, too.

"And," she added with a twinkle, "Geoff wouldn't be that far away. He could come visit you whenever you want."

Kitty dropped her head in her hands and wept with relief.

FOURTEEN

HANK PREPARED BREAKFAST the next morning, quickly and efficiently.

Kitty felt the stress of the last couple of weeks catching up with her. Weariness infiltrated her bones from her neck to her knees. By evening not even the crackle of the campfire logs falling apart could prevent her yawns and the desire to crawl into the sleeping bag in her borrowed tent. Morning came too early and today was not an exception.

Jennifer noticed it too, as the guys, both of them satiated and ebullient, headed out of the clearing and toward the cabin.

"How about you and I go home to Nobleton, sooner rather than later," Jennifer said, "and get you settled while the men finish closing in the cabin? I think this has all been too much for you. You need a warm soak in a bathtub and some motherly attention."

Kitty smiled weakly, the tension humming through every part of her.

"I can take a turn at the wheel if we drive back in your car," Jennifer said. "Hank can bring the camper when they're done. What do you say?"

Kitty threw her arms around Jennifer's neck. "Okay, Mommy," she said. "But—just one more day? I have to prime myself for the rift." The confession embarrassed her, but Jennifer showed nothing but empathy.

"Of course you do, honey. Why don't you invite Geoff for a little walk after supper so you two can talk. I'm sure he'd like that."

Oops. Another talk? Can I handle any more of that?

"Unless," Kitty suggested, "you and I just take off, and Geoff and I do our talking later...?"

"It's up to you, Kitty." Jennifer smiled gently. "I trust you to know your heart."

"Right now," Kitty said, "we should go see if we can be of any help up there this morning. I told Geoff I'd like to help build his log cabin. It's an experience I've never had."

"I haven't either," said Jennifer.

Kitty scurried up the slope, right on Jennifer's heels.

"Help?" Geoff chortled. "Could we use some help, Hank?"

"From the two beautiful ladies sharing this campsite?" Hank said. "Absolutely. Even if only for their inspiration."

"Kitty and I are headed out tomorrow," Jennifer said, "so grab us while you have the chance."

Both Kitty and Jennifer happily discovered how useful their extra pairs of hands could be and how much logs actually weighed.

"Closing in these walls will take half the time it might have without your help," Geoff said, beaming at Kitty.

Jennifer made many trips for snacks and coffee. Kitty was embarrassed—and puzzled—that she wore out faster than Jennifer, considering she was a whole generation younger. It didn't take much for Geoff to persuade her to quit hefting the logs and take pictures instead. Thankfully, the gloves he found for her had saved her city-hands from roughening up. Jennifer, on the other hand, had been wise enough to bring her own.

They worked well past supper time, and they all collapsed together around the campfire, satisfied with a twilight meal and a job well done.

At this late hour, with a canopy of stars overhead, only one more thing was needed. Hot chocolate. Oh, and some comfort from the Word of God.

"You can do the honours tonight," Geoff said as he handed Hank his Bible to make the choice. Jennifer served their hot drinks as they listened to Hank's brief passage of scripture, softly spoken, yet intense.

"By next weekend, or sooner," Geoff said with a nod to Kitty and Jennifer, "we should have everything ready for lock-up and should make you both proud of our teamwork. Then we can take a break, and you can pamper us for the next couple of days once we're back at your place."

Kitty shyly accepted a gentle goodnight hug from Geoff, yearning for the possessive arm Hank extended to Jennifer as the affectionate couple walked to their camper. Thankfully, it was too late now to have to brace herself for another talk with Geoff —tonight.

"'Night, Kitty," Geoff said. "If we don't get done in a few days, or if Hank decides he has to take off sooner, I *will* be there next weekend, for sure. Count on it. I have to see you settled in your new place."

"You'll be there for sure?" Wistfulness softened her voice.

"Abso-tootin'-lutely."

He turned reluctantly. "I'll see you both in the morning. I need my hug before you leave." The joy in her chest was whimpering to be acknowledged. Kitty believed, hesitantly, that God was indeed beginning to confirm His forgiveness in her heart. Even with her misgivings, He was telling her softly that she was His daughter.

Part of her wished she didn't have to go the next morning. Yet the churning of her unsettled emotions confirmed the wisdom of not staying too long around Geoff's pleading scrutiny. Leaving in Jennifer's company was going to make it much easier to do. No one understood her quite like Jennifer.

Instead of waiting for daylight, she packed her bag by the light of the little LED lamp in her tent. This way, she'd have time to tell Geoff goodbye in the morning.

JUST AFTER DAWN, Kitty caught her first glimpse of Geoff standing in the camp kitchen, smiling, confident, his dark waves touched by the breeze, his arms crossed. His waiting stance hinted at a plan he'd already concocted.

Kitty wasn't hungry. She didn't want any of the coffee wafting its aroma into the morning air. The fresh thought of talking to Geoff almost made her feel sick. Yet there he was, reading her mind with expectation lighting his eyes.

"Let's get out of here," Geoff said. "Hank says he'll go warm up the measuring tape without me, so we can take a quick ride up the trail before you two leave us. Come on." He held out his hand, and she went to him as though pulled by a tractor beam.

His hand tightened on hers.

"Stay with Hank, Yukon," he said to his sidekick. He could just as well have added, "I want to be alone with Kitty for a while."

Yukon whined softly as Hank roughed up her neck. "Come on, girl." Yukon looked back once as she followed Hank.

Geoff headed around the corner where the ATV was parked. His possession of Kitty's hand sent electricity up and down her arm. He tugged her with him without speaking, like he was in a hurry to get somewhere. Kitty couldn't find any words either; at least none that could express her mixed joy and apprehension.

Like the gentlemen she knew him to be, he lifted her to the passenger's seat with a flourish, reached in and buckled her up before sprinting around to the driver's side. He revved the motor, and this time she knew what to expect of the rough and rutted logging road. The sun pressing through the trees and the honey-fresh breeze revived her spirits. Anticipation continued to mount as she recognized the road to the tree house. Memories of the intense sweetness of that first mountain experience left her with breathless panic. Her heartbeat quickened with each bumpy metre.

Kitty was sure Geoff planned to reach out to her today —maybe even propose? No, surely it was too soon for that. And she wasn't ready for him anyway—couldn't be ready for a while yet. Was she truly as clean as Jennifer assured her she was?

They stopped under the old ponderosa with the log steps nailed up the tree trunk. Geoff helped her onto the first few steps, boosted her up into the treehouse and followed behind her. Once through the opening and onto the log floor Kitty stood up, wobbling with nervous laughter. He grinned at her affectionately and scooped her into his arms. She stiffened only slightly, then relaxed against his chest.

With a soft sigh he untied her ponytail and sifted his fingers through her hair.

"Oh, Kitty," he said, as an almost imperceptible groan escaped his lips.

He loosened his arms and guided her toward the log railing. "Remember this view?"

She remembered. The sun was once again spreading rainbow colors from the mountainside and beyond the gorge.

He looked down at her with teasing eyes. "Remember what you said about living in a tree house? Or a cabin?"

Oh yes, how well she remembered.

"Not today, of course." she said quickly. "Not this one."

Startled, he looked down at her. Then he grinned. "Of course not. I'll build you a new one."

"You will?"

"Maybe I'm already building it…."

Shyness overcame her, and she stepped back.

Kitty bit her lip when Geoff said, "Do you remember how I told you this mountain makes me feel?"

Kitty shivered.

"How it fills me with hope? That's why I came here after the job up north. It gave me hope. Then you came back into my life like a kiss from God Himself. Kitty, I barely knew what hope was until you showed up and made me forget every discouragement I've ever known."

Probably exaggerated, but Kitty didn't care. She was as close to ecstasy as she'd ever remembered. He slipped an arm around her, and she snuggled close to his strong, fast heartbeat and the muscles rippling over his ribcage.

Kitty looked up and put her fingertips on Geoff's lips. "Maybe you better not say any more right now, Geoff. This is making me a little uncomfortable."

"Please, Kitten, don't be uncomfortable," Geoff said, taking her fingertips in his. "I'm not trying to play games with your mind. I'm serious."

He turned back to the view of the mountaintop she remembered from their trek to Mercy Falls. "Look up there," he said. "That's where I'd like to climb one day. With you. Wouldn't it be amazing to see the world from the top—with God?"

Oh when? Let's do it! Soon? Kitty clenched the words between her teeth instead. How pushy would that be? What if he began to think better of his impulsiveness. He certainly would when she told him the rest of her story—about the part that had been her doing. After all, it wasn't a disclosure of the truth until she'd acknowledged it all. That's what Jennifer's silence to her question had told her the first night they arrived.

Geoff laughed in joyous abandon. He hugged her and danced her around the aging tree house. A very brief kiss held a promise that choked her with anticipation.

"What do you say, Kitty? You with me? Will you think about going all the way to the top of Mount Mercy—with me?"

"Wh…when…?"

"Soon, Kitty. Maybe next time you come—or the time after. But I think it might be a plan to first visit the little church I was telling you about. It's known as Mercy

Chapel." Kitty gasped audibly. "We can figure out how to incorporate that when I see you again. Right now I feel like I shouldn't rush you—or us. Dream about it, sweetheart. Pray about it with me and plan for the not-too-far-away."

Was it possible she could put her self-incriminating accusations behind her? She'd have to. That's what he was suggesting, wasn't it?

The questions in her pounding heart made her falter with a whisper she ignored. "Ye-es... I *would* like to go climbing. With you. *Some*day... soon, I guess..."

Kitty wished he wouldn't look at her like that when her aching heart wept for the freedom to respond. The pain began to pulse like she was being carved with one of Geoff's hand tools.

He appraised her with worried eyes. "Kitty, have I made a mistake? You do care for me, don't you? A little? I was so sure... I thought...."

"Of course, I do. It's just... just... me."

"Kitty!" He groaned with anguish as he reached his arms around her. "My precious one. Do you understand how much I love you?"

Kitty burst into the tears that had been pent up all morning. "No. Don't tell me that. I can't hear it right now!"

"I love you. I love you, Kitty. Surely that doesn't make you feel bad?"

"You wouldn't love me if you knew the truth."

"The truth is that I love you. I know God has put you back into my life and I don't care about that ...your... that Venecia Vale and her dalliance, anymore. Forgiveness goes both ways. I need to be forgiven, too."

"You'll never have enough forgiveness to go all the way around my mistakes. You'll hate me. I'm not sure God doesn't hate me too!"

Geoff shook her, tenderly. "Stop that craziness, Kitty. He loves us both."

Tears that wouldn't quit streaked Kitty's face. Catching Geoff by surprise, she squirmed from his arms and blindly felt her way toward the exit and back down the tree-trunk.

He followed and swung past her to the ground before she was halfway down, catching her in his arms as she made the last long step. He tilted her face to his, and his tortured eyes bored into hers.

"What *is* it, Kitty?" he whispered.

"I lied to you, Geoff. Stop! Don't say any more. I lied to you. That night before I left Calgary, he was too drunk to do anything except collapse. What happened, happened before we went to the shoot. And I let him."

Speaking those words, she wanted to die. The pain in her chest was excruciating beyond anything she had ever experienced. Every utterance sliced her reeling senses.

Slash.

With each additional word, she deliberately twisted the knife inside her soul.

Stab.

"Actually, I encouraged him."

Slash, slash.

Even though that was an untruth, it provided her with enough pain to give her some of what she deserved. She deserved it all and more.

156

Geoff's eyes slowly phased from blue, to navy, to black. They sank into his face until they sat in deep hollows. They weren't even angry. They were dead.

GEOFF'S CHEST FELT EMPTY. "Kitty," he said, "you didn't have to tell me this. I didn't need to know." Then terror gripped him.

Maybe she has a reason for wanting me to know. Maybe I've just been imagining that she cares. Maybe she's trying to drive me away.

"Why *did* you tell me?"

"I'm telling you because I can't walk away and let you think I was raped," she said. "I can't just dump the whole responsibility on him. I was there, too." Her expression was inscrutable.

Was Kitty telling him this because she was sorry? Because she felt compelled to be honest? Or...? He couldn't read her anymore. Did he even matter to her? Or was she relieved? Maybe she actually cared about that scumbag?

Kitty pulled out a tissue and blew her nose. Then another to wipe her eyes. A cloud fell over her face and her tears ceased flowing. Her expression became slowly more closed. Like she was sleepwalking.

Geoff felt like he was sleepwalking, too.

Yet deep in his heart, Geoff knew better. He'd seen it in her compassionate, yearning eyes. He was sure she cared for him—just as much as he did for her.

She loves me. I know she does.

Kitty climbed into the ATV and buckled her seatbelt. He got in without a word. When they stopped at the campsite, she scrambled out in silence.

When Kitty turned toward Jennifer, who was waiting by the camper, she barely acknowledged Groff's goodbye with a flutter of her fingers. He spoke his last words, raspy with grief. "Goodbye, Kitty."

"Hi, you two," Jennifer said cheerily. "Hank and I took your suitcase along with my bag down to your car. Shall we hit the road?"

FIFTEEN

HANK FOLLOWED GEOFF'S hesitant steps down to Kitty's car waiting quietly below the steep grade in the new hours of the morning. The ominous silence felt unnatural.

Hank hugged Jennie passionately, kissed her lightly, and looked reverently into her eyes.

This will be the first time Jennie and I have been apart overnight since we were married.

He chuckled to himself. That was three years ago. No wonder he was feeling separation anxiety! How he loved this woman. He missed her already.

He watched her laugh as she slipped into the passenger seat. She leaned over to Kitty with a question on her features, then they got out of the car and traded places. When Jennie took the driver's seat Hank's smile still lingered as the taillights disappeared.

Only when the car disappeared around the corner was he able to pull his eyes away and follow Geoff's broad shoulders. Geoff was well ahead, stepping resolutely up the incline without a backward glance, until he stopped abruptly beside his Tacoma pickup. Then he turned.

Hank was shocked by the blank expression on Geoff's face, an ashen grey canvass plumbed by two tanzanite stones, blue-black, set in the hollows of his eye sockets.

"Is something wrong, my friend?" Hank asked faintly.

Geoff's voice was as expressionless as his face. "I'm going into town."

"Town? I thought we were currently involved in an insulation project. Are you are planning to abandon me in the middle of it?"

"I have to. It's time to build me a road."

"Wha...at? What've you been smokin'?"

Geoff ignored Hank's uncharacteristic words.

"I have to. Cavey told me last spring he could supply a Cat when I needed it. I'm going to take him up on it. I need it now."

Astonished, Hank ran his hand over his bald head. Geoff must be talking about his old boss at Caveman Road Construction. What he saw in Geoff's eyes unnerved him.

"Now? This very day?"

"This very minute." Geoff said flatly. "Before I explode." Hank cocked his head.

The closed look in Geoff's eyes was not an invitation to discussion. "Hank, I must. I have to grapple with something bigger than a chainsaw."

"Hey, hey. Slow down. Do you not mean Some One bigger?"

"Oh pul...lease. I can't handle a sermon right now. I know what I need, Hank. I need to rip something apart — before I blow up. I know how to deal with myself. God knows me, and He won't mind."

Geoff pulled out his phone impulsively.

"Gotta make a quick call to Kitty so she doesn't worry." It took him just a moment.

Hank recognized a wall that was insurmountable. May as well back off and let God do the talking. Besides, maybe He already had. Perhaps Geoff really did know what he needed right now.

"Very well, then, Geoff. If you do not require my help with this, you are on your own. I shall go back to the insulation under the rafters—and if I am done before you get back, I will start the ceiling logs."

"Leave the insulation for the two of us." Geoff commanded tersely. "Work on the balcony 'til I get back. C'mon, Yukon." Without another word he jumped into his pickup and drove down the mountain, leaving Hank standing, staring after him.

It was nearly noon when Geoff returned hauling a flat-deck loaded with a bright orange excavator, catching tree branches as he maneuvered the rig as close to their campsite as possible.

Hank heard him coming long before he met him at the bottom of the grade. Geoff parked the transport trailer and expertly lowered the deck.

Hank approached in astonishment. The huge Cat glistened in the sunshine.

"That monster looks like it just came out of a sales flyer. It looks brand new."

"It is brand new," Geoff said. "The guys have most of the equipment out on the road—except for Old Clunky, which is on its last legs and in for repair. This is the best and only Cat he had on the lot. He gave me a smokin' deal. Cavey's always known how good I am, so he told me to give this one its trial run before it goes out with his crew. I doubt he'll even send me a bill." Geoff grinned.

The pride he was showing had replaced some of the blackness he had taken with him earlier. He was less like a zombie and more like himself. *Thank God some life had returned to his bones.* Hank's admiration for the young man swept over him in waves of relief.

"You know what you're doing?"

"Watch me," Geoff said as he clapped Hank on the back and leapt onto the flat-deck to fire up the beast. It roared to life, and he backed it down the ramp.

That's exactly what Hank did for the next few hours. Watched Geoff. Watched in awe as Geoff's borrowed Cat dug into the depths of Mount Mercy.

Yukon hung out beside Hank, erect as a sled dog waiting to hear the "mush" that never came. Hank ruffled her ears. "Let's watch for a while, girl," he said. "Then we'll head up to the cabin to do some work while we listen to his racket in the distance."

LICENSE FOR PERMISSION TO DESTROY seared Geoff's gut. Intensity he had never known, on any road project he'd ever done for Caveman Construction, burned inside him. Today this mountain project belonged to him and him alone. Every errant tree was subject to his dominance. His self-focused fury blazed, and the forest around him would have to share it. Power raged from his chest, through his brawny biceps and into the controls.

The Cat's throaty rumble filled the clearing as Geoff surveyed the timbered seclusion with a catch in his throat. Two opposing options argued in his gut. First, to keep his cabin hidden, leaving the forest as naturally wooded as possible. Second, to clear away enough of the timber to accommodate even Kitty's old Chevy. There was no contest. Kitty's Chevy won.

Geoff became one with the excavator's great hoe arm. Power surged into the muscles of his legs, steadying him as he swung and dug and bullied a road through the rocky ground and the unlucky trees, flagged a month ago when he was showing Logan his plan. Every ounce of the machine's force was at his command.

In order to level the steep grade and make it viable for vehicles less powerful than 4x4s, they had mapped an *S*, veering west from the main logging road, cutting east over the ruts higher up, and swerving back west, easing gradually into the meadow beside the cabin.

The motor roared, and the great tracks rolled toward the first huge spruce tree marked for removal. The bucket's teeth dug deep into its base, and the brave trunk yielded its roots like a mammoth tooth from the jaws of the mountain. Geoff felt the pain deep in his belly, right where he wanted it. SHRIEK. The crunch of flailing branches made the air convulse as it fell. Killing this evergreen was a purposeful eradication of the rebuke Geoff felt in his wretched soul. With the grip of the bucket, he balanced the tree and swung it well off the designated road.

It was his own fault Kitty had sunk into depression. He should have been stronger for her. He pointed the Cat at the next proud conifer and stacked it on top of the first. With each sweep of the long arm satisfaction healed him.

A huge ponderosa was slated for sacrifice at the bend toward the west. Like a Roman warrior, the jaws of the excavator wrestled the tree and dropped it, lifeless, to the ground. Other smaller evergreens crackled like kindling. He exalted in his exhaustion with grim pleasure, feeling exactly as he had hoped to feel at the finish—spent and consumed.

Geoff's long experience with Caveman had taught him to cut the road on a perfect incline. For the next step he would need a smaller bobcat. Before any gravel could be laid, he needed to level off the mess he had made and correct the degree of slant. With that much accomplished, he could show Kitty a new way back to the cabin. "Soon I will show her all the way home."

YUKON IGNORED EVERY inviting sound that met her ears and every smell that tantalized her nostrils. With ears erect, she fixed her slanted amber eyes on the monstrous Cat that had swallowed Geoff inside it. That Geoff would come back out she had no doubt.

The one time he had stepped down and around behind the beast was not the time to go to him. He had not whistled to give her that permission. So she stayed. When the monster disappeared from her sight Yukon hardly moved a muscle. The roar and the crushing and the other noises accompanying the excavator all assured her Geoff was still somewhere out there. Yukon simply emitted a few puzzled whines to reassure Hank as he watched beside her. After all, Hank was part of Geoff's pack, so she felt happy enough to guard him. But she *had* whined bitterly when Hank led her back up the hill to go back to building the cabin.

GEOFF WAS DONE. He made one final scan of the last tree that had been flagged and let out a huge sigh of relief. He swung the cab 180 degrees, moving the excavator over the meadow to pull up close to the flat-deck. He killed the engine and took a leap off the track onto the ground. He brushed sweat and dust off his face.

Grinning triumphantly, he pointed two victory fingers into the sky as he watched Hank and Yukon returning from the cabin site.

JOY AND RELIEF SPILLED over Hank as he watched Geoff and Yukon reunite. The dog didn't need a whistle now to recognize Geoff's body language. She leapt at him and yowled in joy, nearly bowling him over, long before Hank was on his feet to welcome them.

"Good girl!" Geoff affirmed her. He grabbed her neck and roughed her up from her ears to her flanks.

Hank stuck out his hand and took Geoff's in a biting grip. "Congratulations, son," he said with a salutation he had never used before. Deep respect swelled in his chest. Geoff had done what he promised—wrestled his demons to the ground. "I think you've leveled the devil for this day, haven't you?"

"I do believe I have," Geoff said as he threw an arm around Hank's shoulder. "What's out there to eat? I'm starved."

Not surprisingly, Chef Hank had steak marinating. Soon sizzling aromas wafted over the meadow and all three of them were diving into buffalo steaks and salad.

As they chatted, Hank saw that Geoff had left his explosive mood in the forest with the fallen trees. Geoff even volunteered, with laughter tingeing his words, "I can hardly wait to see Kitty's face. She's going to love this. Even her poor old car will be able to make it after I get the grading done next week."

"She may have a little trouble," Hank teased, "with the holes and the rocks and the rubble."

Hank enjoyed his private little joke about the potholes. He actually knew more about road building than Geoff thought. He was pretty sure Geoff didn't realize he was getting his leg pulled.

But then, Geoff wouldn't care if he was.

IN A SHORT WEEK Geoff would have the balance of the grading done, and that would be the next step to bringing Kitty home. His old laugh rang over Mount Mercy. The moon was riding the ridge. Geoff could not even remember the rage that had helped him operate the excavator today.

SIXTEEN

THE MORNING BEFORE Geoff became the crazed lone excavator, Jennifer had started the drive back to Nobleton while Kitty curled up on the seat.

Her heart went out to her 'second daughter'. Kitty appeared exhausted. This whole emotional trauma must have caused her more stress than anyone realized. When Kitty disappeared so many months ago, her note indicated she wanted some space but promised to let them know when she was settled again. Now she must be flooded with relief.

Thank you, Lord, for keeping her safe. Thank you for bringing her back to us after all this time. Lord, fill her with true peace.

AS KITTY SNOOZED, the clamour of the cell in her pocket awakened her. She fumbled into the depths of her jacket and mumbled, "Hello."

"Kitty." Geoff's voice was thick with loneliness.

"Geoff..."

"Kitty, you're not driving, are you?"

Kitty laughed. "Not in the state I'm in – which I can't figure out. Jennifer is still at the wheel. How come you're interrupting our escape?"

The urgency in his voice stirred her from her grogginess. "I just had to before my next job. Won't keep you, Kitty. You just have to hear me tell you this. I love you, Kitty. With all my heart. Now you can tell me. If you do love me, I need to hear you say it."

Kitty gasped, and the words could not be contained. "Yes, yes, Geoff. You know I love you! I do."

"Good! Bye for now, then." His phone went dead.

The shock woke her up thoroughly.

"Jennifer," she whispered. "He asked me if I loved him! I think I can drive a bit, now."

Kitty took a brief couple hours at the wheel and then returned it to Jennifer.

KITTY COULD FEEL THE TENSION of the brakes as Jennifer drove into Nobleton. The streetlights had come on. When they pulled up in front of the diner, Hank's sign was shining in welcome.

"Rustic Diner."

"*Country Organic*" flashed beneath it. Kitty tried to grin and open her eyes while stretching her cramped limbs.

"Wakey, wakey," said Jennifer. "We're home."

Best place for Kitty right now was bed. Rather than taking her into Hank's restaurant, Jennifer took Kitty's suitcase from the trunk, flipped on the light at the side entrance and led her upstairs to the apartment where Hank once lived. She gently took Kitty's purse from her hand and placed it on the dining room table.

"Your bed's all ready," Jennifer said. "The kitchen is stocked, but I'm going to go downstairs and bring you up one of Suzie's wonderful coconut muffins and some fresh coffee. She's probably all closed up by now, but we all know where she puts things."

Jennifer patted Kitty's shoulder. "You can have a shower or a soak if you like, or just fall into bed and call it a day. I'll check in on you in half an hour."

She gave Kitty a long mommy-hug, then closed the door and went downstairs to the diner.

Kitty still felt dazed and half asleep. How *could* she have let Jennifer drive nearly the whole way? Well, not to not worry about that right now.

She looked around. It was evident the whole place had been repainted and freshened up. The bedroom welcomed her with a soft blue tone that called gently, "Rock-a-bye Baby." The bathroom sparkled with invitation. If it didn't feel like such a big effort to take off her clothes and run the tub. Why not take a long spa session tonight. Why *was* she so tired?

Instead, Kitty walked into the living room and sank into a tan ultra-suede couch. A matching recliner sat next to it. She moved to the recliner, just to check if it was as comfortable as it looked. With one deep breath Kitty pulled the lever, leaned back, and dozed off again.

Momentarily.

Her hand flipped the lever yet another time. Kitty snapped to a self-conscious start when Jennifer set the promised coconut muffins and coffee on the side-table.

"Thank you so much, Jen." She got up out of the recliner and hugged her. "You shouldn't have to be running up and down those stairs just to pamper me."

"Kitty-Cat," Jennifer said, "it's my pleasure. This couldn't make me happier. I brought up a litre of homo and some cream, in case you want it. They're in your fridge. You can either go to the diner for breakfast in the morning — Suzie will be happy to see you —or find something you like in your own kitchen. Please do what suits your pleasure, as Hank would say. Your new house key and your car keys are on the table. Make yourself at home. And don't be in a hurry. Start with a good rest before you think about going to work."

"Thank you so much, Jen. I'm sure I'll be perkier tomorrow," Kitty said. "I'm anxious to see what Suzie will have for me to do. And learn. I'll certainly need at least some orientation, although I've had lots of experience in this field, and I am a fast learner." She grinned and sat down on the couch.

"I'm sure you are," Jennifer said. "Anyway, I want you to relax for a couple of days first. You don't need to start until Thursday. I sure hope you haven't caught a bug or something."

"Nah," Kitty said. "To tell you the truth, I haven't *ever* been through such an emotional roller coaster in my life. No wonder it's getting to me." She let the words slip off her tongue without editing. Jennifer knew all about it anyway. "I probably needed to get away from the mountain to get a grip on my life. I'm so grateful to be here with you, Jen."

Jennifer joined Kitty on the sofa and hugged her again. "I'm going to love you and leave you," she said. "Take your time in the morning. I'm going to head home to my house and not bother you until tomorrow afternoon. Right now, just climb into bed and sleep it all off."

Jennifer closed the door to the apartment. Kitty could hear her footsteps receding down the stairs. Kitty didn't feel like any coffee or muffins tonight, after all.

When Kitty awoke with a start the next morning, she felt tears wet on her cheeks. She looked upward with a faint sense of daylight, expecting to see the roof of Geoff's tent. Slowly she realized why her cheeks were damp. Engulfed by a deep combination of gratefulness and sadness, she sat up and gazed around the pretty bedroom.

Lord. Are You here?

Something inside her responded weakly in the affirmative.

A deep, desolate sigh escaped, and Kitty decided to act positively. Since she was here at the pleasure of Hank and Jennifer's generosity, she'd better at least act like she appreciated it. Kitty donned a fresh pair of old jeans and T-shirt, grabbed her purse, again feeling slightly nauseous, headed down the stairs, and stepped carefully into the half-seated restaurant below.

The Rustic Diner was as welcoming as she remembered it from the huge double wedding reception Jennifer and Hank had held here three years ago with Jennifer's daughter Becky and faithful, lovable Logan. Only days after their return from individual honeymoon trips, they had turned the place into a festive venue for their belated reception. The friends and family had practically pushed the walls out with excitement and joy. Today, stripped of the party decorations, the Rustic Diner was a new restaurant to Kitty, both elegant and rustic, and warmly inviting. She could learn to enjoy working in a place like this.

A server with the name tag "Barb" smiled at her. Barb led her to a small corner table and left her with a menu and a lemon-rimmed glass of icy water. From near the kitchen, another pair of bright eyes widened in recognition above an even wider smile.

Like a party welcome, the young woman about Kitty's own age stormed her table, landed on the chair across from her and extended both hands in excited hospitality.

"You gotta be Kitty!" she said. "Welcome. I'm Susan. I'm sure you don't remember me from the reception. I was hiding in the corners then, watching you take pictures. Now I'm a permanent replacement under Handsome Hank, our boss-man." Kitty snickered approvingly at the description of Jennifer's *Handsome Hank*. "I've got my Red Seal of Approval recently,"

Susan said. "Jennifer tells me you are going to be helping us, too." Her effervescence bubbled all over her welcoming words.

"So you're the irreplaceable Susan," Kitty said, reaching out her hand for a quick clasp. "What a pleasure to meet you. You look just as sweet as they said you were."

A modest blush crept over Susan's round cheeks. "It's my plan not to bother you right away, as I'm sure you're busy. I just thought I'd say hi." She reluctantly turned to greet a customer at the entrance.

Barb approached with a coffee pot. "May I take your order? Maybe some of our farm-fresh eggs—or yogurt and berries?"

Kitty smiled and said, "You know what... I'm not sure I'm feeling hungry yet. I think I'll just have a black coffee for now, thanks." Barb cheerfully filled the mug sitting in readiness on the pine table and left Kitty to enjoy her quiet.

Kitty lifted the cup hesitantly, gagged, and set it down again. What kind of coffee were they serving here, anyway? It had to be a free-trade variety of Hank's preference. Maybe it had been standing in the pot longer than it should. She'd have to watch that when she started working. Then hunger struck, and she did wish she'd ordered the eggs. *Oh, well.*

Kitty picked up her purse and left. She didn't really need coffee anyway, and she wanted to wander around Nobleton for a little community orientation. The Rustic Diner was situated near the main highway, so she walked to the town center. She could use a few groceries. If she didn't buy too many, carrying the bag would be good exercise.

It was a nice little city. She might be happy working here for a while—especially if Geoff came to see her, as he had promised. Her heart did its familiar flip.

Yes, Geoff. He said he was coming to visit. Next weekend.

Would he, really? After her last awful confession? She'd finally spilled it all, but the aftertaste of her exaggerations, still rancid in her system, made her wonder how he could possibly keep his promise. Then she was shaken by the memory of the moment-long phone call he had made asking her to tell him she loved him. How big was this love he was vowing?

Concentrate on groceries, girl.

Kitty walked into Extra Foods and wandered aimlessly around the store. She had noticed bread in the apartment freezer. What else? Find some fruit. At the end of the orange and banana aisle someone appeared to be offering a demonstration. The tall white sign said, "Fresh Florida Pomegranate Arils."

All Kitty had eyes for were the woman's expert fingers extracting the juicy red seeds from the fruit. She remembered trying to open a pomegranate years ago, frustrated by total incompetence and a bare sip of juice. Never again since then. But now she could feel the saliva flowing, and there was nothing she craved more than a fat clump of ruby pomegranate arils. The demonstrator gave her a sample that filled her taste buds.

Kitty bought nine pomegranates. One to practice on, two to make her an expert, and six more so she wouldn't run out. Plus vanilla ice cream. She'd experiment with the woman's technique when she got home.

With her grocery bag in her hand, Kitty stepped out of the store and carried on down the sidewalk. Her stomach growled. Just a few doors ahead, a handy Tim Horton's enticed her. Probably should have a little snack to last her until she got back to the apartment for more pomegranates.

The rush of coffee hit her nostrils as she opened the door. *What in the world was that bitter aroma?* Not Timmy's, too! And what other smell was fouling up the atmosphere in her favourite coffee place? Soup? Some kind of soup. Maybe she *was* getting the flu! Kitty rushed into the ladies' room, gagging, certain she was going to throw up. She didn't.

"Gotta get out of this place," she said aloud.

Further down the street Kitty took a seat at a bus stop and wiped her damp, hot face. She reached into her purse for a mint and closed her eyes while the flavour cleared her senses. Had she picked up everything she needed —besides pomegranates? Or maybe what she had picked up was a bug. Surely not. What else should she put in her cupboards, now that she had a place to call home for a while. Maybe some Kleenex. Maybe some TP? Maybe…. Oh NO!

Kitty's heart bumped against her ribs and then fell forward. Below that her stomach turned over an imaginary shovelful of thick sludge. She was immobilized, and irrational for long moments. She got up in a trance and followed the sidewalk toward the Rustic Diner.

She needed to lie down.

She had to think.

She was three weeks into her cycle.

She was never late.

"KITTY. YOU DON'T LOOK VERY WELL," were Jennifer's first words when she came up to Kitty's suite shortly after noon. "Do you feel sick? Maybe you do have the flu."

Kitty tried to smile, failing to feel reassuring. "I don't know. I went for some fresh air this morning but didn't stay out long."

"Did you have lunch? Can I get you something?"

"No, that's okay. I just had a quick serving of crackers and an apple. I'm fine for now."

Kitty convinced Jennifer that she just needed to rest some more. As soon as Jennifer was gone, Kitty grabbed her car keys and took a trip to London Drugs. If Jennifer should ask, she'd just say she needed some Tylenol.

This time it was the pharmacy aisles she wandered around in, picking up a box here, a package there, having no idea what she should get. Had she taken some time to Google it, she'd know what to look for. Duh. While she fumbled in her purse for her smartphone, a wise-looking woman in a cotton vest labeled "Pharmacist" startled her.

"Can I help you find something, miss?"

Well, why not. Nobody knew her here, anyway.

"I think I've missed my period. Do you happen to have something to bring it on?"

The clerk raised her eyebrows and, with a knowing look, said, "Come with me." Around the other side of the aisle, she reached into one of the shelves and brought out a small box and said, "This is probably our best first step." Kitty barely glanced at it.

"The instructions are inside," the Pharmacist said. "It's a very simple thing to use." She pressed a calling card into Kitty's hand and added gently, "Just in case you might want to contact a doctor."

With her face flaming and her heart like a block of ice, Kitty pocketed the card and took the box to the counter. She averted her eyes and handed the cashier her credit card.

Back at the apartment, Kitty had just finished reading the instructions when Jennifer tapped lightly on her door and entered the living room. Kitty flung the open box and papers into the night table drawer and hurried to meet Jennifer with a smile.

"Kitty, guess what?" Jennifer's expression made Kitty think of a little girl hiding a surprise.

She waited with questioning eyes for Jennifer to tell her.

"Geoff's on the line." Jennifer set the phone on the end table. "You can take it over in the recliner."

Kitty's facial muscles felt stiff. "I… I'm not sure… I don't think… Jennifer, can you ask him to call back? I can't handle talking to him right now."

Jennifer laughed indulgently. "Oh sure you can, Kitty. After that call in the car, you can be pretty sure he won't bite—if he hasn't already... "

"Jen-ni-fer...."

"Sorry, Kitty." Jennifer said with a small giggle. "I just couldn't resist that. Naughty me. C'mon. Go pick up. Your cell phone didn't respond. He needs to talk to you. I'll be downstairs."

All her chest wiring was on fire. Her heart was pounding and there were no words in her mind. If her crazy new fears were true, she would not be talking to Geoff again for a long time. Like a zombie Kitty picked up the land line and said in a very small voice, "Hello."

His silence was as real as his presence. She could feel his breath. She could hear his thoughts. After what seemed like an eternity his deep, husky voice embraced all of her. "Kitty. I miss you."

What was there to say but, "I miss you too."

He told her about the cabin. It was going well. It should be ready for lock-up by Friday. Hank was a fabulous cook and always made them hungry. Yukon was looking for her. It was lonely on the cabin floor when Kitty was not nearby in the tent. Geoff had a surprise for Kitty.

She didn't ask him what it was. She didn't say much of anything.

"Kitty," Geoff said, "you and I are going to get a grip on our foolishness. I'm coming to Nobleton on Thursday."

"Oh."

No.

There was a tease in his voice. "Is that all you can say? Oh?"

"No-oo. I just thought you might want to wait a bit. It's a long drive. Come later or something, when you're not so busy."

"Actually, this is perfect timing. There's a bit more to do on the cabin, and I need a few supplies. So I thought, 'Why not? I can pick Kitty up at the same time and bring her back for the weekend.' It's all worked out with Hank and Jennifer. While I'm gone Hank is staying on to do some caulking for me and keep Yukon company. He'll be going back home on Sunday, so he can bring you back with him and you can start work next week. Sound good?

"Unless you're too tired." Geoff suddenly sounded worried. "You *are* okay, aren't you? You didn't develop any flu symptoms or anything?"

"Oh, no, no," Kitty assured him. "It's just time for me to get into action, is all. Don't worry if you can't make it right now. We can always catch up later."

Geoff's voice was strong and confident. "If I could catch up right now, I would. But it will have to wait till I get there. Don't forget, Kitten, I love you."

"Okay, bye." The sound of silence deafened her. She hadn't even let him say good night.

When Jennifer bounced through the door, it was evident she and Hank had already said good night. She was all sparkles and anticipation. "So you won't have to wait too long for a visit after all," she said. "I'm happy about that." She gave Kitty a quizzical glance. "You can be happy about it, too, sweetie. Look up. Accept God's mercy and embrace His plan."

"You have any idea what His plan is?"

"Come on, Kitty. His plan is good. Lighten up... I mean with the Way, the Truth, the Life *and* the Light." Jennifer came to her and gave her shoulders a loving shake. "It's time to laugh again."

Kitty tried to lighten up, talking briefly with the server about service orientation she was interested in. Jennifer took her downstairs for dinner, but Kitty ate it in a fog, steeling herself against the smell of coffee, choosing food carefully, and ignoring the worried furrow between Jennifer's brows. When Kitty said she was worn out, they said goodnight early.

The moment Kitty felt her privacy was safe, she retrieved the pregnancy test from the drawer. Yes, the instructions were simple. Three minutes of waiting for the first pink strip left her breathless. She turned her back to the second strip lying on the bathroom counter. The ten- minute wait after that was an eternity. Kitty faced the sink again and reached for the indicator strip. The strip had turned blue.

No *wonder* coffee was making her feel nauseous!

SEVENTEEN

KITTY WAS CONVINCED of one thing only: she had to get out of the apartment before Jennifer showed up in the morning with her encouragement, her loving hugs and her calm thinking… And long before Geoff could come find her. Only one thought had charged her actions after she'd seen it—that little blue line crossing over the long blue one. *Pregnant! Run!*

As far and as fast as possible. Do not pass *Go.* Do not look for a coupon. Do not put your brain in gear. Just flip the dice and make your move.

Kitty was dressed by five a.m. to be sure she'd be ready for the first ferry leaving from the main terminal in Vancouver at seven. Then she could anticipate an hour and a half sailing to feel the breeze against her face and try to clear the churning chaos that had kept her awake most of the night.

She reached the ferry with more than enough time and joined the line driving carefully down the ferry ramp into the bowels of the Queen of Nanaimo's garage. This was the first time she'd be parking her own vehicle. She remembered the cool, dusky sensation. Before now, she had always been a passenger. Today would have been fun if life were still normal. At the very least, safety surrounded her for the moment; she could temporarily avoid the need for further explanation to anyone. Kitty maneuvered her car into position. But the nightmare was only beginning.

She locked her car and quickly made her way up to the deck for sail-away. Kitty wished sail-away could last forever, could postpone her breathing until her nightmare was over. But the nightmare was only beginning. She couldn't even think. Her thoughts made no sense.

Kitty leaned against the railing of the Queen of Nanaimo, barely aware of the wind whipping her hair as the ferry glided into the Straights of Georgia. The seagulls that dipped their wings in overhead paths always called to her; but not today. The mountainous terrain bordering the edges of the straight always lifted her heart with joy; but not today. Today her life was on hold and tomorrow was a black tunnel that left her faith behind. There were no words to describe reality. No immediate encouragement from the Word of God came to erase from her mind the only ugly word she kept hearing. No amount of nauseous ruminating could find any gentler word. It was inevitable.

Terminate!

Her stomach roiled with sludge. Kitty hadn't been able to speak that other gristly "A" word, even in her thoughts. She could hardly tell if her heart was pounding or stopping.

Horror of the impossible unknown kept her in a wide-awake nightmare, churning inside her, all over her, all around her. Kitty wanted to throw up. It could not *be*, could it? Here she was —a Jesus-girl since asking Him to be her Saviour at eight years of age —pregnant. Why hadn't He protected her?

"I love you, Kitty."

Was that assurance real? God loved her? Couldn't He have done a better job of warning her?

Then remorse, excruciating and condemning, seized her heart. Kitty well knew that the choices bringing her to this junction were her own. No one had twisted her arm. Certainly not God. Bad choices brought about bad consequences. She could blame no one but herself.

Unless, just maybe, could the test possibly have given a false positive? Could she redo the test, and then in another day find this to be only a bad dream? Maybe then she could call Geoff and explain her ghastly mistake with Lance. Geoff sounded on the phone as though he wanted to forgive her.

Then a laughter that was not real shrieked inside her brain. Kitty reached both her hands up to cover her ears, then down to caress the special place that a baby began its life— and somehow knew. It had begun.

So she had no choice —did she? She simply could not go on with life in this condition.

She needed to stop it before it *became* a baby.

Unless it *already* was one!

Kitty reached for her jar of pomegranate arils and greedily soothed her misery with a handful of their crunchy sweetness. She was hungry. Shaking the fog from her head, she left the deck and hurried downstairs to the cafeteria, determined to quit thinking.

Kitty hastily chose a bowl of beef-barley soup and a grilled cheese sandwich, surprised that the food tasted so good considering the unpredictability of her stomach. She slipped into an extended wait for the ferry trip to be over.

The ship's sound system made a warning crackle before the message blared, "We are nearing Nanaimo terminal. All passengers please prepare to disembark…"

She seemed to remember there was no hurry, yet Kitty made a hasty move toward the lower ferry and got into her car to wait for the first sounds of the engines. It was a relief to feel amusement when she thought of the words of her cousin Logan. He had been the first to take her on a ferry trip, to visit Vancouver from her home in Nanaimo.

"Listen," he had told her in a hushed voice, in just such an embarkation as now. "Get ready to hear the corn start popping." The first car engine turned over. Then the second. Then a few more, and soon the whole ferry was making popcorn all at once.

Dear cousin Logan. How could she bear his new disappointment in her? From thoughts of Logan, the picture of her mother Olivia joined her in bitterness. She didn't want to entertain thoughts of her mother who had left her as a child.

The ramp made its familiar "crunk" as she exited, headed for Nanaimo following a road that was unfamiliar.

Kitty reached her fingers into the jar that held her pomegranate arils for a handful of their crunchy sweetness. She had scarfed that bowl of beef barley soup and sandwich on the ferry. And her hunger didn't seem to let up. How *could* she need food again when she was so filled with misery and terror? How could she need a*nything*?

She lost awareness of holding the steering wheel. Another handful of pomegranate arils temporarily soothed her misery.

At the next corner the stop light turned green. Kitty realized with a start that she was already inside the city.

Wake up, girl. It's time to go see Grama-ma Nora.

A little lurch of homesickness jumped in her chest. Along with everyone else she loved, Kitty had abandoned Grama-ma, too. She'd seen her only once since her daddy's funeral. She'd wanted to tell her she loved her, to thank her for all the years she had filled in for the real mother who had simply gone away and left her in Nanaimo with her father... the daddy she had so loved.

Her first stop would be the little graveyard in the city. The headstone was small, but its location was easy to find.

"George Alexander Sampson. Asleep in Christ Jesus."

Fresh pansies, recently watered, bloomed on the grave.

Dear Grama-ma. Who else would think to show such love?

Kitty sat on the grass by the grave and revisited her sorrow. But Daddy was in a happier place, so the sorrow was hers alone.

Daddy, I could sure use your hugs and your love now.

Kitty usually felt a hard knot of resistance in her stomach where her mother's tenderness should have been. But today, in the warm presence of Daddy's memory, that knot was trying to melt into a puddle with her tears. She and Daddy and Grama-ma Nora had done just fine, thank you. But now, retching in her impossible nightmare, in her aloneness Kitty began to groan after the mother who had abandoned her.

What would her mother say to her today? "You'll get through this, daughter. Just make a decision. Get it done and get over it. Nothing human there yet. All you have now is a little seed. An embryo barely begun?"

A bitter thought raked her brain. *Too bad my mother didn't get rid of me when she had the chance.*

Or would her mother say, "You can do this, Kitty. This little seed didn't ask to be started."

184

Thanking God for the sweet years she and Grama-ma and Daddy'd had together, Kitty brushed away her memories with her tears and got back into Lizzy to visit her grandmother and her childhood home. Perhaps Grama-ma's hug could do something to calm her turmoil.

Soon Kitty recognized the street next to the one she was looking for. She turned the corner and drove down half a block. The beige asphalt shingles showed above the evergreen hedge, the salmon-colored walls peeked through. It wasn't until Kitty eased into an open spot by the sidewalk that the sign on the lawn saluted her.

SOLD.

Sold?

Oh well, what difference did it make? Sold. What difference did anything make?

Kitty stepped from her car to take a look at the home she'd grown up in. Waves of mixed memories swept over her as her eyes drifted lovingly over the aging bungalow. She had stuffed away the ache caused by her mother's dispassionate goodbye. She had exchanged it for the tender arms of Grama-ma Nora and her daddy's adoration. She enjoyed her childhood, swimming like a fish in the ocean. As a teen she had a great time learning to serve customers, first at MacDonald's in Nanaimo, and then at the restaurant in Vancouver that used to be Jen's Place, and now known as "Mel's Place." Kitty had so much to thank the Lord for.

So why had she thrown away His love and His direction of her life? The appalling mistake of it all ground inside her stomach.

Absently she walked up the wood sidewalk and looked blankly at the door. Nobody would be home, so why was she still standing here?

"Keturah?"

Grama-ma Nora, with her apron still wrapped around her plump middle and her face alight with the love always there for Kitty, walked around the side of the house and spread her arms.

Kitty ran to her with her heart pounding. Her grandmother's clinging hug brought a new torrent of tears. Grama-ma Nora picked up the corner of her apron to wipe Kitty's face, then used the other corner to dry her own, both of them laughing.

"Grama-ma! I thought you were gone!"

TWO HOURS LATER, they were still smiling at each other across the familiar varnished table, worn down by years of cups, plates and soup bowls. Grama-ma had placed crackers and peanut butter in front of them as they chatted. Delicious. But Kitty had to decline the coffee Nora had put on; the aroma was already turning her stomach. Instead, she went back to the cooler in her car and brought back a jar of her ready-to-eat pomegranate arils to share with Nora.

Where had the years flown? Their reminiscence had taken them on a journey from the historic day Kitty's mother had walked away, to the funeral of her daddy, George, a year ago. The memories brought both laughter and tears.

The pomegranate arils appeared to surprise Nora with pleasure.

As pomegranate juice slipped outside the corner of her mouth, Nora said, "Keturah, I sure hope my moving doesn't make your heart feel bad. Without neither you or Georgie around, I felt so all by myself..."

It was plain to Kitty that Nora was lonely for her home on the Queen Charlotte Islands, where she had grown up and raised her own family. She was going back there to make her home with Kitty's uncle, John, now that her first son, George, was gone. John had come to help her pack and had already returned home.

"I hardly didn't recognize you, Keturah," Nora said, "looking like you're from Hollywood with your new hair and all. But I sure can see you're still just my little girl. Too bad your Uncle John wasn't gone back home already. He would love to see you."

Perhaps now was the time to tell it. Her return to Nanaimo was born of the desperate need to share with someone she could trust—share her mortifying, preposterous truth.

"Grama-ma, I'm pregnant."

The cloud of disbelief that fell over Nora's face slowly evolved into an unspoken understanding. She came to the other side of the table and put her arms around Kitty's shoulders.

"I'm so sorry, little Ketura. I'm so sorry." Tears formed in her sad eyes, and she hugged more tightly, taking Kitty's cheeks in her hands. "But don't be worried. We'll help take care of you both."

"Oh, Grama-ma, you are as wonderful as always."

Nora stepped back and looked tenderly at her grand-daughter. "You come back with us to the Islands. You'll be safe there—and the little one will grow up well and happy. We love you, Ketura."

Deep gratitude welled up in Kitty's heart, along with the automatic resistance that sprang forward. This was a beautiful, generous offer she could not accept.

"Oh, Grama-ma. How lovely that would be. But I can't. You understand I would be trying to live in a world I've never known. It just wouldn't work."

Nora sat back down on her chair and her hopeful expression drooped. Though disappointed, she plainly understood.

"I guess...not..." She paused, biting her lips. "But God will look after both of you, somehow."

"There won't be a *'both of us.'* Nora clearly knew what Kitty had just implied.

Nora bit her lip. "Keturah, are you sure you want that?"

"I don't know how else to handle it. It's just too much to expect anyone else to understand. I have to do something intelligent about it. No reason why I shouldn't do whatever I want to. After all, I *do* live in Canada."

Nora's dark eyes misted as she choked on her words. "You have to do what you have to do. But it's not too late to make good choices. Just because the law..." Nora swallowed. "You don't want to be weeping later."

Kitty could barely contain her weeping, now drawing on the bitterness inside her.

Nora hesitated briefly, then stood up and opened a cupboard drawer. She sat down across from Kitty again and passed her a set of keys.

"Keturah," she said. "The moving truck is coming tomorrow. I got everything ready I'm taking to the islands. The people aren't having the house yet for more than a week. You can stay here, if you want to, till the real estate man comes over. Then you can just give him the keys. Could you do that for me?"

Kitty hadn't thought about anything like this, but she could see no better place to go for a few days. "Well... I guess I could do that, if nobody minds. Sure, I'd like to say good-bye to my old home... I guess."

Nora smiled gently. "Good. While you rest up, you can pray. I'm sure the Lord will tell you what to do about -- things."

"I'm sure He will," Kitty said, while confusion raged in her soul.

"Okay, then," Nora said. "You can sleep in your old room. Your saggy little old bed is one of the things that got left. I didn't want to take all my stuff I didn't have room for. We can find some bedding in one of the boxes."

"It's okay, Grama-ma. I have my own bedding in the trunk of my car. Let's not disturb your packing. Save it for when I come to visit you on the Queen Charlottes. After I bring my sleeping bag in, I want to take you out for dinner. That will be better than making a mess in the kitchen tonight.

It was dark by the time Kitty and Nora had finished their chicken at the Chick Inn and were lingering over tea. Nora wore a tender, worried expression.

"Keturah, are you sure you don't want to come home with me for a while?"

"I just can't, Grama-ma. Thank you for offering me shelter in your home with Uncle John, but I have to figure out my life for myself. I certainly didn't plan it this way. But I'll be fine."

Nora looked unconvinced.

"This is Canada." Kitty tasted the acidity in her voice. "In this country, women are no longer prisoners of their own bodies, you know. The choice is mine. I'm free to get rid of anything inside me I don't want, whenever I want to—as long as it's still inside me. That's what the law says."

Even if God put it there?

"You'd have to kill it then?" Nora's forehead wrinkled.

"Well, that's a little harsh, don't you think? What's there to kill except a bad mistake?"

Nora looked like she was searching helplessly for words she couldn't find.

"Not to worry about me, Grama-ma. I'll be fine. Don't think too much about it all. I'm okay."

After all, it is about me, now, and how my life is going to turn out. Isn't it?

She'd made a horrible mistake, but she could choose to be free. Her baby might not have that choice, but in today's tolerant society, what did that matter?

It's only a fetus, anyway.

Nora still wore her worried expression.

"Keturah, do you love this… this man?"

Kitty forced a bitter laugh to cover her revulsion. "Are you kidding me?"

As her grandmother's expression crumpled, Kitty hurried around the table to sit beside her and throw reassuring arms around her, engulfed by helpless remorse.

"I am so sorry. I don't love him, no. But I shouldn't feel the hate I feel. Grama-ma, my life is ruined. Now I have to turn from the man I truly do love." Kitty buried her face on Nora's shoulder and sobbed.

Softly praying in a language from long ago, Nora rocked her granddaughter back and forth in her arms. They sat close together until Kitty got up to pay the bill.

"Who is the one you do love, Keturah?" Kitty gasped in surprise at Nora's unexpected question. It took her strangely long minutes to answer.

Kitty pulled out a pencil and wrote Geoff's phone number on a pad from her bag, shaking her head gently, feeling pulled from within. "Only use it a very long time from now, Grama-ma. A dire emergency, maybe."

Next day, around noon, the driver closed the back doors on the moving van. Kitty and her grandmother wrapped each other in clinging arms to say their final good-bye. As Nora let go of her granddaughter she looked down into the black grocery bag hanging by sturdy handles from her left hand. She reached into the bag to pull out her purse.

"Keturah," she said thoughtfully, "I think I need to give you this now, instead of later some other time. It's the only one she ever gave us." Nora pressed into Kitty's hand a small, framed picture. "You have it."

Puzzled, Kitty accepted the picture and held the image in her gaze. The young woman looked very little older than Kitty was now. She was reminded of herself a few months ago before bleaching her hair to entertain Lance LeFevre. Kitty drew a deep breath and let it out slowly. She recognized the face of her mother.

"Come on, Ms. Sampson," called the truck driver. "I'm sorry to rush you, but we don't wanna miss the next ferry."

Nora climbed into the passenger side and waved sadly at Kitty as they drove away. Kitty stood with filling eyes until the truck had turned the corner and disappeared.

EIGHTEEN

GEOFF DROVE HEEDLESSLY above his self-declared speed limit down Mount Mercy, his heart soaring in gratefulness. His Tundra threw gravel across all of the newly graded access road, speaking the language of joy bounding from his spirit. As the tires grabbed the pavement of the right turn onto Highway 3, Geoff barely braked. At the top of his voice, he sang the boldest hymn of praise he could think of. *"Glory, glory hallelujah; Glory, glory hallelujah...."* Too bad he had to leave Yukon behind—to keep Hank company. If she were here with him, he was certain his empathetic canine partner would also be sensing the Presence surrounding him.

The reason for his heart-song was a simple decision. He had let. It. Go.

He had learned his early lessons in forgiveness at the Rustic Diner where he had found a friend in Hank's then-head waiter, Jennifer. Her unflagging faith made him question the reality of his own. He had unburdened to her the story of his birthmother, a homeless wanderer who died when she bore him, leaving him in the care of the kind woman who had taken her in. Wondering as a teen about his biological father, every beat of his heart had become a stroke of hatred toward the father he had never known.

Just three short years ago he had unloaded into the lap of God all those years of loathing and accepted the Peace that Jesus Christ had poured into his transformed new life. Only when he accepted that Jesus Christ had taken to the cross the sins, not only of Geoff Armistad, but also the man who had fathered and abandoned him, could forgiveness mend his heart. Since Geoff's own acid heart had been forgiven, he had also been able to forgive the man who he was convinced had fathered him and walked away.

With the sweep of God's Holy Spirit over his soul, he recognized that Kitty's mistake should not be held over her, any more than he must bear the ones he had made himself. Irrepressible joy erupted from his soul into God's forgetfulness when he embraced his own ability to forgive.

He was familiar with the verse in the Bible that said, "The past has gone; the new has come." It had rung true to him before; now he thought the fresh recognition of God's redemption would burst his chest. He had to get back to Kitty—if even for just a few hours, to convince her they could make a fresh start. They belonged together. Hallelujah. The Truth had set him free.

He didn't have time today to look for what he wanted: *the ring!* But he could surely find time—perhaps when he was in Nobleton over the weekend—to find it. He planned to take Kitty back to Mount Mercy and up those glorious slopes to place it on her finger. Shivers of hope swept through him. Hope that made him think as an excited little boy once again.

Even if he couldn't expect, just yet, to keep her with him permanently, he had to see her to clear the smog of misery between them. How could he convince her that the unsavoury past, for both of them, was behind them?

Geoff made the whole trip a prayer.

His Tundra continued to float on wings. He planned to stop at the Nobleton Home Depot for the building supplies he told Hank they would need later. What was it, again, that he planned to pick up? Oh, right. He would need more caulking soon. He might think of something else he could use too, if he tried.

No matter how he had to legitimize these extra miles, Geoff could simply not wait ten more days to talk to Kitty—to be close enough to her to make her understand. Whatever happened wasn't her fault. It especially wasn't her fault *forever*. Their loving God had placed them both under the cloak of His indescribable mercy.

By the time he was nearing the Nobleton turn-off, a deep peace had calmed him. His heart, thudding slowly in his chest, was salved with confidence and certainty.

He had left a message on Jennifer's cell not too long ago. He presumed she would be expecting him soon. Maybe she would even have arranged to make his arrival a surprise for Kitty.

JENNIFER PRESSED HER RED EYES with a cold washcloth. Geoff would be arriving soon, and she hoped she could hide the evidence. She'd been wiping tears most of the afternoon.

It was getting late. Geoff had phoned earlier that morning when she was out. He had left a message buoyant with expectation.

"Jennie-Mom!" His deep voice filled the phone. "Surprise, surprise! I'm on my way to Nobleton. Postpone the supper plans if you can. But don't tell Kitty. She's not expecting me until Saturday. I want to surprise her."

Jennifer had decided not to call him back. She'd just let him come here to receive her consolation and mothering.

Jennifer tried to read. Bible first, an old novel later, then gave up and wandered aimlessly from room to room, remembering the last visit they'd had in their home with Geoff. She couldn't help smiling through the tears that dampened her cheeks. Geoff had been so endearing, when his embarrassment over Kitty's visit to his mountain revealed how smitten he was. Kitty was so perfect for him.

So how was he going to handle this new turn of events?

It was getting late when she decided to bake some cookies—Hank's famous "oatmeal crisps." The timer buzzed. Jennifer clicked it off and was taking the last pan out of the oven to set it on the ceramic stove-top when she heard the sound of a motor. A long arm of light seeped through the far bay window and disappeared. Someone cut the engine.

Geoff.

A playful pattern dinged on her doorbell as she hurried to the back entrance and swung it open. Geoff grabbed her with affectionate arms.

"Smells good in here," he proclaimed.

Happiness leaped to her throat. How she loved this big lug. He felt like a son to both Hank and her, and he never failed to raise her spirits. She took his hand and led him to the cookies.

"These are warm." Jennifer presented the pan on the counter. "And these on the stove are hot. Be careful."

"Oatmeal Crisps!" Grinning, he grabbed two with each hand. "I'm starved," he said through a mouth full of cookie.

"Looks like you're ready for dinner," Jennifer said.

196

"As ready as a growing boy can be," he said. "However, I did hope to get here in time to have supper with you and Kitty. Have you eaten yet?"

Jennifer shook her head.

"Good. Take me to Kitty's. I can't wait. Hope she's hungry, too."

Jennifer couldn't hold back all the gathering tears. Her eyes filled and she blinked.

Geoff looked puzzled. "What is it, Jen? Hey, babe. You've been crying."

Alarm appeared in his darkening blue gaze.

Now her eyes overflowed. She dropped her head in her hands and sobs began.

"Jennifer, what is it?" He gathered her trembling shoulders into his arms.

"Geoff..." Her sobs choked her. "Kitty isn't here anymore. She's gone."

"Gone? What are you talking about? Where's she gone to? When's she coming back?"

"She didn't say, Geoff. She just... left."

"Left?" His arms fell to his sides, and he stepped back with disbelief curtaining his face. "She can't have! She knows I'm coming. I promised."

Jennifer had no words to describe her grief. "Her car's gone, too," she told him. Kitty had disappeared well before Jennifer had a chance to tell her good morning.

Geoff exploded like a crazy man, his expression frantic. He snatched Jennifer's hand and pulled her outside and into the cab of his truck. He turned on the motor. Hit the gas pedal. Careened down the driveway. Out onto the street.

Around the edge of town. Slammed on his breaks at the Rustic Diner.

He sat still in the cab and raised his eyes to the darkened windows of the apartment Hank had offered Kitty. He slowly stepped out of the truck and walked around the cab to help Jennifer step out. He held her hand as he led her up the street-lit stairs. At the top he stopped and drew in a deep, harsh breath.

"It's open," Jennifer said.

Geoff opened the door and stepped into the darkness. Jennifer found the light switch behind him. No one was home. The place was immaculate.

Jennifer walked around Geoff's stiff outline and into the bedroom, where the down quilt and pillows looked plumply inviting. Freshly washed sheets she'd left up here this morning were stacked on a chair. The stark emptiness of the room mocked her.

She came back to the living room where Geoff stood without expression. His arms hung at his sides, palms outwards in disbelieving 'why.'

Jennifer bent down and picked up a crumpled piece of paper that represented her own initial response. She moved to the table, sat down and carefully smoothed out the wrinkles.

"Come," she said to Geoff. "You'd better see this, too."

The note was signed in careful handwriting with the signature Geoff had never yet seen. He remained standing as Jennifer handed it to him. She knew what he would read.

Jennifer, Hank, Geoff,

I've realized too late what a terrible mistake I nearly made. I can't just give up my photography to work in a restaurant when I have a mentor so ready and willing to help me succeed. I beg you all to forgive me. I don't want my mistakes to spoil your lives, either. Especially yours, Geoff. You are the kindest, most caring person I have ever known. So I will just retrace my steps, go on with my career and take myself out of your lives. God bless you. Be happy.

PS Please don't try to find me.

Geoff's face collapsed and his hurt slowly changed to despair. Jennifer went to him and wrapped her arms around him.

"Jennifer," he groaned. "Kitty loves me."

Jennifer locked the apartment behind them. Geoff helped her back into the pickup and drove in silence, strictly at the speed limit, back to her house. He obeyed like a robot from another world when she told him to bring in his bag. He sat down and placed his arms on her kitchen table. Slowly his head wilted over his arms.

Jennifer placed a cup of coffee in front of him.

"What do you feel like eating?" she asked gently.

He looked up like he hadn't heard her.

"She loves me," he said. "Her note is lying. If you had heard her telling me the things she did, you would know she hates that life."

"I didn't have to hear what she told you," Jennifer said. "Kitty could never hide it from me. I know her too well. She went back to *her* photography, not to that animal."

"Then what in the world is she thinking?" He picked up his coffee automatically, because it was there. He set it down again and faced Jennifer in bewilderment. "I prayed all the way here. I thought God said, 'yes.' How could I have been so wrong?"

"Are you sure it's God telling you that you're wrong?" He stared blankly back at her. "Geoff, don't believe your fears. You know 'perfect love casts out fear,' so just keep believing what God told you."

Geoff spoke in a whisper. "What if the voice was just an echo of my own?"

Jennifer took his hands in hers. "Let's pray together before I feed you—which I *will* do. You'll stay at our house tonight before you head back. I'm going to ask the Lord to give you peace, continue to guide you as you sleep, and give you some direction in the morning."

He looked as though it didn't matter.

AFTER AN EARLY BREAKFAST on Friday morning, Geoff hugged Jennifer good-bye. They had talked last night—a long time. Nothing made any sense. Nothing they came up with suggested any reasons for Kitty's hasty behaviour.

Jennifer's weeping promise that she would keep on praying and believing lifted his spirit. He had awakened with a new determination to trust. When you didn't understand, didn't have the answers, and didn't know where to go from here, what was there left, but Trust? Trust in the Father whose love was unfailing.

Geoff thought he heard it: *I've got your back, son.*

Geoff didn't even look for a hardware or lumberyard, where he could pick up the extra supplies he didn't yet need. Jennifer would have filled Hank in by the time he got back home, anyway.

That evening at dusk, Hank and Yukon both greeted him the way he'd expected them to; Hank in silent understanding, Yukon with the usual wild abandon—until she, too, realized that quiet was in order. She licked Geoff's fingers, whimpering, and clung to his legs.

NINETEEN

KITTY WAS TIRED in the extreme and very glad she had Nora's house to herself, even if her surroundings consisted largely of blank wall space. She couldn't believe how good it felt to just sleep again in Grama-ma's old place. But when her brain woke up, it was to a nightmare she wished she knew how to forget, or at least to ignore. The nightmare that was slowly materializing into gruesome reality.

Her first panic, back in Nobleton, had come with disbelief, but the horror of the clear truth was worse than the initial shock. A multi-faced ogre was laughing at her. The facts were ganging up on her —her weariness, her increasing appetite, her nausea, her cravings, her unusual aversion to all things coffee.

The truth was that if anything were to change, she'd have to take action. Denial was no longer a possibility. Unfortunately, in her ignorance, she had no idea what that action might be. Before now Kitty had never dreamed of the possibility of an unwanted pregnancy. Things like that just didn't happen to girls like her. Neither, for that matter, did any form of relationship with as suave and unsavory a character as Lance LeFevre. And it was nobody's fault but her own. Regret swept its hot agony over her again.

The high school she'd attended offered special classes to consider teen relationships, and she and her daddy and grama-ma sometimes discussed a few things like that. But nothing had come up then as serious as an unexpected pregnancy. Of course, she knew what the Bible taught about life. Everyone knew "thou shalt not kill." But that was talking about a real baby you could hold in your arms. Until it was breathing, it was only the beginning of a fetus. Wasn't it?

Outside her body there was no life. Was there? Nothing that could survive. So why was she *this* upset? Kitty almost wished she'd paid more attention to those high-school classes, if even for a little insight.

On the other hand, any discussion she might have shared then would hardly be of any help to her present reality.

The next day, Kitty spent most of her time on and near the lumpy single bed that used to be hers. In between her fitful naps, she went back to the city library she'd frequented as a child, surreptitiously searching for information. The photographs she found of developing fetuses only made her stomach churn and ignited a feverish desire to understand more about her condition. None of the unborn pictures did anything but increase her misery.

Why she'd ever want to talk to Lance, she couldn't imagine. But the possibility tormented her. Maybe it was closer to reality to ask, "Why not talk to Lance?" He was the only connection she had to her quandary. Yet the thought of discussing with Lance anything so delicate made her feel queasy. He didn't deserve to know, anyway.

Kitty's fingertips urged her; unbidden, she took the cell phone from her bag.

Then the shock of reality hit her. She *could* call Lance but certainly didn't want him to have her phone number. Kitty walked into the kitchen where a land line telephone still hung on the wall and placed her hand above it, breathing deeply. She picked it up. It was still alive.

She wished Lance's phone number were not so vivid in her mind. Kitty clenched her teeth and dialed his Vancouver number.

No answer.

Relief swept over her. That had been a foolish experiment. She wouldn't make that one again. Lance couldn't help her. She wouldn't want him to even if he could. She wouldn't want him to locate her at all—which could be quite possible if she didn't take precautions to stay hidden. If anyone needed a phone number, Grama-ma was now in possession of Geoff's – but that was just for a possible emergency. Lance would never hear of it.

A rush of panic struck her. She'd better not let anyone find her lazing around in Nanaimo.

Kitty just wanted this to be over with. She had better get out of here early, before anyone caught up with her. She'd call the realtor and arrange to turn in the keys tomorrow.

After that, what next?

Funny she hadn't thought to consult her computer.

After spending half the next night on Google, following link after link, Kitty came up with her plan. She decided to spend one more day and sleep one more night in her free accommodation, then head out on the ferry. Now she had links to a few ideas to ponder, and a few solid addresses in Vancouver of facilities that wouldn't be asking many questions.

Once in Vancouver, her best bet would be to walk into a hospital designated for just such emergencies. All she had to do was make one phone call in the morning, right from wherever she was, and she would have an appointment at a clinic. A short few hours later her mistake would be no more. What could be simpler?

Early in the morning, Kitty met the realtor to give him the keys, then drove her car onto the ferry with the plan to let big, forgiving Vancouver City swallow her up. After that, she could be normal again. Hopefully.

Unexpectedly, when Kitty went back to her computer during that return ferry trip, new horrors introduced themselves; she discovered the gristly truth about aborted baby parts, that they were sometimes preserved and sold. The videos were incriminating. New panic caused new nausea. While she knelt on the cold floor in front of the stainless steel toilet bowl of the constantly shifting ferry, Kitty felt, for the first time in her life, that she could benefit from a dose of alcohol. Which she had no intention of trying.

Good thing her fetus was too infinitely small to have any parts. She hoped.

KITTY DROVE THE TRIP from the ferry, parked her car and didn't stop until midway up the broad stairs of the hospital. A senior lady with a floral handbag shuffled in front of her, clinging to the handrail. On the left, two laughing children, probably pre-school-age, skipped ahead of their mother. A smart-looking gentleman stepped briskly around them all, and up the stairs.

Kitty wanted to turn around and run. She gagged back the sensation of acid reflux and waited to see if there was anyone else going where she was. No-one at this minute. She inhaled and stepped purposefully forward toward the wide entrance door, grasped the handle, and pushed. In the lobby of the clinic, where she was sure all eyes would instantly be on her, no one even met her gaze.

Near a spacious hallway an appropriate sign redirected her. Kitty followed another hallway and two more doors to the next waiting room. She stumbled forward toward the welcome desk and responded incoherently to the questions she was asked before she placed her signature with shaking hand at the bottom of the paper.

Two rows of seats allowed her to squeeze in between an older lady and a younger woman. The most Kitty's confused mind could take in was the fear in the eyes of the teenager beside her. The girl looked like she needed her mother. There was no mother to be seen.

Kitty had no idea how many others shared the double row of chairs. She was alone in a world standing still, as people came and went.

Kitty closed her eyes, and behind them everything she had seen in the library or read on her computer about what she was proposing to do, flashed back to her in visions of horror. Gristly pictures of baby parts screamed in her mind. *Don't you want me, Mama?* The voice in her head was so real her eyes sprang open in daylight terror.

What was she doing? Was this reality?

"Kitty Sampson." Someone tangible called her name. As though in a trance she reported to the desk, and a person in uniform indicated the direction she should go, guiding her into room number three. The attendant calmly informed her to remove her jeans, don the gown and get up on the table.

"Your nurse will be in shortly," she said. "Don't be worried. It only takes about fifteen minutes." She closed the door behind her, leaving Kitty in the darkness of uncertainty and dread.

Her mind careened. Images of two tiny feet wrenched her chest. Feet that appeared doll-like but silkenly soft. Feet that suggested the beginning of the rest of a little body with arms outstretched.

This was ridiculous. She had barely missed a period. There was no baby inside her.

"Don't you want me, Mama?" The plaintive little voice spoke again. Confusion screamed inside her as the vision of tiny arms flailed.

"Sh... sh." Kitty looked up into compassionate eyes, "You'll be just fine." The nurse smiled as she lightly fingered the needle in her hand. "It's local, right? Just double checking. You weren't planning for total anesthesia, were you?"

Kitty gagged and sat up. The nurse put down the needle, grabbed the basin beside the bed and held it under her chin while Kitty wretched, heaving into the bottom of the basin the vomit of her empty stomach.

The nurse handed Kitty a towel and wiped her patient's clammy forehead with another. Kitty saw empathy in the kind face and responded with gasping sobs. Her hands covered tears that could be held back no longer. The fortitude she'd tried to maintain forsook her shuddering body as floods of grief rose in wave after wave.

"You don't have to go through with this, you know."

Kitty heard the words like they came from a TV screen.

I don't have to go through with this?

Did the suggestion come from the hazy blue uniform hovering over her?

A gentle voice reached her through the fog, "Are you okay, child? Would you rather call a halt to the procedure just now?"

Was this truth?

Almost blinded by the light of hope, Kitty swayed wildly. Like a burst of sunshine opening through clouds of sludge, relief overwhelmed her. She opened disbelieving eyes to the empathetic smile of the nurse and allowed herself to be helped off the table to the nearby chair.

The nurse without a name passed Kitty her clothes and disappeared. She returned to lead Kitty to the desk for checkout, then went to call the next patient.

Kitty, almost in a stupor, made her way to the hospital ladies' room. For want of another chair, she sat on the seat of the toilet stool and woke up from her nightmare.

She couldn't very well stay in the bathroom forever. Kitty stood up and tried her legs, surprised that they held her upright as she moved toward the mirror.

"What did I nearly do?" she said to the face she barely recognized in the mirror.

Who was she now? What would she do? What would happen next?

I will be a single mother. That's what will happen. I will have nothing left of this life I have known, but I'll do it anyway.

But my sweet daughter, you still have Me.

Kitty recognized that Voice.

Yes, she did still have Him, her loving, understanding Saviour. She would not go throw herself off the Lionsgate Bridge. She would go on living. She would do it bravely.

She had to go somewhere and think. Kitty didn't feel much *fight* response in her body, but she did feel *flight. Run! Go somewhere. You can't stay here.*

Kitty took a last look in the mirror at the dark rings around her eyes, and the straggling hair falling over her shoulders. She made a long examination of the furrow of dark hair splitting the blonde cascade at its uncertain part. Then Kitty walked out of the bathroom, through the lobby and down the steps of the clinic toward her new beginning.

She located her parked car, unlocked it and stumbled into the driver's seat. She sat. *What did I just do?* What would happen when her relief turned to fresh fear? The implication of her revelation at the clinic, that she could not go through with an abortion, had yet to hit her. If not abort, then what? A new start would have to wait until…? Good question. Until when? And what was she to do next?

Yes. '*Next*' was the correct question. Not next week or even tomorrow. 'Next' was the rest of this morning. Her first step toward anonymity. The beginning of the loneliest era she had ever encountered. 'Next' meant courage.

'Next' meant more than another batch of pomegranate arils.

'Next' meant doing something with this phony hair. Now.

Kitty turned the key and drove half an hour to the only hairdresser she had ever used. Inez, who had coloured her so beautifully blond. Inez, surprised to see her, was booked for the next two hours.

Five blocks away Kitty found a market selling pomegranates. Not fresh pomegranate arils. This type she'd never seen before, arils ready in a jar. She ordered lunch at the corner Wendy's and preceded her fast food with the pomegranate arils someone had already removed straight out of their skin. They were ready to go. Then she scarfed down Wendy's newest burger variation with baked potato and salad. Satiated, Kitty bought some more ready-to-go arils before driving back to Inez's. She parked there, grabbed her pillow and tucked it under her head.

Kitty awoke to a tap on the window where Inez was grinning at her and beckoning her to wake up and get out of the car.

"I can't believe I did that," Kitty said. "I'm glad you had a parking space in front of your shop."

Inez was still chuckling as she washed Kitty's long hair and massaged her scalp. "I'm sure you needed the rest." She wrapped a towel around Kitty's head and led her to the station.

"So what's it going to be? Shall we just touch up this railroad track?"

Inspiration struck Kitty with a jolt.

"I have a better idea. Let's do me red."

"Red?"

Red. Red for determination. Red for my hide-away. Red for my new life.

"Yep. Really red. Blonde was fun, but red might be even funner. What do you think, Inez? Shall I go red?"

Inez laughed indulgently. "Why not? It's your hair."

And my life. Our life. Her hand rested lightly on her tummy.

In another flash of inspired motivation, Kitty remembered dear Becky's flight of fancy years ago when she had her dark curls cut. "Yes. Red. And I think I'll have you give it an extra boost of personality as well. Let's do me a trim, too. Make it a very short bob or something."

"O...kay... It won't be cheap, though. All the steps we need to take will probably have to fit in between my other customers. Are you okay with that?"

Inez was oblivious to Kitty's silent gulp. But Kitty wasn't about to renege. It was a good thing that creep Lance had actually been good for something. She'd squirreled away those random $20 bills he had passed her, and there were still some left in the bank. "Sure. I guess. Just make sure it's really red. Not just pink, brown or orange."

"Like just a little redder than auburn? Like these copper swatches? Just a little less than fire?"

"Make me fiery beautiful," Kitty instructed. "Just blend it in with my roots so if I want to grow it out again, I can just let it."

"Gotcha."

Then Inez paused as if in thought, went to check her schedule and stepped hurriedly back with a wrinkled forehead.

"I'm *really* sorry, Venecia." Inez was sincerely apologetic. "I'm just realizing I don't have *any* time for this long a procedure. I can't fit it in between my standing customers. Just a blonde touch-up would be okay, but going red will take us way more time than that." Inez appeared frustrated. "It's a huge job. I'm so sorry. If you need it so quickly, what would you think about this?

"If I bring you back to a normal blonde today, you could check my wig section and choose an outrageous spiky red wig to cover you up. Would you be okay with something as ridiculously simple as that? I'll certainly give you a break on the charges, and it would allow you to switch between blonde and red at will. What do you think, Venecia?"

It wasn't the necessity for the change of plans that startled Kitty. It was Inez's use of that name, Venecia, that plunged her so abruptly back into the shock of that ugly world.

Kitty considered the idea anyway and soon agreed to the new plan. Kitty let Inez work her in between a couple of kind patrons to become a blonde again. Early in the evening Kitty made her final choice from among the short, spiky wigs she'd handled.

Still in a small daze, Kitty sat back in the chair while Inez carefully taught her how to hide blonde tresses under red spikes. In a few minutes, Kitty was thoroughly educated. She paid and tipped her hairdresser gratefully.

When the appointment was complete, a brand-new, classy, spiky-cut redhead walked out into a new day.

KITTY WANTED SOME more pomegranate arils. So she drove to a kiddie's park she'd seen close by and, with her jar of sweet seeds, parked, and sat down on the first bench she saw. A small family of ducks left ripples behind them as they gathered toward her hopefully. Kitty snickered, thinking that the baby ducks needed her pomegranate treats as much as she did. It felt so good to laugh. Could God's transcendent Holy Spirit be showing approval of that decision she made back at the clinic? She hadn't imagined when she found herself in the terrifying dungeon of death that in only minutes she'd walk out free. Able to laugh again.

Free? Who was she kidding? She hadn't a clue what was ahead for her. The relaxation she'd felt was only temporary denial, she was sure.

Kitty dug in her bag for crackers, and absentmindedly scattered crumbs toward the small pond. She chewed on the seeds of the pomegranate arils while the juice filled her taste buds. She needed a mother herself – or even a Grama-ma – considering the fact that she had never been even a babysitter. And here she was, a make-believe redhead alone in the morning.

Feeding ducks.

With a baby in her body.

A giggling little toddler almost bumped into her leg with his tricycle.

"Toby!" his mother shrieked. "You nearly ran over that nice lady's foot!"

Toby's face scrunched up in consternation as two big tears rolled from his eyes. "Mommy, don't say me that!"

His mother picked him up and snuggled him while he sniffled sadly.

What a relief to have company so alive, rather than the foreboding of death permeating the clinic waiting room. Kitty laughed with a new lightness.

"Oh, he's no danger to me." She looked directly into the contrite little face. "Toby, I'm very happy you're with me in this park. Would you like some pomegranate arils?"

Toby looked puzzled. "Candy?" he said.

His mother laughed. "No, sweetie. They're not candy. They'd probably stick in your throat." She flipped her hair off her forehead and held out a hand to Kitty. "I'm Cheryl. Thanks for being so understanding."

"I'm Kitty."

They spent the next fifteen minutes in small talk as Toby's feet pushed his little no-pedal three-wheeler in safety, back and forth in front of them, regularly bringing his pursed lips to Kitty for a single aril from her stash.

"We come here a lot," Cheryl said. "Toby's dad disappeared long ago so we're usually here by ourselves. But don't feel sorry for us. We have people. We're doing great."

"I'm sorry," Kitty said hesitantly. "That must be hard."

"It's okay. I got used to the idea while I was carrying him and learned so much from the friends who were coaching me. I thank God every day for that care center in Hope."

Kitty's heart lunged. "Hope? What's that?"

"Oh, it's just a nice place a few hundred klicks east of here, near the beginning of the Coquihalla Highway. Nice little city. The director of the center there was just wonderful. I'll be forever grateful to that kind lady." Cheryl looked at her with a question on her face.

Kitty had no reason to run from this friendly person. "Cheryl, I need to go there, too. Can you give me a phone number?"

Cheryl's empathetic surprise was interrupted by the sharp melody of Kitty's cell phone. "Oh, excuse me," Kitty said. "I better get this."

She answered, hesitantly. "Hello. May I ask who's calling, please?"

Kitty felt the colour leave her face. She listened for several minutes before she said to Logan, the caller, "I'll meet you there." Shock anaesthetized her. Logan must have had to inform all the dear ones that he and Becky had a little one on the way. At this news, Kitty gasped with regret. Wouldn't it be wonderful if the two wee ones could grow up together! The monster ground in her chest again.

"Gotta bounce, Cheryl," Kitty said. "My soul sister is in the hospital with a pregnancy that's in trouble. Bye-bye, Toby." She handed Cheryl the last of her pomegranate arils. "You share the arils with Mommy, okay? It was so nice to meet you both."

Kitty looked up gratefully as she pocketed the slip of paper Cheryl handed her. "I've given you the number of the director. She's a wonderful lady. You will love her, and you won't be sorry. I promise."

AS SHE LEFT her new friends in the park Kitty ignored the speed limit. What? Becky was expecting a baby? Kitty hadn't thought she would hear that sort of news at this moment in her life. Why hadn't she been told?

Why haven't I been told? Look who thinks she should be told about anything.

Kitty shuddered as shame poured through her. For all these months she'd been ignoring her sweet Becky, and now she dared think she should have been filled in on Becky's life? What unbelievable presumption. Kitty wished she could zap a plea for forgiveness to Becky's hospital bed and prayed silently instead.

Just keep your mind on the road, Kitty. Get there in one piece.

TWENTY

JENNIFER LARSON SAT quietly beside her daughter's bed in Mary's Maternity Center. The only thing she allowed to creep into her heart was love and the anguished plea to Heaven that drowned out all thought. She held a damp tissue in her hand as she watched Becky sleep. *Lord Jesus, take care of my daughter through this. Take care of our baby!*

Logan's call at 10:00 that morning had shot terror and action through her limbs. After a quick call to Hank, still working with Geoff on Mount Mercy, she ignored the speed limit all the way to the Burnaby hospital. It would be evening before Hank and Geoff could join them, but she and Logan would hold the fort until the others arrived.

When Jennifer reached St. Mary's Maternity ward she was immediately ushered into her daughter's private room. Becky lay pale and still, cushioned, and surrounded by tubes and monitoring paraphernalia. The little red line on the monitor blipped with quiet reassurance. Becky's breathing was soft and steady, and there was no appearance of stress on her features. Her curls tumbled over the white pillow. Her long dark lashes, free of mascara, lay thick over her pale cheeks. Jennifer longed to hold her in her arms. Instead, she stood by the bed, enveloped in prayer.

When Jennifer tiptoed into the room earlier, her first view had been of Logan's broad back as he knelt on the hard floor beside Becky's bed. The first sounds to reach her ears were Logan's muffled pleas, interspersed with bursts of whispered thanksgiving, so focused that he was not aware of her presence until she wrapped her arms around his neck.

Unsurprised, he turned to her with a tremulous smile, and in a voice filled with gratitude, said, "Jennifer... Ma... you're here!"

He got up from his knees and hugged her. "She's going to be okay," he said. "She has to be!"

Jennifer nodded her head firmly. "Absolutely she will. Hank and Geoff are on their way, but they'll be a while. It's a long way to come, but they should make it by six o'clock."

"That's a relief," Logan said. "I know she'll feel so much better with all her family around. I don't think Geoff even knew about us until Hank's recent visit."

"So what happened?" Jennifer asked.

Logan looked more puzzled than certain. "We...ell...obtuse me. I didn't notice how tense she was getting until she woke me up to explain. She'd been spotting for a few hours. I started to panic, but she hadn't been very worried—until pain hit her later this morning. I phoned the hospital to let them know we were on our way and called you after we got here. They put her on a saline drip immediately, and before long, she seemed herself again, though tired. They took an ultrasound, said it was encouraging but didn't tell me much more than that. No-one was telling me anything." Pent-up tears misted Logan's eyes as he wrapped Jennifer in his arms once more. Silent sobs of relief shook all six foot-two of him as he laid his face on the top of her head.

"I've been so worried," he choked.

As he let her go, their smiles reflected mutual hope. God was in this room.

"How about I stay here with her," Jennifer suggested, "while you go have your long-delayed lunch. I'll go down when you come back."

For a brief moment, Logan lingered with adoration at Becky's bedside, then smiled gratefully at Jennifer and left mother and daughter together.

When Jennifer turned her attention back to the bedside, she saw a sleepy smile turning the corners of her daughter's lips. Becky moved languidly in her bed making small stretching sounds as she slowly opened her eyes.

Jennifer broke into a broad smile. "Becky. I'm here, baby." She bent to encircle her waking daughter.

"Mommy." Becky's arms responded weakly. "I'm so sorry. I've made everyone worried. But I'm all right now. We're both good." She lovingly patted the blanket covering the important area.

They were laughing softly together when a knock behind them was followed by steps at the open doorway. They looked up together expectantly and saw her at the same moment. The approaching redhead that used to be a blonde paused momentarily before she rushed to them.

"Kitty!" Becky squealed, and Jennifer grinned and stepped out of the way. Kitty braked her sprint inches from the bed.

"It's you! You're here!" Becky raised her head, holding out her hand. "How ever did you know to come? Oh, thank you. I'm so happy." Becky's dark eyes were too shiny, but they matched the joyous smile she shone on Kitty. "Somebody help me sit up." She reached out her arms.

Their embrace was long and teary. Becky blinked rapidly, ignoring the new hair color.

"What do you think you're doing here in this place?" Kitty demanded maternally, and she wiped her cheeks with her sleeve.

"It won't be for long," Becky said. Jennifer gently eased her back against the pillow, carefully adjusting the tubes attached to her daughter's arm. "I have no plan to stay any longer than necessary."

"You certainly look better than I was prepared for," Kitty said. "It sounded so serious I wanted to hire a flying eagle or something. I thought Lizzy would never get us here."

Becky's face was still pale, but her enthusiastic smile didn't look worried. "All it was, was a little spotting. They just want to take precautions."

"Well, I guess!" Kitty said. "I could hardly believe it when Logan told me you were expecting."

Becky smiled apologetically. "Kit... I'd have given you all the details the time you came to see us... but you were so distraught... I just thought I'd save the news for a little later. I'm sorry..." She teared up again.

"Don't be sorry about anything." Kitty said vehemently. "I'm the one to be sorry. I'm ashamed of how self-centered I was about my own problems when I dropped into your place right out of the blue. You and Logan were simply magnificent. You didn't act any differently than if you'd just seen me the day before... instead of..." Searing memory washed over Kitty's expression.

Jennifer rushed to the rescue with a gentle arm on Kitty's shoulder. "Kitty, you're here now. You're present with us when we need you and that makes us indescribably happy. Forget the might-have beens. The "little man" we're expecting is happy too, now that his auntie is here. He even likes her new look."

Shyness and joy mingled with tears across Kitty's grateful face. "It's a boy?"

"He is!" Becky squeaked. "I'm so thrilled I can hardly stand it."

"But how did you know it was going to be a boy? Ultrasound?"

Excitement lit Becky's face. "Of course! You should just see his pictures. He's getting so big! He's got a heartbeat! And a little... little..."

Kitty laughed aloud. "Guess he has to have a little something if he's a boy. Ooh, it just gives me goosebumps."

The nurse had slipped in earlier to turn on the equipment.

The screen above Becky's well-gelled tummy was alive with delicate activity. Kitty squeezed herself into a small package in the chair beside Jennifer.

Jennifer and Becky exclaimed with laughter and joy while the sonographer pointed out his many little developing parts. His heart was beating with high-speed enthusiasm as the monitor picked up the soundwaves. The profile of his face was rounded and clear. Little arms waved. Little fingers stretched out, until suddenly the miniscule thumb found its way into the tiny sucking lips.

"Ooh." Becky giggled. "Can you believe that! He already wants to suck. And he's only nineteen weeks old. Oh, I wish I could hold him already!"

Jennifer said softly, "It won't be long. There he is, all alive and breathing and active, but just not quite finished. Isn't he a miracle?"

Jennifer turned around for Kitty's response. Kitty appeared to be in another world. Tears ran down her face, and she was shaking. Awe had fallen over her features and transported her somewhere that others were not. Jennifer stepped back in wonder, feeling a poignant jolt in her core. Kitty dropped her head into her hands. Gut-wrenching sobs shook her slim body as Jennifer hugged her, long and hard. Waiting. Wondering at Kitty's deluge of emotion. She doubted it had anything to do with the crazy red wig.

Becky's eyes were wide in empathetic silence.

At last Kitty managed to collect herself. "Do you know what you'll name him?" she barely whispered.

Becky responded immediately with a giggle. "We thought of Hank, but then Mom told us Hank's real name was Hampus and we agreed to pass on that one." The amusement continued until Becky said soberly, "We all want to call him Dawson, after my daddy."

Kitty wept some more. "That's so sweet. His grandpapa now lives somewhere faraway, but another little Dawson will live again down here on this earth." She reached for one of the tissues handy on the bedside table. "I'm sorry, guys, I don't know what's wrong with me today. It's just so overwhelming to think Becky will soon be a mama."

"And," a strong voice joined them, "Logan Kovalik will be the daddy.

Logan returned to the bedside just in time to see the ultrasound fade away and the nurse take her leave. "Daddy," he mused. "Daddy of little Dawson Logan Kovalik. Unbelievable." His soft laughter lightened the mood as they shared the wonder of the moment—even though Kitty's tears kept requiring the assistance of more tissue.

A short time later a new nurse came in to inform them that Becky could be discharged the following morning. But only with strict instructions for required behaviour. Logan and Becky wrapped each other in rejoicing arms.

JENNIFER WALKED WITH KITTY down to the cafeteria to have supper. They picked up their trays and stood in silence in the line-up, carefully making their choices. As they paid for their meals and carried them to a table for two, Jennifer's persistent intuition wanted to beg Kitty to communicate. Surely Kitty must be feeling the pull of her pleading and empathy.

That something was very amiss was clear. Clearer now, by far, than it had been when Kitty escaped from Nobleton without an explanation. Since the morning Jennifer discovered Kitty's note with its pathetic pretense, her mind had been inundated with a dozen unlikely excuses for Kitty's weird behaviour. Now, having watched Kitty's excruciating pain with the exposure to Becky's ultrasound, Jennifer was beginning to narrow down the possible explanation to one that had not occurred to her until now. Could Kitty be *pregnant?*

Jennifer observed her with a breaking heart. Kitty could barely swallow her soup, let alone make her vocal chords respond. Besides, how could Kitty explain anything without having the willingness to admit she needed help? Her earlier escape had revealed her stubborn independence. Without swallowing some pride and exposing the shame she must feel, Kitty would keep running. Jennifer was certain enough of Geoff's honour to know the baby was not his. That left only one unsettling question. Whose?

Even Kitty's love for Geoff wasn't stopping her obvious angst. Or maybe she was running *because* of her love.

Kitty sat at the table choked-up and teary-eyed. She picked up her spoon to negotiate another bite, when Jennifer's cell buzzed.

Jennifer's heart soared with joy at the sound of Hank's voice. "Okay, good," she said. "Hurry fast. We have a nice surprise for you when you get here." As she hung up, Jennifer smirked delightedly. "The guys are making great time. They'll be here in less than an hour. What a surprise you'll be."

"That's nice," Kitty said flatly.

Jennifer recognized the lie. Then panic struck her heart.

She couldn't help pleading, "Kitty, talk to me."

Kitty smiled wanly. "Gotta hit the washroom, Jennifer." Kitty gave her a light hug as she stood and passed her. Then she turned back and hugged her once more, this time fiercely.

"I'm sorry, but it may be a while before I see you all again. Plan for me to be blonde again before you know it. Take care of my little cuz until he gets here, okay?" Kitty picked up her purse and jacket and hurried toward the restroom.

Jennifer's mind was awash with truth. Hank was on his way. But Kitty knew the other important part. Geoff was on his way.

She won't be back. How are we going to be able to help her?

TWENTY-ONE

GEOFF FELT A LONELY heartbeat as he climbed the stairs into the hospital well behind Hank. And it seemed to take an inordinate amount of time to get to Becky's room and the few family members waiting there with Logan. Where was everybody else? Where was Jennifer? Where was Kitty?

He had missed meeting Kitty?

Had she actually been here and already left?

He made a futile trek around the hospital corridors and parking lot outside feeling like a foolish schoolchild playing hide-and-seek. He returned to the lobby with pretended nonchalance and went up to Becky's room. Trying to cover the heaviness that told him Kitty was lost again. He needed to appear calm to his loved ones.

"Becky can go home tomorrow," Logan informed them with ardent relief. "We'll see you as soon as we can."

Jennifer clung to Hank's side gratefully. "I'll go back with you today," she declared, then turned to Geoff. The good-bye hug she wound around Geoff's neck imparted the depths of her understanding. "I'll be praying for you," she whispered.

Geoff nodded, then led Hank and Jennifer to the far end of the hospital parking lot where his pick-up waited. He spotted a motel that would accommodate the three of them for the night and signed for it.

Early next morning they began the trip back to Mount Mercy. Geoff had already opened himself to Hank's empathy. Last night they had thoroughly covered the topic of Kitty's flight from Nobleton and pondered her self-incrimination. Hank seemed as baffled as Geoff about Kitty's disappearance but could add very little to clear their understanding. Kitty had shown no change of mind about severing her budding relationship with Geoff. If she'd had any intention of reconsidering right now, she would never have flown the scene so determinedly. It was hard not to be resentful of her penchant to disappear.

They drove most of the trip to the cabin listening to CD's, some of which were cheerful. But most of them encouraged prayerfulness. Geoff had his CD container full of both kinds, plus others positively boisterous. He also carried some Bible talks that he informed them would take his mind off Kitty—for all of 20 seconds at a time.

Hank was taking his turn at the wheel when he said, "I've been pondering these latest events and have concluded that Jennie and I may as well remain at Mount Mercy for another few nights," He turned warm eyes on Jennifer. "If that suits you, my love, we can leave Becky safe home in Logan's tender care, and we'll keep Geoff so occupied at the cabin he'll have no time to reflect." He turned to Geoff. "What is your pleasure?"

Geoff lifted his slumping head. "Sure," he said. "Cabin certainly still needs more work." He turned his eyes to Jennifer. "If you don't mind not getting home this weekend, Jennifer, that suits me well. I'd appreciate it."

By Saturday Geoff and Hank finished insulating the cabin and fashioned some window trims. Geoff placed the locks into the awkward log openings and played with the keys to be sure they were a perfect fit. They approved each other's work with wan smiles and concluded that most jobs had been crossed off the list.

Geoff abruptly stood straight beside the strong sliding front door. He avoided anyone's direct gaze and asked no one's advice when he said, "This cabin, from now and always, will be known as *Mercy Manor*."

A FEW DAYS LATER Hank and Jennifer were ready to leave. Jennifer's mind was a tumult of possibilities. Or w*ere* there actually any possibilities? If Kitty refused to be found, hiring a detective wasn't exactly the answer. Should they spend another day doing – what? Wondering? Just one more day.

Hank and Jennifer started saying their good-byes that evening. They planned to drive away early next morning, leaving their prayers and encouragement hovering over Geoff, somehow including his dog Yukon, the slopes of Mount Mercy, the walls of Mercy Manor and the silence of the absent Kitty.

GEOFF WAS RUBBING HIS EYES next morning when he heard Hank revving the motor. No one had mentioned breakfast when Hank and Jennifer drove away. Geoff didn't even think to be embarrassed about it. He still wasn't hungry himself. He needed spiritual nourishment, not food.

Geoff was still echoing his friends' prayers as they left in their camper.

"Oh, God," he groaned, "Bless those two completely. You've been so good to us all. You've been merciful to both me *and* Kitty. I know I can be merciful to Kitty, too. Why can't she feel mercy to herself? Father, God, *why* did she write those lies? I don't believe for a moment she meant what she said. How am I going to find her? What am I going to do? Where *is* she?"

With dry eyes and numb heart Geoff began a triangular walk with Yukon at his heels—to the fresh drinking water spring, to the outhouse, to the tent where Kitty had slept. The spring, the outhouse, the tent. Spring, outhouse, tent. Spring…

His cell phone buzzed in his pocket.

Kitty!

He snatched it. "Geoff, here."

"Geoff Armistad?"

He deciphered the shaky vibrations of a male voice. *No. Not Kitty.*

From hopeful outer space, Geoff came back to earth's reality. "Armistad speaking."

"I'm looking for a Venecia Vale," the voice replied. "I got this phone number by way of her grandmother. I thought she might be with you." He stopped as though someone should enlighten him.

A slow prickle slithered up Geoff's spine and the answer originating inside his head sounded like someone had spoken for him. "To whom might I be speaking?"

"Oh, yeah. Sorry. Name's Lance LeFevre. Call me Larry. Like to talk to her if she's there."

"You must be kidding," Geoff hissed. "What makes you think Kitty'd want to talk to you?"

"Don't get your shorts in a knot," the voice returned groggily. "Kitty – Venecia – Kitty's my good friend. 'N fact, she left a message for me coupla days ago. I wasn't there to pick up, and I had to track it down all the way to Auntie Bee's Nest. She's a good friend, you know. Thought I could help. I heard from her grandmother that she was looking for a medic. You got any idea why she'd be doing that?" His laugh masked a mild sneer.

Geoff's heart lurched. She *was* sick, after all.

"Kitty's sick? Who told you that? What's wrong with her?"

"How should I know? Haven't seen her since she stole my car."

"What did her gramma say?" That he had to engage this jerk in conversation infuriated Geoff. "Where is she now?"

"Well, why d'you think I'm calling? If I knew, I'd be right where she is."

Like—You'd better not be!

Larry LeFevre seemed to know how to play with the conversation. "Well," he said, "if you don't know 'ny more than I do, I migh's well hang up. I got the impression she was lookin' for a hospital. Good plan. If she thinks I'm going to foot her bills, though, she's got another think coming. Tell her that if you see her."

Geoff inhaled in stunned silence. When he found his voice, he repeated inanely, "What's wrong with her?"

Lance snorted. "You're not really pretendin' you don't know? Obviously, she seems to think she needs a clinic. Just wanted to let her know I'd foot the bill for a cruise afterwards, if she likes."

Creeping fury began to burn Geoff's reacting muscles. "You scum!"

Lance laughed again. "Actually, you may as well foot the bill for the cruise yourself. It's probably yours, anyway."

Geoff had not yet collected his crazed emotions, but his voice was controlled. "Hang up, LeFevre. Be thankful you're not here. When I find you, I'll take your head off."

This time Lance laughed outright. "Don't be too sure it makes any difference now, dude. B'sides, no need for bad blood between you'n me. I don' know what you wanna do with Venecia Vale, but she's not my concern anymore. Why don't you just have her?"

Geoff pushed his third finger in fury at his phone and immediately realized he'd been duped as the cell disconnected. Shame flushed his face, with only the trees to observe.

He firmly clicked into the recall and heard Lance say, "Lefevre."

"I gotta say sorry, Larry. That was juvenile of me."

Geoff heard a snicker just as Lance clicked off his own connection.

Geoff held the dead phone in silence. Frustrated emptiness enclosed him.

Not since his teen years had Geoff felt such wrath. This beast who had violated his precious Kitty was not fit to live. The need for revenge rising like a geyser inside him seared his throat and raised his eyes toward the horizon. The acknowledgement of his powerlessness spewed its rage across the distant vista.

In its grip he was helpless.

"God, help me!"

Yukon tipped her head and questioned his agony with amber eyes.

Help came in the form of the empty woodlot near the campsite. Geoff grabbed the axe and began swinging until perspiration ran down his back. The logs he cut would last until winter, he was sure. He threw down the axe and collapsed beside the stump Kitty had hugged. He had to get a grip!

Geoff felt sick. He stood up and swept his eyes over the achingly lonely home-site. His lack of understanding, the absence of knowledge, his uncertainty, all dug holes in his gut. He wanted to weep. The relief of tears would not come. His gaze took in the quiet cabin, moved down toward his half-finished road and back.

Yukon clung close as Geoff absently ruffled her ears. Every breeze whispered, "Kitty."

Was it lunch time? He didn't know. And didn't care.

Then slow resolve began to stir his veins. He simply could not allow this evil inside to defeat him. A plan evolved.

He closed the doors of the cabin and tent and locked anything lockable, like his truck.

Geoff located his backpack in the corner of his tent, threw into it some emergency supplies—matches, flashlight, water container. He carefully placed his Bible in the front pocket, along with a notebook and mechanical pencil. It would take him more than two hours to get to the treehouse on foot. He'd take his time and veer along the gully, headed in the direction of Mercy Falls. He'd start pushing upward beyond the falls, keeping his eyes lifted *'unto the hills'* and stretch out in his sleeping bag as soon as it got dark. If it rained, it rained. He carried a small lightweight tarp. At sunrise, he'd decide how far to continue

232

the climb. He'd like to touch the waters of Mercy Falls—or at least view her in all her glory and share her roar—before winding eastward again toward Sunset Ridge. He would make no plans. He just wanted to wander around in Creation, read the Word, hear what God had to say to him, and feel His comfort.

Jesus had spent forty days and nights fasting in the wilderness to battle the enemy. Good plan. Geoff wanted some wilderness, too, to challenge his weak humanity. He probably wasn't up for forty days, but he could handle a few nights, at least. Inside him was a deep urge to fast. Anyway, his need for food right now was non-existent. Yukon could take care of herself with rabbits and other small creatures teeming in the forest. For him there was an abundance of icy cold spring water.

He located his quiver and slung it with his backpack over his shoulder. He grabbed his bow, tucked his phone in its pocket, whistled for Yukon and struck upwards into the heights.

The Holy Spirit was already bringing transcendent waves of comfort.

Geoff savoured the quiet as he walked – until the intensity of his inner peace overwhelmed his being, and he couldn't help reaching spirit arms toward Kitty in her distance. Waves of hot tears flooded his face.

He was helpless, indeed, but God was not.

TWENTY-TWO

LOGAN GAZED ADORINGLY AT BECKY, snuggled up mid-morning on the couch in their Nobleton living room while the sun streamed in the window. It was just a few days after their return from Mercy Manor.

"You feeling okay?" Logan brushed his hand lightly over her hair. His voice, this moment held no concern, only the honour that never failed to show. Especially now, since Becky had recently returned from a check at the hospital, he was constantly aware that baby Dawson was developing in that special space made just for him to grow.

"You know how I feel when you're close to me," she said. A small giggle affirmed her own obvious love. Logan widened his arms in the beginning of a hug, almost missing the sound of a rustle from outside in the distance.

"Who's that?" Becky warded off the hug as her eyes widened, lifting toward the top end of the driveway.

Logan momentarily tightened his arms in response, then let go to check what Becky was looking at through the top of the window. His forehead creased and he squinted.

"Hey, honey. It looks like Kitty's back!" He jumped off the sofa and ran to fling open the front door. He saw a woman with long blonde hair and an expectant expression on her face.

Logan's lips fell open but no words were forthcoming. The lady's smile was more of a question than of greeting. Her voice was barely a whisper. "Would, would someone here know Kitty Sampson?"

It didn't take Logan very long to consider whom he was talking to. She hadn't seen him for a long time—from an occasion when she would hardly be concentrating on him.

Logan's greeting was cautious. "There is no Kitty Sampson around here at the moment. Welcome, though, whoever you are! Obviously, you're not Kitty, but you sure look like *someone* we should know." He stepped toward the blonde facing them from the top of the sidewalk and took her hand in his so tightly she gasped.

"I guess you don't recognize me yet."

Olivia Sampson's eyes sprang wide, then clouded as she dropped her head toward her view of the sidewalk. She responded like she couldn't speak, and Logan let her writhe in her misery for what must have been for her a very uncomfortable space of time. Then he gave in. The implication of her presence was too positive to hold out against.

No matter what, Logan was glad to see Kitty's mother. He would accept it as a time for gratitude. He gently took her shoulders in his hands.

"Auntie Olivia! Oh Auntie, Auntie. Why has it taken you so long? Poor Kitty has been waiting forever!" There was no pent-up animosity in Logan's heart. Olivia's attitude, now obvious in his beautiful aunt, was begging forgiveness. How could Logan feel anything but gladness?

Olivia's hands covered her face as her shoulders shook and tears poured through protective fingers.

IT TOOK THE NEXT two hours, flying by like only one, for Olivia to be convinced by Logan's warmth to accept the possibility of a new future. Arriving at Logan's door, Kitty's mother was thankful to acknowledge that she was, indeed, Logan's aunt Olivia. Only a few months ago Olivia was sure her presence would have spurred Logan to fury. She was beyond thankful for his unexpected gentleness. Olivia, who had long ago left her daughter Keturah in the lonely arms of Ketuah's daddy George, was now here trying to find the daughter she had abandoned. Each year she was away must have increased Logan's disgust of her. Yet here he was now, showing no signs of rejection. Each year had only increased her own misery, and her hatred of the drugs that had captured her. Her heart squeezed with thankfulness that Logan seemed to be leaning toward forgiveness.

Olivia reflected on the goodness of God when she thought about the kind people who embraced her after her addicted partner's death, leading her to faith in Christ Jesus and His unimaginable love for a lost drug addict. Tears of gratefulness stung her eyes. Jesus had even protected her from the relapse that so many recovering addicts experienced, and now here she was, finding her way back home.

Olivia had never met Becky, much less shared with her the story of her own daughter, Logan's cousin Kitty. Kitty, she learned, had become one of the young servers at Jen's Place. That must have been about the same time that Logan claimed Becky's promise to marry him. Whatever story parts had taken place those years ago, Becky seemed today to be pleased by the return of her new aunt, Olivia.

Olivia watched Becky scurry from the living room and return in her housecoat with a plate of what she termed *surprise cookies,* while Logan showed his expertise at the coffee pot. Olivia could hardly still the awe bubbling in her heart, now that she had come back to the country where she was hoping to hear about her daughter, and to find so little reproach from the nephew she had also left. Yes, Olivia had been certain, Keturah would be somewhere out in this Canadian West, where she'd abandoned her years ago -- and now she wasn't sure where that might be or what might have taken place in between. Coming back, although her heart had shuddered in fear of the reception she deserved, Olivia was still hopeful that she and Keturah could find each other again.

"I'm so thankful I found someone so soon," Olivia said. "I'm so glad you didn't boot me out into the wilderness like I deserve. I know you'll be able to help me find her, although I don't know why you should, considering what I've done."

"We all want to find her." Logan said. "There have been many strange pieces added into this puzzle since you left her, way back when."

Olivia had not yet heard him tell what he might know about Keturah's life. He didn't live in Keturah's part of the country. Logan may not even have gotten to know her. The only words Olivia heard Logan say were, "I hardly know Kitty's story, myself, Olivia. For one thing, years ago, I had to go searching to realize I had such an adorable cousin, I did find her, but since those days I haven't been a big part of her life."

When Olivia finally accepted the fact that nobody *actually* knew where Kitty might be, she agreed with Logan that a trip to Mount Mercy might be the next best step. "You'll need to give me some good directions," Olivia said.

"No, no," Becky demurred. We'll need to go with you. It's a tricky place to find."

Logan recoiled. "Sorry. Becky. You will not be going to the mountain after what you've just been through. Olivia and I will go in her car. I'll leave ours here in case you want it for anything."

Too surprised to object and too moved by Logan's concern to try, Becky made her own suggestion. "Okay, then, you can start in the morning. And in the meantime, we have a nice room for you, Olivia."

"What if she's not there?" Olivia looked concerned. "You called it Mount Mercy?"

"In that case," Becky said, "you can meet Kitty's *Geoff* instead, and give him a hug."

"Keturah has a Geoff? That's nice. I won't keep him long," Olivia assured them with a laugh. "But I do need to meet this Geoff to be sure I approve of him, or we'll find her someone else."

Becky laughed. "That's not a very likely possibility," she said. "I'm pretty sure that's going to be a done deal. Just hurry back home to us."

Aunt and nephew left early in the morning. Along the drive, Olivia stopped to fill up her thermoses and add some fruit and sandwiches to the cooler in the car.

Logan nursed his phone as they were nearing their destination hours later. He tried Mount Mercy's unpredictable cell area several times. But even as Olivia breathed in her admiration of the drive to the cabin, the distant mountains were still not answering Logan's urgent phone call.

"Geoff can't be that far away." Logan complained about the silent cell as they pulled in to Short Stop Motel for coffee. "I'm pretty sure we'll get a connection before too long."

"We'll catch up to him soon," Olivia stated confidently.

"But," Logan warned, "not even Geoff may know where to find Kitty! Anyway, before we find Kitty, we'll need to find Geoff."

TWENTY-THREE

BERTHA MADDIGAN WIPED her hands on her apron and reached for the landline noisily returning her call. Her heart did a small flip as she snatched it to her ear.

"Auntie Bee's Nest. May I help you?"

She barely recognized the strong voice. "Officer Robert McCain here."

"Mr. McCain! Thank goodness it's you! Thank you so much for answering my call. Someone's at my door. I'm afraid it's the same guy that's been pestering me today about Kitty."

"Kitty Sampson?" Concern colored his voice.

"Mm—hmm. He's scruffy and suspicious looking. It may be just my imagination, but he makes me kinda worried. He called about an hour ago for the second time — and now he's at my doorstep!"

"Don't let him in till I get there. Hang on. I won't be too long."

ROBERT MCCAIN HAD BEEN having a difficult time getting out of his mind the visit he'd had with the precocious Kitty Sampson -- alias Venecia Vale. Not too long ago he had left her in safety at *Auntie Bee's Nest;* she was carrying one of the cards he had given her should he be needed.

Bertha's call today left him shaken. McCain had heard the fear in Kitty's voice a few weeks ago, the day he had stopped her on the highway and concluded she was not a car thief. But when she told him her story and spoke Lance LeFevre's name, the fear that spilled from her voice had been authentic. Heart pounding now, he pushed the accelerator of his unmarked car, soon reaching Auntie Bee's Nest.

A tattered sedan was parked beside Bertha's boarding house. A lanky fellow in a wrinkled, tie-less suit leaned against the driver's door, dangling a cigarette between his lips.

Robert McCain parked his vehicle beside the sedan. He turned his long legs toward Auntie Bee's front door as the owner of the vehicle spit out his cigarette. McCain pulled a card from his pocket and passed it to the driver of the sedan.

"May I see your ID please."

Larry LeFevre pulled out of his slouch, demanding, "Whoa, whoa! What's this all about?"

"You got my card," McCain snapped. "I want to know what you think you're doing parked beside this lady's house."

"Since when is there a law against parking?"

"You tell me." McCain didn't add that he thought LeFevre looked drugged.

"There isn't, far's I know. I came to see a friend of mine who lives at Auntie Bee's, but Auntie says she doesn't live here anymore so I need to find out where she's at."

Grimly Officer McCain stomped up to the front door with LeFeve following. He gentled his demeanour when Auntie Bee hesitantly eased open the door.

"Yes, Officer McCain?" She looked worried,

Lance LeFevre followed tightly behind McCain. "You ask her, Officer. She thinks Venecia is out west in the mountains."

"No, no. I don't know where she is."

"Didn't you say she went to find Geoff?"

"I said nothing of the kind. I've barely talked to her since she left."

"Well then," said Lance, "I'll follow some leads and have a go-look-see myself. No law against that, is there?" He turned away from the officer, toward his own scruffy-looking vehicle.

McCain paused. The only quick thing he could think to do was follow LeFevre. He considered another unusual move. "Okay, LeFevre. I have an offer for you. If you have any concerns about getting very far east in that old rattletrap of yours, I can follow you up in my car. Or, if you'd rather, how about asking me for a ride and we can go up together in my vehicle and see if we can find her. I know the name of the motel they will be close to. We should be able to make phone connection somewhere along the route."

The suggestion was preposterous, yet Lance jumped at it.

"Good stuff," he said. He brazenly headed for McCain's car and opened the door. "See you, Auntie Bee. I'll say hello to Venecia when I see her." Lance stumbled into the passenger side.

Robert McCain smiled encouragingly at Auntie Bee. "What do *you* suspect, Ms. Bertha? Do you think we might find anything driving west? Does this hitchhiker know anything we should know?"

Auntie Bee looked uncertain. "I don't know, Officer McCain. When Kitty left, she sounded like she had something specific in mind. I suspected that someone special named Geoff was parked out in the mountains. and she might be stopping at a motel called The Short Stop. But I'm only guessing."

The officer squeezed her hand and said goodbye.

Robert McCain gazed quizzically at the hitchhiker who slumped beside him in the passenger seat. He generally had a pretty good take on this kind of character, but this morning his sharp mind was feeling like it had gone for a nap. For one thing, what would they ever find to talk about for so many hours on the road? Wouldn't need to for a while anyway, he surmised, watching Lance snooze as his thin frame slouched against the window.

After a couple hours of travel, McCain concluded coffee was in order. As he pulled over to a small snack stand beside the road, Lance stretched elaborately, then grinned in apology.

"Hey, good idea." He turned the door handle and said, more firmly than McCain would have expected, "I'll get this. Want a burger or something?"

The food was welcome to both men. They took a seat on the wooden bench and munched voraciously until McCain stood with a sincere thank you to remove the garbage.

"I'm more awake, now," Lance said, returning from the rest-stop. "I hope you won't mind hearing me gab for a bit as we drive."

"Well, of course not." McCain agreed. "Planning to practice so you can explain to a lawyer?"

LeFevre's face flushed, and McCain felt almost ashamed as they returned to the vehicle.

"I'll try to keep it short," Lance said. He actually looked much brighter than he had. "The only reason I need to gab is to catch up with Kitty – I'll use her real name from now on. I want to apologize to her. I haven't told this to anyone else, McCain. Just you. You strike me as a decent guy, and if I don't get to talk to Kitty, I just want you to tell her how sorry, sorry, sorry I am. I was dead drunk when I did what I did to her. I didn't mean to."

McCain's eyes widened and he made a slight nod.

"See, here's the deal. A very old friend of mine has been praying for me for months. I paid attention off and on for a while, between binges. And kept on getting drunk again. When I woke up the last time, he said some more things about the love of God and why God cared so much about me. His words hit me hard. Something that was in the little Bible he gave me, and what I remembered hearing him tell me, completely shook me up.

"So, McCain, if you're a Christian, please tell Kitty when you see her, that I'm planning to be one now, too. If you don't know what I'm talking about, tell her anyway."

Lance choked and determinedly continued. "Officer, she doesn't know that I'm done for. I've known for two months or so that my teen cancer has come back, and this time it's terminal. I was too chicken to tell her. I'm ashamed of that. Kitty is the only woman I have every cared anything for, but even so, I'm not man enough to do anything about it. So the main thing is that you tell Kitty I'm sorry -- and it's better if you don't let her try to find me. I'm pretty sure I'll be gone by then anyway. Dead. But I do understand that I'll see her again, for sure, when we all meet in the place where they say that the Good God makes everything right again.

"Will you do that, McCain? Can I count on you to tell her for me how sorry I am?"

Robert McCain nodded his head but could find no words to speak.

His sad job seemed finished. Lance seemed to think so too. "Tell Kitty I'll be forever sorry. I'll get a little more cash for her too, to Nora's PO box. I pray she'll be happy in spite of me ... and especially if she actually does have our child inside her. You can tell Armistad to take care of their future – if he will. Seems like a good guy."

"Yes, I've no doubt he is."

"I'm okay now, McCain," Lance said as the officer turned on the ignition. "I just needed someone to unload on, first. Anyway, I really don't think Kitty's anywhere up here today. As long as I can count on you to give her my message one day soon, I think we may as well go back to Auntie Bee's where my wheels are parked."

"Maybe let's just finish the short drive we have left to go," McCain suggested, "only in case we miss someone and are sorry." Robert McCain turned his vehicle back onto Highway Three and headed toward Mount Mercy. He wouldn't be surprised if Lance had seen him using his sleeve on his tears.

LeFevre still wore a pensive, sorrowful expression and seemed to want to add a few words to his first confession. "After beating that first bout with cancer in my teens, I got cocky enough to think I had the world by the tail. Even played around with drugs, too, for a while." His hollow eyes searched the hills with memories. "But I realized that the cancer demon was coming back again with a vengeance. I felt it about the same time I made that bad decision to take Kitty to the Calgary photo-op. Made me pretty mad. Still am. But it's not like I don't deserve it."

"Not so sure about that, LeFevre." McCain's steady voice broke the silence with a catch in his throat. "I doubt if you deserve it any more than the rest of us do. We've all tried to run our own lives and gotten ourselves into trouble. I've had plenty of opportunities to try to do that. Long ago I left a beautiful wife behind me, being too career-oriented to give her the attention she deserved. By the time I woke up to what I was allowing to happen, it was too late. And still, they tell me God loves me, too. I hope that's true. If He really died to take on Himself the punishment we *do* deserve, then what we will both be getting is something *neither* of us deserves—His Mercy." Robert McCain seemed to be looking for his own re-birth.

As he drove past a motel named Short Stop, he began to search the side of the road more intently. A few klicks further, he suspected they were nearing a suitable location for this Geoff to have camped. His attention caught a driveway that appeared freshly cut. Could it be signaling Mount Mercy?

GEOFF WAS NEARING the cabin he could soon call 'home', relieved that Hank and Jennifer's call had finally connected with him on his way back down Mount Mercy. And thrilled that they would be there to greet him.

Geoff had been at the tree house several hours, praying. Sometimes facing the log floor on his knees. Sometimes looking over the log walls into the distance. He wanted to talk to God where he could most keenly feel the presence of Kitty. Her loveliness, her pain, her sorrow wrapped him most poignantly in the place where they had first shared the mountain's call together, where he had been so freely delighted by her sweetness.

The treehouse whispered her name. "Kitty." But then, so did Mercy Falls. So did Sunset Ridge. So did the whole of God's creation.

He couldn't travel anywhere on this expanse called Mount Mercy, whether by ATV or on foot, to anywhere that Kitty was not, without being gripped by aching need to reach out and touch her. Yet today he could find her nowhere on Mount Mercy. He didn't have a clue where she was. Neither did Yukon, who clung to his legs with plaintive whimpers. This situation was all wrong: Yukon understood that, too. Besides, it seemed futile to try to reach *anyone* by phone on the mountain right now. That, of course, included Kitty.

Yet his walk into the wilderness with his Saviour had done for him everything he had hoped for. Far more than he deserved.

Then suddenly, he discovered his cell phone finally did want to work..... as did Logan's. They yelled their buddy greetings into the technology and shared their comments for just a few moments. Geoff said he was nearly home.

Logan whooped.

Geoff was soon at the cabin looking for Logan's vehicle. When he also saw Hank's van parked beside Mercy Manor his chest leapt. He sprinted ahead. This was double delight—both Logan and Hank. He laughed with pleasure, yelling and waving his arms.

There was a second woman down there moving at Jennifer's side. When he saw the long shock of blonde hair his laughter switched to glee. "Kit-tee," he screamed, running blindly toward the cabin. But this gorgeous blonde in navy denim who seemed to have turned up out of nowhere only *looked* like Kitty, even in the distance. Geoff threw off the disappointment he felt.

He should have known better, anyway. He was pretty certain the woman he saw was none other than the long-lost Olivia. He would soon receive an introduction to Kitty's mother.

Right now, he had other things to consider. The bigger concern was yet *another* car parked beside Hank's, and two other guys who seemed to be hanging in the background.

He'd never met either of them. One appeared to be a uniformed officer with an authoritative air. The other was a puzzling derelict slinking behind him, no handcuffs visible.

Geoff was sure he would not be surprised to hear the guy's name. This had to be Lance.

The antagonistic words they had shared earlier on the phone repeated themselves in his reluctant ears. Lance dared to come here to Mount Mercy? And he had with him a uniformed officer! Or did the officer have him?

Calm, welcoming Hank had already met the newcomers and had turned all of those there into a chatting circle of friends. The one who must be Lance was attempting to move into the background as far as he could, for which Geoff was thoroughly grateful. He would like to postpone a face-to-face discussion with that guy as long as possible. How had he even dared come here?

Olivia already seemed to be garnering everyone's attention. They were all deeply attentive to the story she was telling. From a distance, Geoff watched her, entranced, as words bubbled from her lips while her face registered sad, changing emotional responses. She appeared to be sharing a deeply personal story. Geoff paused, entranced... As he came near enough to join the gathering, it didn't take him long to throw down his jacket and backpack, wipe his brow and turn his attention to the lovely lady who was speaking. Olivia appeared to have been having no hesitation in sharing the history of her shameful abandonment of her little girl, Keturah. Her words would become part of Geoff's life forever.

Geoff saw that Hank had placed the coffee pot on the propane stove and turned up the heat under the pan. Hank had no reason to realize how much Geoff needed food; this was his simple welcome habit coming to the fore. Hank's welcoming glance met him as he moved to embrace him.

"Thank you, Hank. You have no idea how much this preparation will nourish both my system and my soul." Then Geoff turned his attention directly to Olivia with an open grin. "You must be Olivia. And I see our wonderful chef has already shown his hospitality."

With a Kitty-Smile that turned Geoff's heart over, Olivia said, "We couldn't even have made the turn up the hill before he would have switched on the stove. Geoff, I feel so honoured to be here with you all at Mount Mercy and met by such generosity."

Hank's steaks were already sizzling.

Olivia was a woman of deep tenderness. In two hours together around the campfire eating elk steak, she shrouded Hank and Jennifer, as well as Geoff, and even Lance and his officer companion, with the essence of the loneliness, anguish and guilt she had experienced while Kitty had been left motherless with her father and grandmother. Yet Olivia showed no self-pity, only remorse.

After that, the reality of Olivia's newly developing faith, reviving itself after many years of ignoring its call, brought them together in spirit, rejoicing with forgiveness and gratefulness. She made them feel like family. Like *Family*. Even Lance and his companion seemed to be clinging to her words.

GEOFF LONGED FOR KITTY more than ever, now that he had listened to the painful sharing by Kitty's mother of her search for the daughter she had left behind. Olivia had explained that she had now been sober for a full year. God's power was so overwhelming!

Olivia wept as she told them how her second companion, the one who had introduced her to drugs so many years ago, had utterly succumbed to the world of the drug lords and recently passed away, leaving her alone somewhere in Portland area. Now she was coming home to search for the daughter she had never abandoned in her heart. Her first shock was the discovery that Kitty's father, her husband, George, had already been laid to rest.

Officer McCain and Lance LeFevre listened in silence, and Geoff had no intention of trying to include them yet. He knew the time for communication would certainly arrive. They all wept, and together thanked God for so many undeserved blessings.

In the middle of their unexpected happiness, Logan's cell rang.

Logan grabbed it to his ear. "Becky!"

His happy smile faded, and wrinkles creased his brow as he strained to hear. "You're not feeling well! The spotting has started *again*?"

Becky's voice escaping from the line answered slowly. "I'm okay, Logan. But you maybe better come when you can." Her words came more weakly as Logan strained to hear what she was saying.

"She's tricky to hear," Logan said. "I think she says she's spotting again. She wants Jennifer, and she wants Kitty, too. But she can't wait any longer. She wants to take the car and try to meet at St. Mary's."

She wanted Kitty? They must locate Kitty.

"But sweetheart," Logan said into a silent receiver, "we don't know how to *find* Kitty"

Olivia's voice, both strong and courageous, directed, "Sure we do. I've been in touch with Nora before now. She's been talking to Kitty. Logan, we'll call Nora for some information. We'll tell her Becky is back in the hospital and wants to see Kitty."

Logan looked up frantically and handed Geoff his phone.

"Becky, sweetie." Geoff said. "We love you and will be with you soon. Right now, you need to do what I tell you, or Logan will be a basket case. We'll all be praying every minute. Listen carefully. Call an ambulance, give them Logan's name, and relax. Get yourself to the hospital, and we'll be with you before you can blink your eye. Got that?"

The answer at Becky's end must have been favourable. Geoff smiled in relief and passed the phone back to Logan.

Jennifer and Hank elected to remain temporarily at Mount Mercy in case Kitty showed there, while Olivia and Logan would follow Geoff back to Vancouver. The tail of the short caravan would be occupied by Lance LeFevre and Robert McCain, who opted to return to Vancouver with the rest of the family.

Geoff felt his resentment rise in fresh anger. Where did this LeFevre guy come from? Why is he still hanging around us?

The Spirit of the Lord checked Geoff again with fresh severity. Isn't this exactly what your recent hike was about? Getting some love and forgiveness into your heart for Lance LeFevre? Have you forgotten so soon? Get a grip!

"When you're looking for Kitty," Geoff called, "Look for a gorgeous blonde like Olivia. Kitty is not dark-haired any more like she used to be. And, I have no doubt that in spite of everything, Olivia will make Kitty her first priority."

Even as they drove in caravan toward the hospital, they knew this would be a difficult trip.

KITTY WAS DEEPLY GRATEFUL that the rush in her spirit had quieted. All she needed to do in the next few hours was relax and begin her way toward Hope. What a beautiful name for a beautiful city to make her calming place. HOPE. She'd never been there before, but she knew it was in the far east of the valley beyond Vancouver and promised to be easy to find.

Cheryl. She also had her friend's card and on it, directions to Home of Hope with the phone number. Every step of this new way God was leading, felt better than the last. Yes, she could joyfully love this baby she was carrying. She would learn how to forgive his father with the mercy God had shown her. She would be the best mother any child ever had. She wouldn't have to do it alone. Jesus was walking beside her.

Kitty considered where she wanted to stop: the little coffee shop where Officer McCain had escorted her. She had been so grateful he had extended mercy on her when she had been able to convince him she was not a car thief. Now she simply wanted to savour the comfort of that forgiveness.

Kitty soon had the coffee in her hand and its warmth filling her throat. Many questions inside her wanted to be asked, but Kitty decided that she had no obligation to find answers for them just yet. Since the Lord was with her, she'd just bask in the knowledge that, yes, His mercy was real, just like Geoff had tried to convince her. But even if that mercy was not enough to overlook the weakness that had led to this crazy day, it was still enough to see her through the hard places ahead – all by herself, if she must. *Thank You with all my heart, Heavenly Father.*

The waiter walked by in the distance. Kitty waved and smiled as he brought her a water refill.

"Thank you so much," she said. "I'll take a muffin with me for the road. Not very far to Hope, is it?"

"Few hours," was the answer that would have sent her on her way. Then Kitty's cellphone buzzed.

It was Logan. "Kitty! I can hardly believe I got you! How good to hear you speak. I'm so glad Nora still had your phone number. Kitty, this is not good news. Becky is in the hospital for the second time. She's spotting again. We are praying that our wee Dawson is not in danger. Becky is calling for you. Can you come?"

There wasn't a moment of hesitance. "Yes. Yes, I'll be there. Bye."

"Kitty," Logan warned. "Be expecting Geoff. He'll be there, too. He can't *not* be."

MANY HOURS LATER, by the time the members of her extended family had gathered at her bedside, Becky was no longer alone. Close to her side was a gorgeous young woman who had arrived with what appeared to be a cropped head of brilliant, spiky red hair which shocked everyone that had known her—either first dark-haired, or recently, blond.

Logan and Geoff arrived with Olivia the blonde to introduce her to the redhead. The silence between the two was almost visceral. Kitty lifted her head to Olivia as though she' been born with her short, red, audacious clip, but her eyes were wary and even hostile. "How nice to have you visit. As you will see, there are unsolved problems in this group, so it may not be necessary for you to stick around."

Olivia's face blanched. Silence descended as shock froze the room.

Kitty recoiled as though she had awakened from a daze, and her expression changed. "I'm sorry," she said weakly. "Please forgive me for saying that. It was wrong."

Logan was oblivious to their words. Through it all, he only held lovingly to Becky's side. It was difficult to tell if she was awake, and Logan had little interest in anyone other than Becky.

"Look," Logan said. "You guys should go have a bite to eat. I'm not hungry yet."

McCain and Lance, almost invisible, stood back near the wall where they had sneaked up. Lance, with hanging head, acted like he didn't know where he was. Robert McCain appeared quite out of place. When he saw Kitty, he gave her a nod, as though expecting Lance to tell her goodbye. Dazed, that's just what Lance did. He caught Kitty's eye and took a step toward her.

He stopped at the same time she did, and whispered, almost on the run, "I'm saying goodbye, Kitty. I'll be forever sorry. I'm going to get a little more cash for you to Nora's PO box. I'll love you forever, and I pray you'll be happy in spite of my stupidity, and especially if you actually do have our child in your body. Please let Armistad take care of your future – if he will. He's a good guy. And Kitty, please remember me as Larry. "*Lance*" isn't real."

Their eyes met in slow agreement.

Then both men vacated the place they were not needed. With a puzzled expression and a daring glance, Larry said as he left, "Keturah, maybe you should accompany your mother to the cafeteria. And I do like your hair." Then Kitty's brain woke up.

There was a change inside her.

PERHAPS KITTY BECAME AWARE of her red, red wig. Something seemed to underwrite a braver, stronger, newly-born spirit. Her shock seemed to be over. Even Geoff's careful presence did not terrify her. Kitty took Olivia's willing elbow as they found their way to the cafeteria. None of them were very hungry, but they tried to smile as they attempted small talk.

After the group had finished ordering coffee and a few small snacks, Olivia seemed to find it impossible not to try to explain her abandonment of her little girl. "My Keturah – I think I'll call her what you all do -- Kitty. She has a wonderful father, whom God has already called Home to be with Him. Even though I was so mixed up, and so deep in drugs that I was useless, leaving Kitty in her real father's care was much wiser than keeping her in the drug mess. I'm glad I left her in Nanaimo. I am so grateful for Nora and her son."

"God has been merciful and forgiving to us all," Geoff said. He looked directly at Kitty for the first time since coming down from the mountain. "Right, Kitty? God doesn't hold any grudges, does He?"

Kitty found it hard to speak. "No, He doesn't. But ... it's kind of hard for God's people not to hold them ...."

"Yes. I guess that could be." Olivia said. "Which people, Kitty?"

Kitty bit her lip. Olivia's eyes twinkled.

"Come on, Kitty," she said. "Do you think that loner I've heard about -- Geoff Armistad is his name, right? -- you really think he's holding a grudge against you? He understands why you ran away, don't you think?"

Kitty couldn't hold up her face toward Geoff. Neither could she keep her tears from beginning to trickle again.

"Ah, Kitty," Geoff said. He reached out his arms and pulled her to him. "It's about time we accept mercy from each other, put the past behind and start new under God's wings. Don't you think so?"

Awash in tears, Kitty could only drop her head in embarrassment. Olivia looked unashamedly happy as Geoff held Kitty in his arms. His voice was tender. "You can find it in your heart by now to extend your mercy to me, can't you, Kitty?"

Kitty choked as she tried to answer. "Me extend mercy to you? Geoff, you don't need any mercy. It's me in the way. I just need to be out of your life so you can get on with yours. How could you possibly not be utterly disgusted with me?"

Geoff shook her gently. "I'm not disgusted with anything about you except your exaggerations about the relationship Lance forced on you. It was just one of those things that happened. I forgave you for that. Now Kitty, it's your turn to let it go. Take my hand and let's both go forward."

No answer.

"Kitty." There was authority in his voice. "I love you. You know that. I've told you before. Do you love me?"

More tears were rising. "Geoff, you know that I do."

"Then accept my mercy. I'll accept yours. Let's be one."

"But, Geoff, I pretended.—I lied. And I didn't do enough to stop Lance in his actions. I knew, long before things went too far, that I should have quit right then. How can you forgive me for that?"

"So you didn't put the brakes on soon enough. God forgives you. So, I can too."

Kitty turned away from Geoff's pleading face. "But, Geoff. I was going to have an abortion. I stopped in the middle of that when I probably should have just continued. Now look at the mess we're in!" Kitty began to weep.

Geoff let her sob in his arms until the shaking subsided, patting her when he could, hushing her with tender whispers. "Kitty. I know you wouldn't want to kill your baby. Now listen to me. When we marry, that baby will be mine, too. We'll be parents together. In fact, we'll both have to adopt this child. Am I right?"

Kitty's mouth dropped open. She was not yet smiling, but the happiness had reached her eyes as they filled with the dawning of truth. Geoff's arms tightened fiercely as he snugged her head into his chest.

Olivia was almost close enough to extend her arms to both of them. Geoff loosened his arms from Kitty's shoulders.

Kitty found enough courage to look into Olivia's eyes. Her own animosity evaporated as Kitty's mother showed only longing love. Their expressions joined with desperate need. Kitty and Olivia shyly reached their arms around each other in the relationship they had just renewed. Tears began to flow. Hesitant giggles emerged.

"Mommy!" Kitty wept through her hug. "You look just like me!"

"Keturah, baby! You're so grown up!" Olivia grabbed a napkin, and both mother and daughter shed tears without restraint. Geoff swiped at his own eyes.

Softness engulfed the three of them, and remained -- until Logan walked toward them, ashen faced, from the direction of Becky's room.

At that moment grief and faith met together under the same ceiling. Logan spoke words barely discernible. "Baby Dawson is gone. Becky is sedated." Logan crumpled into the nearest chair and dropped his head on his lap.

Hesitance immobilized them all, until Olivia moved. She took Kitty's cold hand to Geoff and settled it in his broad, warm one. Then she began the move that left Becky and Logan quiet in their sad considerations. The others followed.

Geoff took Olivia's wise example to exit and walked Kitty outside into the fresh air around St. Mary's Hospital. Geoff settled Kitty on a bench at the edge of a small children's playground. He looked into her eyes and then knelt on the grass before her.

"Kitty, you heard what Larry said back there. I didn't realize until that moment that I had forgiven him." Geoff reached out his hand softly to the place where the new little one was forming. "But yes, I have forgiven, and if you can do the same, we can together accept this gift as from God. I don't understand God's process today, why He keeps one but takes the other to be with Him. But someday I probably will. I will accept this as God's plan if you will."

TWENTY-FOUR

FORTY-EIGHT HOURS LATER MANY of Hank's friends had begun to gather back at Hank and Jennifer's *"Welcome Home."* A waterfall of sorrow and calm and love cascaded over them. Logan had brought Becky from the hospital on the third day after delivery. Becky and Logan had never expected to know the unspeakable grief of such an experience. Hank and Jennifer's place became the Shelter of Love during these hours of sorrow.

Ultimate empathy covered them: "Gram" Olivia, "Auntie" Kitty, and "Uncle" Geoff. So far no one had yet tried to reconnect with Robert McCain. There were several other dear friends of the family who also needed to hear about this unexpected parting.

Hank accepted the responsibility of locating the uninformed and letting them know, beginning with Robert McCain, who passed on the message to Auntie Bee and LeFevre.

After the closest ones first gathered to share in early prayers of grief, the Heavenly Father's promised strength made Him abundantly real. His Word was true, even when the *'why?'* remained. His presence was with them. He understood.

As they consoled each other, Geoff made a suggestion he had undoubtedly been thinking about for a while. "Shall we contact Pastor James at *Mercy Chapel*? Wouldn't it be beautiful to give it all to the Lord in the woods under that little pointy church roof? We'll rent a comfortable wheelchair just in case Becky needs it for a while, although I know the Lord is rapidly giving her fresh strength."

Becky nodded her head with tear-shine in her eyes. Choking, she said, "Yes. And I'd like us to find a dear little burial spot under the trees close beside Mercy Falls. When we finish the service, we'll carry his tiny little urn to a spot Geoff can choose. Geoff knows Mount Mercy better than any of us right now."

Geoff gulped, nodded and joined Becky's tears. "If no one has any objections, I'd say, why not us guys arrange that, and the ladies can plan the memorial service?"

"Okay." Kitty said. "Geoff can use the flute I once heard him play in the woods."

Hank added, "And we all know Logan will be willing to play his guitar."

"And Pastor James can play that little piano in Mercy Chapel," Geoff volunteered. "God will help us all the way."

BECKY CLUNG TO DAWSON'S TINY URN. A week later, on the day of the memorial service at Mercy Chapel, the comfort of the Holy Spirit settled over them all. Pastor James spoke the Word of God with humble faith, bringing blessing and stillness to everyone there.

Dawson Logan Kovalik's tiny frame was enclosed in the box that was his urn. With eyes that had never opened nor had seen any of this world's light, God's little one would probably now be in the midst of unspeakably wondrous Light. Light beyond understanding to mortal beings – and shining invisibly forward. However, the method that God prepared the future glory of such young creations was known only to Him. Wee Dawson would be looking at the

Light of the World, long before the rest of his family would recognize him in the arms of Jesus.

Becky held Dawson's little oak urn in her arms. Its cover, artfully adorned with up-tilted hummingbird's wings, filled her with peace. Her original grief had softened -- only a little -- but it had entered into the next season of the glory she knew was coming.

God was *here.*

Every memorable song, chosen by the women, brought spiritual rest as they sang the comforting words of praise. Geoff's flute whispered in solo. "Because He Lives, I shall know tomorrow..." *What a heavenly promise.*

Logan with his guitar had joined the accompaniment of the worship time, but he was also coerced into singing alone, in his versatile baritone. He sang to his son, too little to have seen the light of day, but large in the eyes of the Heavenly Father who saw his child like no other could.

Safe in the arms of Jesus,
Safe on His gentle breast,
There by His love o'ershaded
Sweetly my soul shall rest.

The group tears that accompanied the beautiful rich voice of Dawson's daddy were as natural as the flowing waters of Mercy Falls.

In silence, they left the church. A few other church members who heard about Geoff's hurting loved ones had joined them to commemorate the day.

Geoff, strong and proud, led the little parade to a low rock bluff, close enough to Mercy Falls to view the stream as it began to drop over the crest.

Inside the opened root of what would one day be a live, growing memorial, Pastor James tucked wee Dawson's urn and closed the opening with a small hibiscus. The cross Logan had brought reached slightly above the floral grouping, with the words that proclaimed:

Dawson Logan Kovalik, designed by the Father, belonging forever to Christ Jesus.

KITTY AND BECKY HUGGED farewell shortly after the lunch in the woods near the memorial site. Well before this official commemoration, Becky had wept her heart out and placed her loss in the hands of her Heavenly Father. But her longing to go back home with Logan sent them quickly on their early evening drive back to Nobleton.

After the Kovaliks left, Kitty and her mother met in the dark beside the fire pit next to Geoff's *Mercy Manor*. Neither blonde nor red head could wait much longer for privacy.

The hour of the memorial had begun for Kitty with a closed-up heart still troubled by resentment. But she could not absorb the loving words of Pastor James without freeing her mother from blame. Kitty ran her hands through Olivia's blonde sheaves of hair, so reminiscent of the ones she had months ago made her own persona. Olivia crinkled her fingers through the red brilliance of Kitty's spikey clip. She crunched the bent, crisp waves and laughed as though she understood it was hiding Kitty's own hair. Then they both shared their relief in giggles.

Olivia Sampson had never forsaken the name of the man whom she had married and who had fathered her child. Even with her alcoholism and dalliance across the border, she had never abandoned the fleeting hope that she would one day be reunited with her family.

It was only a year ago that Olivia found the indescribable peace of forgiveness for her unplanned faithlessness. She'd unexpectedly found release from her addictions when a new acquaintance convinced her that God still loved her. A friend that could only have been sent by God, she was convinced. Now, to have so quickly located the forgiving daughter that was Kitty, Olivia's soul was overwhelmed with gratitude.

As they reminisced far into the night, Olivia made her thankfulness to Geoff quite obvious. Olivia was convinced that she, personally, deserved nothing. And yet the blessed love of God was pouring over her, as well as her daughter, Keturah.

Olivia's heart was breaking for her daughter. Having recognized Kitty's unmentioned condition, she hoped that somehow, some way, she could be a strength to her daughter, although right now she felt as though she had never ever *been* strong, herself, and had no right to expect such a blessing.

"Keturah." She tentatively squeezed Kitty's hand conveying her understanding with overflowing eyes. "It's okay."

Her thoughts went to Larry LeFevre. Her prayers followed. Tears trickled slowly down her cheeks. Poor guy. He, too, was simply another of Satan's mistreated, mislead pawns.

Geoff hovered paternally, then helped Kitty and Olivia cuddle up on the benches next to the fire pit, bringing them hot chocolate and a new view of life.

Olivia snuggled close to Kitty's side and wrapped a gentle arm around her shoulder. "Kitty," she said, "How do you think Larry will make out?"

Kitty squeezed her eyes shut. "Mama, I sure don't know. I don't think I care much, either." An inner gasp checked her words. "And yet I guess I do -- at least a little. Our mess was not all his fault. My greed had something to do with it."

She paused and turned her anguished eyes into the ones that searched hers. "Mama. You know where I'm at, don't you?"

Olivia squashed her daughter to her. She held tighter. And tighter. Then the tears flowed as Kitty returned the embrace, and both of them sobbed for long minutes.

"Mama -- to think I almost aborted my precious baby!"

Almost an hour later, promising to meet again the next day at the Short Stop Motel, Olivia said good night to *her* precious baby while Geoff waited in the distance.

AS OLIVIA DROVE AWAY, Kitty stood still by the fire pit and watched Geoff come near to her.

"Kitty, my sweet," he said. "Jennifer and Hank have gone home to Nobleton. You'll have to put yourself to bed in the tent again tonight. Maybe tomorrow morning we could meet Olivia, and she could help us plan our wedding?"

Kitty gasped and threw her arms around Geoff's neck. He hugged her very lightly and let her go. "Sleep well, my precious. We will plan in daylight, OK?" Even with the mischievous look in those midnight eyes, he kept rigid arms and turned firmly toward the tent he considered Kitty's. Kitty had slept there last night, and so she would tonight.

"Breakfast whenever you like in the morning. Okay?"

COFFEE WAS READY soon after sunrise. Geoff and Kitty walked to the ridge, holding hands. As they admired the rays rising to meet them, Geoff pulled out his cell phone. "What do you say we call Olivia and take her to breakfast at the Short Stop?"

Grinning, Kitty nodded vigorously.

The threesome met just as the coffee shop opened. Olivia threw motherly arms around her daughter, then shyly transferred them to Geoff's shoulders. "I'm so glad you're in this picture," she told him.

"Me, too! You've no idea, Olivia, how terrified I was that Kitty might never come to me again. I think I have to give you full credit for her courageous attitude."

Geoff turned back toward Kitty, the woman whose love had captured him so completely. He lifted his arms to her shoulders, then dropped his hands to her waistline, curving them lovingly downward over the home of the child he had fully accepted.

"Mommi-O." He directed his words to Olivia. "I have a request for you. Will you please pray right now for the child Kitty is carrying and dedicate his little being as both Kitty's *and* mine. I want to adopt this wee one, just like God has adopted me. I want to be a *real* father. We'll soon probably know whether it is a girl or a boy, which will make not a speck of difference to our love. He turned toward Kitty with the question in his eyes. And she responded with the deep glow of her joy.

266

The waiter interrupted them with his order pad. Olivia's blessing first focused on the arriving food, and then more fully on Geoff's warm prayer for the coming family. Even Kitty appeared to have forgiven the truth of Larry LeFevre's paternity. A new family was born by simple acceptance, in the reality of God's kind of adoption. By the miracle presence of the Holy Spirit.

"And dear Lord, please hang close to Larry in this difficult time," Geoff said. "Fill him with your comfort and presence this very moment and every minute ahead."

Real tears were wiped as Geoff added, "Kitty, you know how much I love you. I've forgiven you your mistakes, just as I know you have forgiven me mine. God has showered us all with His mercy and cleansed us totally by the blood He shed on Calvary. So, there should be no reason we can't get married right away, should there? Like how about two weeks from yesterday, the day when little Dawson was laid to rest. And I can hardly wait for the future joy we'll all know when we finally meet together in God's Eternity.

"Is thirteen days enough time?"

Kitty was speechless, but acceptance shone in eyes of joy.

"Sure it is," Olivia said firmly. "There is no point in waiting any longer."

"I know I'm crazy," Geoff continued. "But if you don't object, Kitty, I will see that there's a noon reception provided after Pastor James marries us at Mercy Chapel. I also plan to have a cozy tent waiting for us up higher. We'll say goodbye to our good friends after our lunch. We'll take a quick lift in the tracker up to the top of Mount Mercy and stay there at least part of the first night watching the moonlight. The next night we'll be cuddling up beside the Big Upper. What do you think?"

Kitty could hardly conceive of Geoff's imaginative picture. She gasped when she considered a Heavenly Father this forgiving and loving. She could hardly absorb the mercy pouring from Geoff. His love had not been simply temporary. His generous forgiveness was real and permanent. Geoff's assurance of actually reaching the Upper Mercy made her shiver with anticipation. "What do you think?" Geoff had asked.

Olivia's expression was as jubilant as the tone of her voice. "What does Kitty think, you ask? She thinks she is the luckiest woman in the whole wide world! C'mon, daughter! Show this wonderful man what you think."

Kitty threw herself into Geoff's open arms.

He hugged her tightly, then guided her into a seat beside Olivia. "I have another surprise for you, Kitten. Olivia can share this with us. You'll never believe it."

He became silent, almost irritatingly so, with only a hint of his teasing chuckle.

"So?" Kitty said. "Tell me what I won't believe so I can believe it!"

Geoff drew a sober expression. "Kitty, tell me, are you missing any of the lovely photography you've taken lately?"

Kitty's eyes widened in horrified shock.

What? Lovely photography?

"What are you talking about? Those are gone! I cleaned out every last one of those awful things! Why did you bring *those* up now when I was feeling so forgiven?"

268

Kitty collapsed near Olivia on the bench, shoulders shaking in silent denial.

Geoff's reaction was almost as shaken as Kitty's. He grabbed her and stood up with her in his arms, apology exploding. "No, Kitty! No! I've made you misunderstand. Not those old things. I've found your *good* picture."

"I didn't have any good ones anymore. I was sure I emptied that case completely. Those pictures weren't me, anyway!"

Geoff shivered and patted Kitty's back. "Shh, shh. Sweetheart. It was *one* shot only. It wasn't in your photo case. It was still in your camera!"

"Camera?"

"Yes, Kitty. You must have snapped it on the ridge when you fell. I'm dying to have it finished. It reminds me so much of Tom Thompson's pine tree art that it leaves me breathless. You just watch, Kitty. They'll be chasing you down the highway to the museum as soon as we expose it!"

Kitty had no words left with which to respond. Her breath seemed to leave her as Geoff put her back into Olivia's arms.

Olivia squeezed reassuringly while her head gently moved in puzzlement. "Sounds okay to me, Keturah," she said. "Don't worry. As long as Geoff's taking charge of it, just let him do it. We have a wedding to prepare for."

TWENTY-FIVE

KITTY SPENT THE NEXT two days tagging along with her mother and Becky, shopping in Vancouver's wedding malls. The three friends came up with several unusual ideas for a wedding. Knowing Geoff's mountain plan, Kitty concluded that she needed a two-piece wedding dress. The silk jacket, separate from the fish-tailed skirt, would sport a lace peplum curving over the bodice and hips. Appropriate for the most modest wedding of the season. The exchangeable part would be pants.

Kitty's plan was to change into her afternoon outfit just before the lunch celebration and cake cutting. She would exchange her skirt for comfortable silk pants and top them with the same lace jacket she'd worn for the ceremony. Becky, her maid of honour, ordered an ocean-blue gown, without pants, similarly styled to Kitty's wedding dress. Olivia blended in with a teal gown styled to match the trio.

Becky followed mother and daughter with giggling approval. "It's going to be the most memorable wedding in the world! Especially when Geoff and Kitty take off in the tracker for their honeymoon!"

THE DAY BEFORE THE WEDDING, Geoff approached Kitty with a sober expression. He found her hand and tugged her into one of the trails near Mercy Manor. He paused under the branches of one of the surrounding pines, an inscrutable expression in his dark eyes.

Kitty became aware of Geoff's gentle fingers sifting through her short red locks, and her thoughts were drawn to what he might be thinking. "Geoff, do you wish I were really a red head?"

"Ah, Kitty. I'd love you if you were purple or green or chokecherry. I don't think you made these changes for Larry anyway. Or anyone else." His finger ran along the part in her hair that was already trying to become original. "But if you want to do something just for me, I'd love it if you wanted to become authentic once more. Even just for a while." Kitty looked gratefully surprised.

"You would? You mean the *original* me? The one you had almost forgotten? Okay, Geoff, my love, starting today that's how it will be. I'm going to turn back into Keturah. But while we're waiting, I'll have to be your blonde wife. Sometimes your red one."

Geoff's embrace tightened. "Remember, Kitten, I will love you eternally and forever, no matter what colour you feel like being." His expression remained concerned. "And Kitty. Let's consider this as we are joined together. Let's both, together, forgive Larry LeFevre."

Kitty's wide eyes softened in acquiescence. She nodded her head as Geoff continued speaking.

"Kitty, I think you should hear this now, just so we go with complete understanding into our forever covenant. Evidently no one has been aware of Larry's condition these last few weeks. You didn't realize he was sick, did you?"

Kitty's eyes widened in shock. "Larry? Sick? He was so busy being drunk I wouldn't have guessed that he had a different problem! What's wrong with him, Geoff?" Her face expressed sudden empathy.

"Robert McCain just called me."

"They're not coming?" Kitty's face dropped. Geoff tightened his hug around her shoulders.

"Officer McCain will be here, yes. But he just called to say Larry LeFevre won't. Larry has gone to be with his Heavenly Father, Kitty. We're all still in total shock. McCain says that Larry left word for him at the funeral parlour. His internment had already been carried out. Larry is at peace at last.

"Robert McCain is on his way now, to be with us."

Tears coursed down Kitty's cheeks. She could hardly comprehend what Geoff had just told her. Huge waves of what could be considered forgiveness swept through her body.

Or maybe it was remorse. How she hoped that this man had found peace in God's love. She could not help but question her own responsibility. Could she have done more, while he was still with them, to show the love of Christ to the father of Geoff's adopted child? She wept.

NEXT MORNING THE RAYS of sunrise beamed in approval on the beautiful Mountain of Mercy, its little brown church, and the joyful celebration that was planned for the 50-seat chapel. The three ladies joyfully brought three shades of hair to the celebration: blonde, brunette and red.

Hank chose a tux to walk his new daughter down the short aisle of the small church to meet his favourite son. At exactly eleven o'clock, Pastor James gave the introduction on the baby grand piano, then played the full wedding march in triumph. The music that was planned moved every heart there. Hank gave away his new daughter with solemnity unusual for him.

Pastor James' words to the couple were both wise and filled with humour.

Then, at the moment he asked the important question, "Do you...?" The breathing in the church seemed to disappear in a hallowed silence, until the sacred kiss sealed the promise.

Instead of an immediate march, Geoff and Kitty stood motionless while Logan joined Pastor James on the piano with his guitar rendition of *"Mine Eyes Have Seen the Glory."* Slowly the small congregation lifted to their feet and began to raise voices in worship that would not be held back – *"Glory, Glory, Hallelujah,"* they sang, until the last *'Hallelujah'* rose in high praise, concluding, *"His truth ... is ... marching ... on ..."*

After long minutes of quiet, Geoff and Kitty, unspeakable joy on their faces, held hands while they led the worshippers from the chapel into the garden as the piano continued to ring.

KITTY SLIPPED AWAY to exchange the fan-tailed skirt for her silk pants. She hurried back to participate with everyone else, thrilled to see the enormous variety of diminutive finger treats and other nameless steaming hors d'oeuvres their friends had produced. Protecting her yellow rose bouquet, she also joined Geoff moving around the tables for the next hour passing out hugs and wedding mementos, still feeling like she was in a storybook. A table of unopened gifts stood next to the church steps.

Before she left with Geoff, she slipped Olivia her red wig.

GEOFF AND KITTY disappeared together and returned with the tracker, packed and prepared, and including a joyful Yukon in the truck-box. The bride, now blonde, had already found her seat in the get-away vehicle. The guests stared in shock at the blonde they already knew. The blonde Kitty was back.

Olivia, the mother of the bride, ran through the stunned crowd wearing a red wig that had been pushed over her swirling hair before the laughing guests realized what had happened.

Then brunette bridesmaid, Becky, lovely in her ocean blue gown, ran toward the mountain vehicle clutching the yellow rose bouquet Kitty had carried.

Geoff grinned, and while standing up in the tracker, lifted his deep voice.

"Thank you all, dear friends, for joining us in our holy ceremony. Please ignore our levity with hair today." Chuckles danced through the crowd. "I had almost forgotten my Kitty was blonde."

He grinned. "For a while I found myself fearing this celebration might not happen 'til Christmas, but Kitty's mother, Olivia, gave me courage to believe it wouldn't take that long." He turned his face to Olivia waiting at the side of the tracker and winked at her. "Watch, now. See this lovely yellow bouquet in Kitty's arms. In less than a minute it's going to fly. Who's ready to catch it?"

Kitty held it above her head, encouragingly high, and shook her blonde locks, laughing.

Like a soccer player, she rolled her arms, squeez
yellow rose bouquet and flung it high above all their h

Making a flip, the bouquet dropped downwi
falling neatly into Olivia's open arms while the red wig
off her head. By the time the friends realized what had ju
transpired, the yellow rose bouquet had been captured
hopeful arms. A roar of approval rose up.

And the cheers continued to lift.

BUT GEOFF AND KITTY were not aware of the
rising cheers. The Tracker, with Geoff at the wheel and
Yukon guarding Kitty, was already headed around the
corner and up the mountain.

MERCY FALLS, hidden in the distant peaks, was
calling to the newlyweds.

THE END